P9-CEN-025

DISCARD

The
Silence
of the Rain

The Silence of the Rain

Luiz Alfredo

GARCIA-ROZA

Translated by Benjamin Moser

Henry Holt and Company

New York

Henry Holt and Company, LLC
Publishers since 1866
115 West 18th Street
New York, New York 10011

Henry Holt® is a registered trademark
of Henry Holt and Company, LLC.

Distributed in Canada by H. B. Fenn and Company Ltd.

Originally published in Brazil in 1996
under the title *O silêncio da chuva*
by Companhia Das Letras, São Paulo.

Library of Congress Cataloging-in-Publication Data

García-Roza, L. A. (Luiz Alfredo)
[Silēncio da chuva. English]
The silence of the rain / Luiz Alfredo Garcia-Roza;
translated by Benjamin Moser.—1st American ed.
p. cm.
ISBN 0-8050-6889-9
I. Moser, Benjamin. II. Title.
PQ9698.17.A745 S513 2002
869.3'42—dc21 2001051523

Henry Holt books are available for special promotions and premiums. For details contact: Director, Special Markets.

First American Edition 2002

Designed by Margaret M. Wagner

Printed in the United States of America
1 3 5 7 9 10 8 6 4 2

The Silence of the Rain

PART I

The
Two Arts

He examined the gun delicately, as if it were a rare object. He felt its weight—ran his finger along the barrel—opened the drum—spun it around—flipped it shut and tested the trigger. Eyes shut, guided only by touch, he put his fingers around the grip, not pointing at anything. The words inscribed on the barrel—DETECTIVE SPECIAL—made him think of old crime movies. He took six bullets out of a box and slid them into the drum one by one. He shut it, placed the box of bullets and a cloth in the drawer, and put the gun in his briefcase. The money and the envelope were on the table. He placed them in a different compartment of the briefcase. He glanced around the office, picked up the briefcase, unlocked the door, and went out.

In the next office, he said good-bye to Rose, his secretary. He bumped into Cláudio Lucena by the elevators. He wished he hadn't quarreled with him, but now it didn't really matter; they'd often fought and it had never affected their friendship. By the time the elevator reached the bottom, all bad feelings had disappeared. They chatted outside for a minute and went their separate ways.

He walked down Rua São José toward the parking garage. He wasn't in a hurry; he had no doubts. His parking place was on the second floor—he reached it by the escalator in the shopping arcade. He'd parked close to the door. The darkness in the garage contrasted sharply with the brightness outside. The garage was still pretty full.

He got in, put the briefcase down on the passenger seat, and sat thinking about what had been going on. He felt peaceful. He opened the glove compartment and took out the cigarettes that had been sitting there since he quit smoking, about two months earlier. He lit one and took long drags; after such a long abstinence, each puff gave him a little buzz—not enough, though, to cloud his mind. He finished the cigarette, rolled up the windows, opened the briefcase, took out the gun, pressed the barrel to his head—and pulled the trigger.

1

Espinosa crossed the street slowly, eyes downcast, hands in his pockets, and headed for the plaza. The sun still burned hot in the spring afternoon. He found a bench facing the port; behind him was the old building occupied by the newspaper *A Noite*. Under a big ficus, he let his ideas weave their own web.

Not many people—besides Espinosa and some beggars—would consider the Praça Mauá a good place to sit and think. The beggars had eyed him warily at first, but gradually got used to him. He never went at night, respectful of its metamorphosis when the clientele of the Scandinavia Night Club or Disco Florida showed up.

He focused on the cranes in the port, allowing his thoughts to take shape. While he had long believed such moments of solitude essential to reflection, now, on the bench, he realized this simply didn't apply to him. His mental process was mainly a dreamy flow of pictures alongside entirely imaginary dialogues. It seemed he was incapable of sustained rational thought—a failing that, for a policeman, was embarrassing, to say the least.

The square was small and located in one of the busiest parts of Rio, but it allowed him to escape the claustrophobia of the station house. Tuesday wasn't such a bad day, especially compared to weekends, when the station was packed full of hookers and pickpockets from the port. That was his clientele: hookers, pickpockets, drunks, and junkies, the small fry of the port's underworld. The real crimes, committed in the offices downtown, never reached the First Precinct—even the high-class prostitution in the buildings right next to the station were safe from police action. And murders were rare downtown.

2

Even though it was a Tuesday afternoon, almost every seat in the auditorium was filled when the moderator introduced Bia Vasconcelos. They had first met a year ago, when she was on a panel where Júlio had given a talk; since then they'd bumped into each other on three occasions, two openings and an art event in the Parque Lage.

Tonight, as always, she was dressed simply but elegantly. Her thick black hair came just below her ears, showing off her face and neck. She was thirty-four, as graceful as a dancer. When the debate was over, Júlio invited her for a beer downtown. On the way out, they were hit by the glare of the September evening and the roar of a jet taking off from Galeão. In the car, a feeling of intimacy quieted them both. They didn't speak until they were leaving the campus; during the trip there was more silence than talk.

They parked on Avenida Chile, near the cathedral, and walked to Rua da Carioca. On the packed sidewalk, people were hurrying another chaotic day to its close. Outside the Cinema Íris was a handwritten announcement of "Two Films and Two Shows with specially selected Girls"; another heavily illustrated poster advertised a film called *The Orgasm Exterminatrix*. The crowds and the music pumping from the record stores made conversation impossible. They got to the Bar Luiz at five minutes to five. They chose a table for two by the wall. Next to them, a tourist was scrutinizing a city map; at another table, farther off, a group of people were talking; behind Bia, a tall, light-skinned black man in a sleeveless silk T-shirt—wearing a necklace, a bunch of rings, and two silver bracelets on each wrist—was arguing in a low voice with a blonde.

A six-foot screen of wood and fluted glass protected the art deco interior of Bar Luiz from the street. The upper part was open, allowing customers a view of the old colonial houses across the street, with their stone facades and small wrought-iron balconies. Júlio had eyes only for Bia. For the first time, they were face-to-face, a few inches apart. They ordered beer and sausages; Bia could hardly open the plastic wrapping around the silverware. Júlio helped her; their hands touched. They talked, learning little things about each other; under the cramped table their knees occasionally brushed.

Bia's beauty wasn't—not all of it—immediately obvious; its new and unrevealed facets were constantly coming to light. For Júlio, each new aspect was like an epiphany. They kept to small talk: the graphic arts course she'd taken in Italy, his two jobs (teacher at the architecture school and professional architect). The encounter lasted about an hour. At six-fifteen, Bia said she had to go and refused Júlio's offer to drive her home. They said good-bye; their lips touched lightly.

3

At eight, when most of the cars on the second floor had been driven away, the fat man breathlessly informed the attendant in charge of that floor that there was a dead body in the car next to his.

"You sure he's dead, sir?" asked the attendant, feigning indifference.

"A guy with a hole in his head and bloodstained clothes didn't just fall asleep at the wheel!"

The word "blood" can be more shocking than "death." The attendant came out of his booth and looked toward where the man was pointing.

"I can't abandon my post."

"Is this a fucking boat? Get someone else and call the police! I'll take care of the car."

" 'Take care of the car'? Didn't you just say the guy's dead?"

"So nobody messes with it. Don't you get it? The guy's dead. Maybe murdered."

The word "murdered" was more effective; the attendant abandoned his booth and yelled up to someone upstairs.

The parking attendants were soon joined by some curious onlookers who had come out of nowhere. The group quickly shrank when, lights flashing, a military police car arrived. The area was cordoned off and the remaining onlookers were sent away, leaving only the attendants and the man who'd discovered the body. The police station in the Praça Mauá was informed of the incident and learned that the victim was an important executive in a large downtown company.

When Espinosa got there half an hour later, the patrolman reported what he had discovered and handed him some business cards found in one of the man's jacket pockets; the other pocket was empty. The dead man had no money on him. The cards had enabled them to identify him: Ricardo Fonseca de Carvalho, forty-two, executive director of Planalto Minerações. His address and phone number were on the cards.

The fat man, sitting inside his own car, was no longer breathless but looked tired. He jumped when Espinosa's face appeared at the window.

"Good evening, sir. I'm Inspector Espinosa from the First Precinct. I understand that you found the body?"

"Yes, sir."

The fat man got out of the car.

"Could you give me your name, address, and phone number?"

He spoke calmly, somewhat wearily, not in the least intimidating. Despite all his years as a cop, Espinosa had never adopted their lingo. His colleagues found his reports, with their almost literary style, somewhat opaque. His clothes weren't standard-issue either; he never wore the uniform adopted by younger detectives—sneakers and leather vests.

"My name is Osmar . . . Osmar Ferreira Bueno. I already gave all that to the other policeman."

"Mr. Osmar, I know that you've had a very unpleasant experience and that you should be home, but your testimony is very important. I'd like you to tell me exactly what happened, from the moment you saw the car."

"Well, there's not a lot to tell. I went to open my car door and saw the guy in the next car slumped over the steering wheel. He didn't look asleep, so I thought he'd had a heart attack. I banged on the window a few times, but since he didn't budge I opened the door. The inside light went on and I saw the blood on his clothes; I walked around and saw the wound to his head from the other side. I shut the door and ran over to tell the attendant."

"Did you touch the body or pick anything up?"

"No. He was obviously dead, so I didn't touch anything."

"While you were talking to the attendant, did anyone else get near the car?"

"No. I ran off and got back fast. The parking lot was practically empty, so I could have seen anybody getting close."

"Thank you, Mr. Osmar. We'll be in touch."

The executive obviously had been robbed. No one goes around with absolutely no money, especially not a man dressed like that in a car like that. The size of the wound indicated that the gun must have been a .38. The bullet had remained lodged in the brain. There were no signs of a struggle, and the key was still in the ignition. In the ashtray was a single recently extinguished cigarette. There was no ash. The back seat and the trunk were empty.

Leaning on the wall of the exit ramp, gazing over at the Convent of Santo Antônio, Espinosa tried to reconstruct the scene. He imagined a few possibilities, all based on one fact that seemed clear enough: the murderer was sitting next to the driver when he or she fired.

First scenario: the murderer is hiding in the back seat, waiting. It's almost completely dark. The victim opens the driver's door—the light goes on—the murderer surprises the executive and forces him at gunpoint into the car. He hands over his money and a few other things, then tries to fight back and is shot. The murderer leaves through the passenger door and goes downstairs without being seen.

Second scenario: the murderer is lurking outside the car. The executive approaches; the murderer points the gun at him and forces him into the car through the passenger door. The murderer gets in immediately and orders him to start the engine; when the executive leans forward, puts the key in the ignition, and turns it, he gets shot in the head.

If that was it, the lock on the driver's side would be down, but it wasn't.

There was still the question of motive. He dismissed attempted kidnapping as highly unlikely. The place wasn't right: there was only one exit; the businessman could have made a dramatic escape when they stopped at the ticket window. Besides, kidnappings were never carried out alone, and there was no sign of a second assailant.

Third scenario: the executive knows the murderer. They come together to pick up the car. When they get in, he or she puts the gun to the executive's head and fires. He or she grabs his wallet and the watch—to make it look like a robbery—and leaves by the emergency stairs.

Espinosa didn't take these imaginary scenarios too seriously and didn't try to commit them to memory. As the investigation progressed, he knew, other possibilities would arise, none of which would even vaguely resemble the original ones; eventually they would all merge to create other, more complex, scenarios. He walked down to the car. The forensic expert was placing various instruments and labeled plastic envelopes into a case.

"I'm taking these away to check 'em out," he said. "So far there's not much to tell you. The gun was pressed against the victim's temple when it was fired, and it was probably a .38. He died instantly. No sign of a struggle, no fingerprints. I'll know more after a more thorough examination."

"Thanks, Freire. We'll talk tomorrow."

As he was leaving, he turned back to Freire:

"One more thing. Any trace of lipstick on his lips or face?"

"Not that I could see. The pathologist can find out."

Fourth scenario: on the way to the parking lot, the businessman meets a girlfriend. They kiss and walk together to the car. The executive opens the passenger door for her, walks around the car, gets in, and—before he turns on the engine or the lights—is shot.

By half past nine, there wasn't much more he could do. The café on the first floor of the parking lot, next to the escalator, was closed. (If Ricardo Carvalho had stopped in for coffee before going up the escalator, someone might have seen him.) But all the shops and bars were shut, the streets deserted. And there wouldn't be anyone at Planalto Minerações either.

A fifth scenario—suicide—didn't even occur to him. No gun was found in the car.

4

Espinosa made it a rule never to say certain things over the phone. He stopped by the station, picked up his car, and went to talk to the executive's wife. On the way to her home in Jardim Botânico, he thought of more possibilities.

When the doorman asked his name, Espinosa flashed his badge and said he'd rather arrive unannounced.

"It's the penthouse, sir. Just press P."

Espinosa didn't reply. The elevator was lined with mirrors and—unless someone else had just gotten off—perfumed.

He had to ring the doorbell twice, which made him think the doorman had buzzed to warn her that the police were coming. But that theory crumbled when the door opened. The beautiful young woman who answered seemed completely at ease.

"Dona Bia Carvalho?"

"Bia Vasconcelos," she replied firmly and, seeing Espinosa's confusion, added:

"I use my maiden name."

"I'm Inspector Espinosa, from the First Precinct."

"Has something happened?"

"Yes. I'm afraid I'm not bringing you good news."

"What's wrong?"

"May I come in?" Espinosa asked without answering.

"Of course, please, come in. But what's wrong?" she asked, almost whispering.

"Your husband is dead," said Espinosa. "Murdered."

Bia Vasconcelos turned pale and reached for something to steady herself. Espinosa grabbed her arms and helped her sit down on the sofa. For a few seconds, she simply stared at something between the wall and the ceiling.

"I'm so sorry," said Espinosa. "But there's no way to break news like this gently."

"How did it happen?"

"I could tell you how he was found, but not how it happened. Would you like a glass of water?"

"Yes, please, the kitchen's through there."

Espinosa soon returned with the water.

"Do you need a tranquilizer or anything? Would you like me to call someone?"

"No, I don't need to take anything, but could you call my father? His name is Alírio Vasconcelos, and his number's on the first page of that book."

Her hand trembled as she pointed to the address book by the phone.

While Espinosa was dialing, she turned to him and said:

"Please, let me tell him myself."

Espinosa heard a voice answer and carried the phone over to where she was sitting.

"Daddy . . . Ricardo's dead . . . murdered. . . . Yes, murdered. . . . I don't know yet. . . . Yes, I'm fine. . . . A policeman named—" She turned to Espinosa. "Sorry, what was your name again?"

"Espinosa, Inspector Espinosa from the First Precinct."

"Inspector Espinosa," she repeated.

"My father wonders if you would mind waiting for him to come over? It'll just take him a few minutes."

"Of course. No rush, I'm not in a hurry."

She repeated this to her father and hung up. They sat for a while in silence. Bia Vasconcelos gradually recovered her color and asked what time her husband had been murdered and how. Espinosa described approximately when and, as gently as possible, how he had been found. She sat staring at the same point between the wall and the ceiling. Then, without being asked, she said flatly:

"I was having a beer with a friend right around there at that time."

"What time was that?" asked Espinosa.

"Between five and six. I left right after six because I wanted to drop by the studio before coming home."

"And did you?"

"No, I went to the movies instead. I needed to think a few things over, and the theater's a good place for that."

"How was the movie?"

"You have a very courteous way of interrogating people, Inspector."

"I'm not interrogating you. You just mentioned having a beer with a friend and going to the movies."

"Without the friend," she added.

Espinosa didn't probe further. He asked a few questions about her husband's habits, wondered if he had any enemies, if he'd said anything that might have some bearing on the crime, if she'd noticed anything strange about him when he left home that morning.

"Did your husband usually carry some kind of briefcase?"

"Yes, he has a leather briefcase he takes with him everywhere."

"Could you describe it, ma'am?"

"It's brown leather, the usual size, with two or three compartments inside and his initials engraved on the outside."

Her voice was gradually calming down. She remained seated. Espinosa became aware of soft music coming from somewhere in the bookcase—classical music. He couldn't identify the composer. After a few minutes, the doorbell rang.

Alírio Torres Vasconcelos was about sixty, with a deep voice and a broad chest. He enfolded his daughter in a long embrace, introduced himself, asked the inspector to give a detailed account of what had happened, which Espinosa did, though he omitted some details. From the questions the father asked and from his reactions to the answers, it became obvious that he hadn't really liked his son-in-law. Finally, he asked what immediate steps needed to be taken.

"I'm afraid," said Espinosa, "that someone will need to identify the body. But that can be done tomorrow."

And with that he left the father alone with the daughter.

On the street, he suddenly realized he hadn't eaten anything since a sandwich at lunchtime.

5

The mineral-exploration company Planalto Minerações occupies the twelfth floor of a building on Rua do Ouvidor, near Avenida Rio Branco. The smoked-glass facade protects the occupants of the luxurious offices from prying outside eyes. The air-conditioning maintains a civilized temperature, keeping the tropics permanently at bay. The elevators are spacious, silent, and swift. The closed-circuit television and an efficient security system ensure that both the First and the Third Worlds are held at a safe distance.

News of the murder had preceded Espinosa. In reception, two young women were chattering excitedly; their excitement only increased when Espinosa flashed his badge.

"Good morning, I'm Inspector Espinosa from the First Precinct. I'd like to talk to the director of the company."

"Dr. Daniel Weil is the president, but he's not in yet . . . he usually gets here around ten," one of the women replied breathlessly. "Would you like to speak to one of the directors?"

Cláudio Lucena, executive director of the company, must have been about the same age as Ricardo Carvalho. He was athletically built and elegantly dressed; his somewhat high-pitched voice seemed out of keeping with his otherwise masculine appearance. He received Espinosa with an unconvincing pained look on his face.

"Inspector, what a tragedy. How could something like this happen?" he said, getting up and extending his hand.

"That's what I'm trying to find out," replied Espinosa.

"Sit down, please," said Lucena, indicating some comfortable-looking black leather furniture.

Espinosa noticed that everything was black, gray, or white,

pictures and ornaments no exception to the rule. Despite the lack of color, everything was in excellent taste. Seeing Espinosa looking around, Lucena remarked, "Our offices in Brazil and abroad are all decorated exactly the same. Our president says it's a way to make sure we always feel at home wherever we are. Dona Carmem, two coffees, please," he said into the intercom.

Sitting down in the armchair opposite Espinosa, he said:

"Inspector, I'm ready to help in whatever way I can."

"Thank you, sir. When did you last see Ricardo Carvalho?"

"We left together last night, at six forty-five; we stood outside chatting for a few minutes and then left in different directions. I got a cab on Avenida Rio Branco and he went to get his car in the garage. I must have been the last person to see him alive."

"The next to last, I hope, Mr. Lucena."

"I mean the last person who knew him, Inspector."

"Why do you think the murderer was a stranger?"

"I really don't know, except that I can't believe anyone who knew him would have done this."

"Do you always go home by cab?"

"Yes, it's more convenient."

"Why didn't you get a ride with your friend?"

"He lives in Jardim Botânico, I live in Leme—they're in different directions."

Carmem brought in a tray with a silver coffeepot, two cups, two glasses of water, and a plate of cookies. Conversation stopped while the coffee was poured. Then they were left alone again.

"Did you know Ricardo Carvalho well?"

"Well, we worked together, but we were also friends: we went to each other's houses and took a few trips together with our wives."

"What was he like?"

"An excellent businessman, absolutely devoted to the company, ambitious, uncompromising. As a friend he was loyal and very helpful. Everyone in the company respected him."

It sounded to Espinosa like the man thought he could have been describing himself.

Lucena paused, then added: "I just don't understand how someone could have done this."

"Did he have any enemies outside the company? You said he was uncompromising."

"Well, that might be a bit strong. He was a skilled negotiator and didn't like to lose. But nothing that would justify murder."

"Nothing justifies murder."

"Of course not. I was just thinking of a motive."

"Did Ricardo Carvalho ever say anything that might have some bearing on the crime?"

"I can't think of anything, to be honest, Inspector, besides theft. I can't see what other motive there could have been."

"How was his relationship with his wife?"

"Bia's a wonderful person—much too good for Ricardo."

Realizing he'd spoken strongly, he added:

"Oh, don't be surprised that I should say that about a friend, Inspector, especially about a friend who's just been brutally murdered. But it's absolutely true. There was no one like Ricardo for making money, but when it came to personal relationships he was a disaster."

Espinosa's furrowed brow invited Lucena to continue, although his high-pitched voice and pretentious tone were irritating.

"Ricardo didn't care much about people."

"Not even his wife?"

"Well, a beautiful, intelligent, cultured wife was an important accessory for him. But he could do without love—I think he even considered it dangerous."

"And how did she feel about that?"

"Bia's got her job—she's an internationally renowned designer—so they lived in totally separate worlds. Their paths crossed less and less."

"Did those worlds involve extramarital affairs?"

"For him, definitely. As for her, I don't think so. She's very proper; if she fell in love with someone else, she wouldn't stay with her husband."

"I was thinking more about casual affairs."

"Oh, that's not Bia's style; she's not easily seduced."

"Have you ever tried, Mr. Lucena?"

"Inspector, Ricardo was my best friend and my wife is a friend of Bia's."

"That sounds more like a justification than a reply, Mr. Lucena."

"No, I never tried to seduce her."

"One more question. Do you know if Mr. Carvalho kept any guns at home?"

"I'm not sure. About a year ago, when we went to the beach for the weekend, he took a revolver with him."

"Could you describe it?"

"I really only glimpsed it. I know it was a revolver, but I have no idea what kind."

"One last thing. Was he carrying anything when you last saw him?"

"Only his briefcase."

"Are you sure he had it on him?"

"Absolutely."

"Thank you, Mr. Lucena. You've been very helpful."

"If you need anything from me, Inspector, please get in touch. I want this murderer to be found."

Dr. Weil, the president and CEO of the company, still hadn't come in. The secretaries and the other employees could add little to what Mr. Lucena had told him; Rose, Ricardo Carvalho's secretary, hadn't come in; she had apparently called earlier to say she wasn't feeling well. So Espinosa would have to return to Planalto Minerações on another day. The idea didn't exactly fill him with joy.

6

Not many people showed up at the wake. Alírio Vasconcelos and Elísio came with Bia. Elísio, the director of her gallery, was like a brother to Bia. The son of one of Alírio's former employees, he had lost both parents when he was only nine; Alírio had raised him like his own son. He studied at the School of Fine Arts and, even before graduation, was put in charge of the Torres Vasconcelos Gallery. It had been hard for Bia to convince him that it was okay for him to leave, that she could sit through the night with only her friend Teresa for company. Ricardo's parents, again on Bia's insistence, also left before the wee hours. Only Bia and Teresa remained.

After a first cup of coffee at the café in the chapel, the two friends sat down, facing the coffin. Liberated from the morgue, the body had been made up to look like a sleeping movie star.

"So, my friend, does this mean that God is as good as people say?" said Teresa, as if commenting on the success of a fund-raiser.

"Teresa!" replied Bia, shocked by the harshness of the remark. "Ricardo was my husband, and we still cared about each other."

"Honey, the only thing your late husband cared about was money."

"You're being cruel."

"But not dishonest. Or unfair, for that matter."

And she went on:

"I never understood how a pretty, intelligent woman like you, with excellent taste, could have married someone like him."

"In the beginning, he was really kind and sweet to me," replied Bia, slightly embarrassed.

"As kind and sweet as when he cradled a gold bar in his hands."

There was no anger in Teresa's voice; she remained perfectly calm and friendly.

"Look, let's talk about this some other time. It doesn't feel right to be talking about him while he's lying dead right in front of us," said Bia softly, as if talking to herself.

"Fine. Not that he ever treated you so delicately, when he was alive."

That was the end of it. They started talking about Bia's speech at the architecture school and the days when they had lived together in Italy.

They had met in Milan. Bia was studying at the Istituto Europeo di Design, while Teresa was finishing her law degree. Teresa's parents were Italian immigrants and so she had a right to Italian citizenship, which made it much easier to live in Milan and travel around Europe. When she came back to Brazil, she never bothered to transfer the credits, and ended up marrying a lawyer twenty-two years her senior. She lost a little of her vivacity, but remained intelligent and talkative.

In the morning, when Ricardo's parents came back to the chapel, Bia and Teresa went home to change clothes and eat something. After nine, a few friends began to arrive; around ten, Ricardo's fellow executives and a few employees showed up. Daniel Weil was huffing and puffing.

"My dear, such a tragedy. We're so profoundly shocked by this brutal crime. I've insisted that the investigating officer keep me informed of his progress. And you can count on me for anything, anything at all."

Lucena tried a more personal tack, but Bia was unreceptive. Alírio Vasconcelos kept his distance, wary of any contact with these men. Like theirs, his life had always revolved around money; but unlike them Alírio didn't regard money as all-important.

As she listened to people drone on about "irreparable loss" and "irreplaceable people," she suddenly noticed the man standing by the wall opposite her, carefully observing the scene: the policeman who had come to her house. She didn't see him again during the ceremony.

When it was time to close the coffin, Bia approached it, studied her husband's face for a while, then removed her wedding ring and placed it on his body. She did not cry or embrace or kiss the dead man. When the funeral was over, and the directors of the company came to pay their respects, she only said:

"Thank you. You've been so kind . . . and so efficient."

In all her words and gestures there was a disconcerting ambiguity.

The only person who seemed genuinely sad was Rose, Ricardo's secretary. Several times, she tried to approach Bia and twice even began to speak, but was interrupted by people anxious to give their condolences to the widow. By half past eleven, everything was over. Or so they thought.

7

Bia stayed home all afternoon, haphazardly putting away some of her husband's things, more to get used to the idea of his death than to try to impose a new order. She had given the maid the day off; she didn't want anyone around, especially someone who had seen so much of her married life. Right before noon, her father had called to check on her and ask if she wanted to have lunch with him. No, she didn't. She'd rather stay home. Later, Rose called.

"Dona Bia?"

"Yes," she said, recognizing the secretary's voice. "How are you, Rose? Thanks for coming to the funeral."

"I wouldn't have missed it for the world, Dona Bia . . . I mean, I wish I hadn't had to . . . I mean, that he hadn't died . . ."

"I know how fond of Ricardo you were," said Bia, extricating Rose from her embarrassment.

"Dona Bia, I've got to talk to you. There are some things you should know."

"Rose, Ricardo is dead. I don't care what he did."

"No, it's not that," Rose said quickly. "It's about his death."

"Yes?"

"I can't talk from the office, not right now. I'd prefer it if we could meet," Rose said.

"The police are investigating, Rose. There's nothing we can do."

"I think I might be able to help. That policeman was in the office yesterday afternoon and wanted to talk to me and said he'd come back tomorrow. But I'd like to talk to you first."

Then, in a very low voice:

"Please, Dona Bia. I need to talk to you personally."

"All right," said Bia. "When?"

"Today. I can leave in a few minutes, catch a bus, and come right over."

"Fine," said Bia.

She put the phone down. It was a quarter to six. Rose had been to the apartment a few times with documents for Ricardo's signature. She was young, pretty, cheerful—and extremely discreet about anything to do with the company or Ricardo Carvalho. It must be really important.

On the living room table, she spread out the illustrations she had brought from the studio for her new book. The final illustration was still only halfway done. She toyed around with it for a bit but couldn't concentrate and kept checking the time. At eight, the doorbell rang. It was the doorman.

"Dona Bia, a gentleman asked me to give you this envelope."

"Who was it?"

"He didn't say, ma'am, but he insisted I give it to you right away."

"Thank you, Waldir."

As the doorman was leaving, she said, "I'm expecting a young woman named Rose. When she gets here, tell her to come straight up, please."

She didn't open the envelope; she knew who it was from. She was exhausted. Every muscle in her body was tense. Her neck and shoulders ached. It was a cool night, and she decided to relax with a hot shower. She told the doorman she'd be in the bathroom if anyone needed her. She turned on the shower and let the water fall on her back. She was still tense, but she felt a lot better. She put on a baggy T-shirt, got a beer from the fridge, and sat down on the living room sofa to read Júlio's note.

This might have been a really nice moment, if it weren't for what had just happened. When her husband was traveling or out at a business dinner, she often spent the evening alone in that comfortable room, reading, listening to music, thinking about her work, or just thinking. She lived in the penthouse of a modern building, the back of which looked out onto the Parque Lage. At night, the muffled roar of the traffic down below on Rua Jardim Botânico was overpowered by the croaking of the toads and frogs in the park. The apartment was comfortable and furnished impeccably. She had chosen everything: her husband knew what was expensive, but not what was good. She opened the note.

Bia,

I heard about your husband's death a few hours ago. I'm so terribly sorry. I can't bear to think of you suffering. Please call me if you need anything. I hope to see you soon.

With love,

Júlio

She was confused. She was definitely attracted to Júlio; she hadn't felt so comfortable with a man in ages, and life with her husband had become difficult. She knew about Ricardo's affairs, but she also knew how superficial he was. He didn't have real friends, just a network; women were nothing more than a constant reminder of his power to seduce. She really doubted if, even once, he had ever genuinely liked anyone, including her. Júlio was a different story. He belonged to a different world, closer to her own. But Ricardo was barely in the grave, and his life was still as present as his death.

She reread the note. With every reading, the meaning grew fuzzier. Júlio's words got mixed up with memories of Ricardo; images of both men merged. She woke up the next day on the sofa, with the lights still on and the note on the floor next to the beer can. Her body ached even more than the night before. Rose had never shown up.

Two days without working: why sit home waiting to calm down? She sipped her coffee, flipped through the newspaper, got ready, and left. It was Friday. A hesitant, silent rain was falling.

8

The Torres Vasconcelos Gallery's solid reputation in the art world was mainly due to Elísio Sclar's intelligence and sensitivity. It had an equally solid reputation with the banks, but that was because of the support of Alírio Vasconcelos's company, Gráfica Vasconcelos, one of the largest manufacturers of diaries, calendars, and printed labels in the country.

The old two-story house in Leblon had been completely renovated to house the gallery. The walls on the first floor had been knocked down and the side windows blocked up to create one big exhibition room. Everything was white, except a row of black leather benches. At the back of the room, an open staircase with broad steps of peroba wood led to the second floor, where works of art not on display or waiting for auction were stored.

A driveway led to the building behind the house. The three-car garage was on the first floor and Bia's studio was on the second. It had a picture window that looked out onto a huge mango tree in the garden behind the main house.

The studio was big enough for a drawing board and a large worktable cluttered with jars (brushes, spatulas, felt-tip pens, colored pencils). The only wall without windows or doors had bookshelves crammed with magazines and art books. Beneath the window that looked out onto the drive was a chest of drawers for storing paper. A three-seat sofa, comfortable enough to sleep on, completed the furnishings. In the back were two doors that opened onto a bathroom and small kitchen. The studio had its own phone, answering machine, and fax. You accessed the studio by stairs on the side of the building.

At the studio, Bia found only the night watchman and the caretaker. Her father stopped by every morning on his way to work, but neither he nor Elísio had arrived yet. The red light on the answering machine was blinking. A message from Júlio, one from her publisher. Júlio had left the message before he heard about Ricardo's death and made a discreet reference to her talk at the school.

Elísio and Alírio usually arrived around nine. Bia put the coffeepot on and tried to organize the papers and books she had used to get ready for her talk. The computer, containing two versions of the presentation, was gathering dust on the table. She wouldn't let anyone clean the studio; the caretaker was allowed to deal with only the bathroom and the kitchen.

Elísio was the first to come in.

"It's great to have you back," he said happily, trying to assess Bia's emotional state.

He was one of the few people who could tell how she was really feeling.

"Elísio! I guess you're the first friendly face I've seen in the last forty-eight hours."

As she said this, her father, who took longer to climb the stairs, came in, still out of breath.

"And what about me?"

Bia kissed her dad and then her almost-brother warmly.

"Coffee? I just made it."

Outside, a tentative rain continued to drip; the mango tree was blooming, and the smell of coffee filled the studio. The atmosphere was perfect for a personal conversation, but they drank their coffee and talked about Bia's work and the next auction. No one mentioned Ricardo.

When they had left, Bia called her publisher and then Teresa. Both calls took longer than she would have liked. She didn't try to call Júlio; he'd probably be at the university. She dealt with a few more things and then called Planalto Minerações. Cláudio Lucena's secretary answered.

"Dona Bia? How are you?"

"Fine, thanks, Carmem."

"Did you want to speak to Mr. Lucena?"

"No, I wanted to speak to Rose; she was going to bring me some of Ricardo's things."

"Rose hasn't come in today," Carmem said. "When she left yesterday, she said something about going to see you. Maybe she thought she'd stop by today instead."

"Thank you, Carmem."

When Bia hung up, she felt a slight throb in her forehead and a little tremor in her hands. The tremor stopped at once, but the throbbing grew gradually worse. She took an aspirin with some more coffee and sat on the sofa for a few minutes. The rain was heavier now. She decided to try to work, but the next two hours were totally unproductive. She couldn't stop thinking about Rose.

For lunch, she ordered a salad and some orange juice from an organic restaurant down the street. Maybe the headache was from not eating anything the night before and having had only coffee that morning. While she waited on the swivel chair at her drawing board she looked around, studying each object as if for the first time. She felt at ease in the studio; it was hers alone. Ricardo had been there only once, to see what it looked like, and had stayed only about fifteen minutes. He'd left no mark; there were no souvenirs, not even a photograph.

When her lunch arrived, she ate the salad mechanically, barely tasting it, although there might not have been much to taste. She brewed some more coffee and walked around the room with the cup in her hand, skirting the drawing board and the table, nudging a few objects, opening an art magazine that had come in the mail. Just when she was entirely absorbed by the mango tree's green leaves—the phone rang. She wasn't sure if she should let the machine get it or answer herself. She picked it up.

"Dona Bia?"

"Speaking."

"Inspector Espinosa. How are you?"

"Fine, Inspector. What can I do for you?"

"I was hoping I could speak to you alone this afternoon. It won't take long; I can be there in about forty minutes. Okay?"

"S . . . sure. I was about to leave, but I'll wait."

"Thank you. See you soon."

The pulsing in her head, which had stopped, started again. She had never had anything to do with cops before and didn't really like them. She took another aspirin with some more coffee and told the caretaker to bring the inspector to the studio as soon as he got there. There was no point in trying to work, so she lay down on the sofa, closed her eyes, and waited.

A few minutes later, the phone rang again, but she let the machine get it. It was Júlio, saying he couldn't find her anywhere and would try calling her at home later. The call made her slightly more nervous; she went over to the window a few times. The rain had stopped.

Espinosa got there a little sooner than he'd said, a sign that he was in a hurry. A bad sign, she thought. From the window, she saw him walk slowly over to the studio. He didn't seem to be in a rush now. He stood for a while at the top of the staircase, admiring the mango tree. Bia was waiting for him at the door.

"Do you like mangoes, Inspector? These are really delicious."

"And from the amount of flowers, it looks like you'll have a good crop."

"I'll send you some."

"Thanks, but not to the station—policemen can't always be trusted."

The brief dialogue at the top of the stairs helped relieve the anxiety of waiting.

"Come on in, Inspector. Can I get you some coffee?"

"Sure, thanks. Not too much sugar, please. What a lovely studio."

While he was drinking his coffee, Espinosa wandered around the room, studying everything in it: the make of the brushes, the boxes of pencils, every shelf. He wasn't so much investigating as appreciating. Finally, he said, "The brushes and paints are magnificent, but I really love the colored pencils. Brings back childhood memories—not that my pencils were Caran d'Ache."

"Do you know much about art, Inspector?"

"Not really . . . unless, like Thomas De Quincey, you consider murder one of the fine arts." He added: "Have you read Thomas De Quincey?"

"I'm afraid not, Inspector. What did he write about?"

"About crime and his experiments with opium. He had a real passion for murder, though he himself was a very mild mannered Englishman who wouldn't have hurt a fly. He *wrote* about murder; he didn't practice it himself."

"Is he your favorite author, Inspector?" she asked with a slightly ironic smile.

"He's a fine writer," Espinosa replied, "but not my favorite."

"Any writers who don't just write about opium and murder?"

"Oh, yes. I love American literature: Hemingway, Steinbeck, Faulkner, and especially Melville. 'Bartleby the Scrivener' is a masterpiece, and not a word about opium or murder," he added with a smile.

Bia was disconcerted. She hadn't decided if he was a dunce or uncharacteristically sharp. Just to be on the safe side, she decided to assume he was that rare bird, a cultivated policeman.

"But you didn't come here to discuss literature and art, did you?"

"Unfortunately not," he answered. "I'd much rather talk about your art than mine."

While he spoke, his gaze kept skipping around the room.

"Have a seat, Inspector," said Bia, indicating the sofa.

"Thanks." He sat down. "What do you think of Lucena?" he asked suddenly.

"He's a clone of my husband . . . my late husband. You just have to talk to him to know exactly how Ricardo was. Same gestures, same way of speaking, same clothes, same values—maybe even the same lovers. After a while, you couldn't tell who was copying who."

"I've already spoken to him, and to be honest, when he was talking about your ex-husband I thought he was actually describing himself. Can you imagine that he'd want to see his friend dead?"

"Certainly not, Inspector. Lucena wouldn't shoot my husband for some psychological motive. Anyway, I thought it was a case of theft."

"Maybe," said Espinosa, examining some brushes bunched together in a wooden jar. "Your husband dealt with gold and diamonds, both highly explosive substances."

"But not reason enough for Lucena to kill his best friend, Inspector."

"How much does Rose know about his business?"

"A lot, I guess, but not everything. Even I don't know everything."

"Have you talked to her since your husband's death?" The question sounded like a statement.

"I saw her for a second at the funeral."

"But not since?"

"No. She called yesterday afternoon, wanting to come see me. She sounded upset and said she had something important to tell me. I thought she wanted to gossip about Ricardo's affairs, but she said it wasn't about that. She insisted on seeing me rather than talking on the phone."

"When did she call?" asked Espinosa.

"Right before six. She said she'd come by my house after work."

"Did she mention any document?"

"No. But why are you asking me this? I'm sure she'll be glad to cooperate. She was very fond of Ricardo."

Espinosa paused for a few seconds and then said in the same tone:

"Rose has disappeared. She didn't go home last night and she didn't show up for work this morning. No one has seen or heard from her since she left the office yesterday. Did anyone else know she was coming to your apartment?"

"No, I didn't tell anyone about it, but she might have said something to someone at work. Maybe to Carmem, Mr. Lucena's secretary: they're friends and share an office. Rose lives with her mother. Did she go home or leave a note?"

"We just know that she never got to your apartment. I spoke to the doorman and he assured me that you had no female visitors yesterday evening."

Rose had been gone for less than twenty-four hours. In normal circumstances, this would not be very worrisome. In the present situation, though, Espinosa was worried.

"If Ricardo was killed for his money, what connection can there be between that and Rose's disappearance? You don't think she's been killed, too?" asked Bia, almost in a whisper.

"I don't know. I hope not. Call me immediately if she gets in touch with you again."

9

Instead of going back to the station, Espinosa went straight to the park. He wanted to get an idea of how many people were around in the late afternoon and early evening. Welber, a young detective on his team, had been put in charge of checking out the surrounding area.

The park, bigger than a soccer stadium, was thickly wooded; the ground was covered with dense undergrowth. It was crisscrossed by narrow walkways all converging on the mansion that housed the School of Visual Arts, set back about a hundred yards from the street. By day, the park was filled with children and their mothers or nannies; by night, it was frequented by lovers and students attending classes at the school. The massive wrought-iron gates, which provided the only access for cars and pedestrians off Rua Jardim Botânico, were open until ten-thirty at night. There weren't enough groundskeepers to cover the whole park, and there was almost no way to tell who came and went.

When Espinosa arrived, Welber was sauntering down the avenue of trees toward the art school. He looked like a vacationing student: polo shirt, sweater around his shoulders, jeans, sneakers. The look was only thrown off by his untucked shirt, which concealed the gun in his belt. Since the benches in the park were wet from the rain, they sat in the car to talk.

Rose's call to Bia had provided Espinosa with another scenario. If what Bia said was true, Rose would have boarded the bus downtown and gotten off at the stop opposite the park. If someone she knew had been waiting for her, they might have coerced her into the park with them. Rose gets on downtown—six-fifteen, six-thirty—the bus is crowded; no one notices the young woman jammed in between all the other passengers; they're not paying attention. As the bus turns onto Rua Jardim Botânico, she finally gets a seat, but by this point it's almost time to get off; shortly afterward, she rings the bell. Then the possibilities multiply. Rose gets off, walks to the corner, turns right toward Bia's building. It's getting dark, a misty rain is falling, but she doesn't have to go too far; she keeps her head down, covering it with her purse to keep her hair dry. She doesn't see Cláudio Lucena, who grabs her and forces her into a car.

Or on the other hand: Rose gets off the bus and finds Bia waiting for her by the park gates. Bia, in a hooded, waterproof cape, offers the secretary an umbrella and suggests they walk around the park so they can talk without being interrupted; her father's supposed to be there any minute. Rose agrees, and they go down one of the walkways, which, given the time of day and the rain, are deserted. When they're far enough from the avenue, Bia takes a revolver from a pocket in the cape and fires it point-blank. She hides the body in the thick undergrowth or pushes it into the lake; the roar of the traffic had disguised the shot. Bia walks home and waits for the doorman to leave his desk for a minute so that she can slip back in unseen.

In a vaguer version, with an even fuzzier cast of characters, Rose doesn't even get the bus downtown.

"Sir, you're not listening."

"Sorry, Welber, go on."

"At Planalto Minerações, they confirmed that Rose left at six-fifteen. Considering the time she'd need to catch the bus, the rush-hour traffic, and the distance down here, she could have gotten here between seven and seven-thirty. The bus stop is right across from the gates. It's also the closest one to Carvalho's building."

"Did you find out anything from the park employees?"

"No, nothing. I showed them pictures of the secretary and Carvalho's wife, but no one remembers seeing either of them. The cleaning people leave at five, long before Rose could have gotten here. Another problem is that the courses at the school change every day. So the people here yesterday between seven and nine aren't necessarily the same ones who come today. I picked up a copy of the course catalog from the registrar and figure that our only chance of finding someone who could have seen Rose would be next Tuesday. So the likelihood of getting any useful information is about zero. The doorman confirmed what Bia said. She got home around noon and didn't go out again; around eight, a man left an envelope with the doorman and he delivered it personally."

"Did he know him? Had he been to the apartment before?"

"No, he doesn't think so. He didn't leave his name and said he didn't want to go up himself; he just asked for the envelope to be delivered immediately."

"Could he describe him?" asked Espinosa.

"Not really. Around forty, tall, good-looking, deep voice, well-mannered is what I gathered. He said he could recognize him."

Welber paused to emphasize what he was about to say.

"And something interesting. The people in the building don't have a reserved place in the garage. When they get here, they give the keys to the doorman, who parks their car. Most people get here between seven and eight, and the doorman has to get up several times to repark the cars. So our lovely designer could have slipped in during one of those absences."

"Yes, that's interesting," Espinosa remarked. "But I really don't think someone intending to kidnap or kill someone would do it so close to where they live, in a public place, when they just got a phone call from the victim arranging to meet upstairs."

"It could be," continued the young detective, unperturbed, "that someone overheard the conversation, left before Rose did, and waited for her at the bus stop to prevent her from speaking to Bia Vasconcelos."

"A third possibility," said Espinosa, "is that this is all an incredible coincidence and her disappearance has nothing to do with Carvalho's death. But I don't believe in coincidences like that. Try to find out at the company who she might have told she was coming here or who could have overheard her phone conversation. I need to talk to Dona Bia again and find out who sent that note."

Espinosa didn't mention another detail to Welber. It struck him that the doorman said the guy had asked for the note to be delivered "immediately." That might be the doorman's way of intimating that Bia Vasconcelos was home at eight, the likely time of the secretary's disappearance.

After a rainy day, the damp air in the park made it seem colder. The warmth of their bodies and their hot breath had steamed up the windshield. As they were talking, Welber had been doodling; the words now resembled a kind of lace. When they stepped outside again, Espinosa became aware of how thin his linen jacket was. They said their good-byes and Welber went to retrieve his own car from the parking lot.

Espinosa wandered up and down the avenue for a while. Groups of kids walked toward the School of Visual Arts with large portfolios, rolls of paper, canvases, and shoulder bags. He could see the back of Bia's building from there. There was a light on in the penthouse. He was cautious by nature, but just then he felt an urge to ring her doorbell and ask: "Who sent you that note?" He was also worried that his impulse had nothing to do with the mystery but with his desire to see Bia Vasconcelos again. He needed only to walk out through the gates, onto Rua Jardim Botânico, turn the corner, and walk a hundred yards in order to see the only woman who had really made an impression on him since his marriage broke up. He liked everything about her; he resisted the idea that she was involved in those deaths. What was she doing now? He walked slowly through the park, imagining: Bia watching

10

Júlio had been sitting in his car for forty minutes watching the people going in and out of the gym across the street. The facade was glass but he couldn't see the whole second floor. At regular intervals, a line of women in tight, colorful clothing passed by the window, clapping their hands above their heads and kicking rhythmically. Everything there annoyed him: blaring music, stereotyped movements, lurid leotards, exuberant health, no smoking.

He was about to leave when Alba bounced out in a green-and-purple leotard, black leggings, white leg warmers, and sneakers, with a backpack slung over her shoulder. Her smile faded when she saw Júlio crossing the street in her direction.

"Hey, baby," he said, slightly awkwardly, and Alba's face changed completely.

"Don't you 'baby' me!" she said, prodding Júlio in the chest. "You dump me for a whole week to go fuck some rich bitch and then you've got the nerve to come call me 'baby'?"

"She's not a rich bitch," protested Júlio. "She's an internationally renowned designer."

"Oooooh, an intellectual," Alba sneered. "So you spent the week talkin' about art, huh?"

"You don't understand—"

"No, you don't get it, you little intellectual piece of shit. Just remember, you're a so-so brain and a so-so fuck. Plus you're not exactly loaded. So you really don't have much to offer."

She huffed off, thumping his arm with her backpack.

He thought about what she said as she vanished around the corner. He didn't know which hurt more: the so-so brain or the so-so fuck. He wasn't worried about not being rich, although he understood what she was getting at. When Alba had opened the gym with three partners, ex-classmates from the School of Physical Education, she didn't have any money to put in, so her contribution was the architectural plan drawn up by Júlio, which made her a minority shareholder. "Your design's not even worth a fourth of the capital," she'd say when she wanted to hurt him.

The scene underlined the difference between the two women, although Júlio had to admit that Alba had every right to be angry. Her figure was sculpted by daily doses of aerobics, but she was nowhere near as elegant or beautiful as Bia. Nor, for that matter, as cultured: why did she have to talk like that? There was a vast cultural gulf between the Istituto Europeo di Design in Milan and a gym in Ipanema. He stormed off in the other direction.

It was Thursday, two days since Bia's talk and their meeting in the Bar Luiz. The more he thought about Bia, the less he thought about Alba. Next to Bia's discreet elegance, Alba looked like some brightly colored, squawking parrot. But she was there—habit had made her available, familiar. Júlio could have predicted her little scene. She'd probably call that night or—at the latest—the next day, apologize for throwing a fit, and then everything would start over like it always did. He didn't have the nerve to tell her that Bia's husband had been killed. Alba would assume that he was about to make a play for the wife. And she'd be absolutely right, he thought. Anyway, she was a romantic, and murder would only get her going. He wouldn't wait for her; he'd call first and invite her out for Chinese.

He didn't want to hurt her. They'd met a little more than two years ago, a year before the gym opened. Since then the relationship had been good for both of them. Once when he'd been thinking about it, he'd decided the word "satisfactory" summed it up. She's probably right, he thought now. Maybe a relationship that's just satisfactory is by definition boring. Boring brain, boring in bed. "Habit breeds mediocrity." He said this last sentence out loud, attracting a few stares. It was six and the streets of Ipanema were packed. Tourists laden with shopping bags were returning to their hotels; as he walked he noticed that the crowded buses were moving even more slowly than he was.

11

It was past nine when he got home. He took a long shower and then called Alba, who answered after the first ring, sounding perfectly normal. One of the good things about her was that she never stayed mad. She loved the idea of Chinese. "So healthy!" They had made their peace by the time they reached the restaurant. Bia wasn't mentioned once, although she was very much there the whole time. Júlio kept waiting for the moment when the thought would be put into words, but it never was. There wasn't that much to talk about; the sequence of events was entirely unsurprising. When they left the restaurant, she would say: "Your place or mine?" He would choose to go to her place, not because it was closer or more comfortable but for strategic reasons: in case of an argument, he could easily bail. He didn't know whose fault it was that their relationship had atrophied: hers or his, for underestimating her.

Her apartment was at the rear of the building, on one of the upper floors, looking out over a hillside slum only about a hundred yards away. From her window, Alba could see samba dancing, gunfights (the wall of her building was pockmarked by stray bullets), family arguments, the collapse of shacks in the rainy season, and the fireworks that announced the arrival of a fresh supply of drugs. Occasionally, she'd witness the show put on by the police going up the hill with a TV crew, finding "yet another major haul of drugs, arms, and munitions" and the imprisonment of a few child thieves labeled as dangerous bandits. The following day it would be the lead news story.

But that night things didn't go according to schedule. Alba didn't ask where they'd spend the night—Júlio suggested her place; the slum was quiet; and the expected argument about Bia never materialized. They made love as usual and went to sleep. The next morning, after flipping through the paper and drinking her coffee in silence, Alba suddenly asked:

"So who killed Bia's husband?"

"How do you know about that?"

"It was on TV, and then I saw it in the paper."

"I don't know, it was probably an attempted robbery or kidnapping."

"The news said they haven't ruled out revenge killing or a crime of passion."

"That's what they always say when they don't have anything to go on." Júlio shrugged as coolly as possible. He said a quick goodbye: "Gotta run, babe. I've got to drop by my apartment before I head to school."

On the way, he tasted the sour aftertaste of Chinese food. At home, he shaved, changed his clothes, and called Bia's apartment. She'd already left, so he tried the studio. The machine picked up. It was the last day of the Week of Art and Visual Perception. He went to the university. Another boring Friday.

12

Espinosa hadn't cleaned his apartment for the last two Saturdays. His cleaning lady said he didn't really need to clean so much as get organized. This, she said, had to be done before she could get down to cleaning. Espinosa had instructed her to clean everything but move nothing; she thought this was impossible, mainly because of the books. He thought she was absolutely right.

He lived in the Peixoto district in Copacabana, in an old three-story building with no elevator. His apartment was on the top floor, facing the square. Apart from the books wildly scattered everywhere, it was in reasonably good order. The other residents knew he was a cop, although he'd never actually told any of them.

His family had been the first to move into the building back when, its white walls still smelling of fresh paint, it was a clean slate. Their old home, with all his childhood memories, had been in the Fátima district downtown. In fact, most of his memories—childhood or otherwise—were related to the house in Fátima; few memorable things had happened to him since they'd moved all those years ago. He realized now how few vivid memories had been created since they had lived in that old house, when his parents were still alive. Then, the only death that had touched him deeply was that of a puppy, a gift from one of his dad's friends. The very intensity of those memories, infused with the smell of rain in the garden, made him feel he could recall every instant of those childhood years. He couldn't say that about his first few years in Copacabana, which had been almost entirely forgotten.

His father had died a little more than a year after his mother, and the images of the two funerals had become confused in his memory. He was fourteen. His maternal grandmother had moved into the apartment in Peixoto to take care of him and his education. With her came the books. She was a proofreader. The books linked their two worlds; his love of reading and his perhaps overdeveloped fantasy life both dated from those days. Their relationship had not been without its difficulties, but it had always been lively. Just before his twenty-first birthday, he was summoned to have a talk with his grandmother. She said she'd stayed longer than necessary and felt it was time to go back to her small apartment in Flamengo, where she stored the rest of her books and her personal history. "I'm leaving before the roles are reversed and you have to take care of me." She didn't live much longer; she died from her best part, her heart. With her he lost his only known relative, and ever since he'd been responsible for his own survival. His inheritance was his parents' apartment, his grandmother's books, and just enough money to cover the funeral of the only person he'd loved for the past eight years.

It was Saturday, so he decided not to call Bia Vasconcelos before eleven. He started gathering the books piled by the armchair and the sofa, on top of the table, by the bed, on the bedside tables, and on the chairs. He intended to make bigger piles along one of the walls. Nothing definitive, but a start. It proved to be slow going because he kept stopping to reread pages he happened across. By eleven, he'd built a shelfless bookcase by lining books up along the wall and separating the rows with other books, lying flat. The pile was waist-high and took up the entirety of the only bare wall in the room.

He stood for a while, contemplating his feat of engineering. He washed his hands, which were black with dust, and called Bia. The machine picked up, and he left a message. The next half hour was unproductive. Realizing she must be asleep but finding himself unable to do anything else until he'd spoken with her, he abandoned his attempt at sorting out books to wait for her to wake up. Just before noon, the phone rang.

"Inspector Espinosa?" asked the now familiar voice.

"Yes. How are you, Dona Bia? Sorry to bother you on a Saturday morning."

"No problem, Inspector. Any news?"

"Not really," he answered. "Could I drop by your apartment? I won't be more than five minutes."

"As long as it's just five minutes. I'm having lunch with my father. Is it something important?"

"I promise it'll only be five minutes."

"All right. I'll be here."

"Thanks, I'll be there soon."

The previous night's rain had washed the air clean, and it was a beautiful spring day by the time he arrived at Bia's apartment. She was dressed and ready to go out; her face bore no trace of the week's events.

"Good morning, Inspector. Don't you ever get any rest?" She said this with a friendly tone; her smile seemed genuine.

"Well, I do, but sometimes I wish I didn't."

He continued: "If I'd gone to Rose's apartment on Thursday night instead of going home and waiting to question her the next day, she might not have disappeared."

"How can you think that, Inspector? How were you supposed to know she'd disappear or that she had important information?"

"Dona Bia, my job is to have such suspicions. But I made the mistake of resting. Anyway, I don't want to use up my five minutes talking about things we already know."

"I have more than five minutes now, Inspector. My father said he'd come pick me up. We can talk until he gets here."

"I just need to know one thing," said Espinosa. "Who was the man who left you a note on Thursday night at eight?"

The atmosphere chilled immediately; warmth gave way to defensiveness. She stiffened, and her smile vanished.

"Is that important?" she asked coldly.

"It might be. I don't know yet." Then: "Was it the man you were with in the Bar Luiz on Tuesday?"

"It was."

"I'm sorry, but I need to know his name and, if possible, his address and phone number."

"His name is Júlio Campos de Azevedo. He teaches at the architecture school. We were both at an art conference at the university, and he gave me a ride back. He very nicely invited me for a drink. It was the first time we'd gone out together. I don't know where he lives; I only have his phone number."

All this was delivered in a flat monotone.

"May I see the note?" asked Espinosa.

"I'm not sure where it is. I'll have to look."

"I can wait."

She found the note and handed it to Espinosa. He read it several times and remarked:

"For someone who's only been out with you once, ma'am, he expresses himself very intimately, don't you think?"

"He's just being nice, Inspector. Not everyone's a policeman."

He noted the name and number and left, certain that he'd blown it. Until then, he'd played the courteous, understanding policeman. He didn't know if he'd managed to conceal his attraction to her. From now on, though, she'd probably see him as a busybody cop trying to invade her privacy. The way she'd said good-bye left little room for doubt.

He found a pay phone and called the number she'd given him. Júlio's recorded voice told him that he wasn't home, but gave instructions—"if you'd like to send a fax . . ."—and repeated the message in English and French. International business or a way of impressing clients? He immediately called the station and asked them to trace the address. The reply surprised him: they were practically neighbors. Júlio lived a few blocks away, on Rua Santa Clara, in a two-story house that served as both home and office. A visit to the house and a quick chat with a neighbor of Júlio's confirmed this.

He spent the rest of the afternoon dealing with his books at home, or at least trying to make it look as if he'd tried. After an hour, he realized he was just shifting piles. Rearranging the chaos.

Scenes begin to insinuate themselves into his mind, always involving Bia and a man, presumably Júlio. Espinosa had never met him, so he was a very vague figure, only acquiring more character—closely resembling Espinosa himself—in the more amorous scenes. He grew hazy again when the couple was plotting Ricardo Carvalho's death or luring Rose into a trap. The scenes gradually gave way to isolated images. Toward the evening, he'd almost convinced himself that it was highly unlikely that two young, good-looking (he was sure Júlio was good-looking too), successful, cultured people would carry out a murder, possibly two, running the risk of spending the rest of their lives in prison. After all, there wasn't any indication that this was what had actually happened; the whole thing was just a figment of his imagination.

It was now night and the room was dark. He'd lived alone for a long time. He turned on the light, went into the kitchen to check out the fridge, and decided instead to go out for a pizza.

13

Júlio thought about every moment since his meeting in the Bar Luiz with Bia and concluded that something had changed. Ricardo Carvalho's death had opened a new distance between them. She didn't return his calls or acknowledge the note he'd left with the doorman—nothing suggested the more interested woman he'd talked to at the bar. On the other hand, he understood that a husband's death was cause enough to shake any woman and make her shrink back temporarily.

He was confused and scared. Bia wasn't just any woman: her mere presence could push him to the edge. He felt like she was asking him to do much more than he possibly could—without ever actually demanding or requiring anything at all. He didn't know what to do next; he didn't even know if he should take the initiative or wait for her to get in touch with him. Then there was Alba, body sculpted by aerobics and head sculpted by TV soap operas. A sweet thing, who only wanted to be happy forever—which, Júlio thought, meant getting married and having kids. Júlio was thirty-eight, had been married twice and had two kids, and didn't have any intention of going down that road again. He'd never been very daring. Until now, his life had been marked by prudence, rarely exceeding the circumscribed limits he'd set for himself. The combination of teaching college and professional practice gave him the stability he needed for what he thought was a life without ugly surprises.

Since it was Sunday, he let himself stay in bed until noon. Without Alba, he could turn himself over to thoughts of Bia without feeling bad about it. He drank a strong coffee, got dressed (he didn't like to sit scruffily at home, even by himself), and was starting to sort out the materials he'd need for his class when the doorbell rang. Annoyed, he imagined it might be Alba. He didn't feel like seeing her. Still, he tried to smile when he opened the door.

"Professor Júlio de Azevedo?"

"That's right."

"Good afternoon, Professor. I'm Inspector Espinosa, from the First Precinct."

Júlio was so surprised that the whole sentence didn't quite click; he only registered the words "Inspector" and "Precinct" as he squinted at the badge Espinosa was holding up.

"Excuse me," he asked. "Inspector . . . ?"

"Espinosa."

"From the police?"

"Yes," said Espinosa, without repeating the precinct number. "Can we go inside? I'd like to speak with you for a moment."

"Please, come in."

"I'm sorry I came without calling first, but we're practically neighbors and I thought I'd stop by to see if you were home."

"Of course," said Júlio, as if having a police officer stop by on a Sunday afternoon were the most natural thing in the world. "Would you like some coffee, officer? I just made some."

"Sure. With only a little sugar, please."

(Kindness or a way of getting over the scare? wondered Espinosa as he looked around him.) The two rooms were separated only by an arch. The first room was smaller, but comfortable and decorated in good taste. The second looked like an office. From his seat, he could see a drawing board and a table with a computer and a printer. Júlio came back bearing a tray with two espresso cups and two glasses of water, which he put on the little coffee table.

"What brings you here, Officer?" he asked, clearly already over the shock.

"A meeting, a note, a death, and a disappearance," Espinosa replied, as if he were giving the minutes of a co-op meeting.

"What?" said Júlio, smiling. "Could you be a little more specific?"

"Let's start at the beginning," said Espinosa. "You know Bia Vasconcelos?"

"I do, we're friends, but what does she have to do with this?"

"How long have you known her?" Espinosa continued, ignoring the question.

"For exactly a year. We met last September during a conference at the university. We ran into each other at a couple of gallery shows, and I saw her again a week ago, when we were both on the panel at this year's conference."

"That's it?" asked Espinosa.

"Yes. What are you trying to suggest?"

"You didn't meet last Tuesday downtown at the Bar Luiz?"

"We didn't meet at the Bar Luiz," Júlio replied. "We left the conference together, I offered her a ride because she didn't have a car, and I suggested we have a beer to relax after three hours of speeches and debates."

"And when did you leave?"

"Around six."

"An hour before Bia Vasconcelos's husband was murdered."

"What does one have to do with the other?"

"That's what I'm trying to find out, Professor. What did you do after the meeting?"

"I went to the Papelaria União, on Rua do Ouvidor, to buy drawing materials."

"What did you buy?"

"Some tracing paper and ink."

"Do you have the receipt?"

"Of course not, I don't keep receipts for everything I buy."

"And on Thursday, early in the evening, where were you?"

"In Ipanema, at a friend's gym. Then I went to Jardim Botânico to leave a note for Bia. I heard that day about the death of her husband."

"And did you hear anything about the disappearance of the secretary?"

"What secretary?"

"Rose, Ricardo Carvalho's secretary, vanished on Thursday, around seven-thirty, on her way to Bia Vasconcelos's apartment."

"I'm hearing about it now, Officer."

"You don't think it's strange that you were in the same place at the same time as both of these unfortunate occurrences?"

"From what I can tell, both the crime and the disappearance took place in very busy areas, where there were thousands of people around. I was only one of them."

"Surely," Espinosa went on. "But you were the only one, as far as I know, who was in both places. You could have heard from Dona Bia that on Tuesdays her husband left work around six-thirty. The Papelaria União is practically next door to Planalto Minerações; you could have followed Ricardo Carvalho into the parking lot."

"Very clever, Officer. And what did I do with the secretary? Did I kill her too?"

"I'm not saying you killed anybody. I'm just pointing out coincidences and imagining scenes. Not even hypotheses, just fantasies."

"And what's your fantasy about the secretary?"

"In her case, you would have had to have the help of someone who knew she was going to Dona Bia's apartment on that day and at that hour."

"Your fantasies, as interesting as they are, Officer, don't take into consideration an important question: why would I kill two people I didn't know and whose deaths wouldn't help me in any way?"

"The contents of the note you left for Dona Bia suggests an intimate relationship."

"But only suggests," Júlio replied. "In fact, there isn't any intimacy at all between us. I'll say again that the only time we've ever been alone together was at the Bar Luiz on Tuesday afternoon. I agree that the note had a certain tone, but that's just how I express myself. Besides, Officer, I can't believe that in this day and age you think that just because a man is interested in a married woman it follows that he goes out and starts killing husbands and secretaries."

"You're right. Lots of businesses would have to close their doors," said Espinosa, smiling. "But, like I said, they're just fantasies."

And getting up to go:

"Just one more thing, Professor. After you left the note with the doorman, what did you do?"

"I went home and then went out with the girl I mentioned before."

"The one from the gym?"

"Yeah."

"How could I get in touch with her?" Espinosa asked. "Just off the record, nothing that would worry her."

"I must have a card from the gym somewhere," Júlio said, heading toward the other room. In less than half a minute he was back, with a card between his fingers.

"Here you go, Officer. Her name is Alba Antunes."

"Thank you, sir, you've been very kind. And thank you for the coffee—it was delicious."

Júlio walked the inspector to the door and watched him as he walked toward the street. He was perplexed and scared. Ideas came and went in a blur. It was as if he were in some bizarre fairy tale. Who was that guy? A cop, surely, but what did he truly mean by that visit? Did he really suspect something or was he merely playing a cynical game to try to extract some information? Was he a corrupt policeman trying to lay the groundwork for future blackmail? Or a maniac who enjoyed abusing his authority? It

14

When he got to the gym, at around nine in the morning, several groups had already paid tribute to beauty. The receptionist, who didn't appear to need to work out at all, looked at Espinosa as if he were something out of an album of old family photographs. After a quick once-over, she decided he wasn't a candidate for the activities offered by the Ipanema Health Center. He didn't look like a tax inspector—he didn't have a briefcase. For the same reason, he didn't look like a salesman. He could be the husband or boyfriend of one of the students, despite his age.

Thrown off guard by the receptionist's inspection, Espinosa took the initiative.

"Hello. I'd like to speak with Ms. Alba Antunes."

"Who can I tell her is here?" stuttered the secretary, looking surprised that Espinosa could speak.

"My name is Espinosa."

"And what company are you from?"

"What do you mean?"

"You're not here from any company?" insisted the girl.

"In a way, yes," Espinosa replied, smiling, "but I'm here about a private matter."

"Just a minute, please, I'm going to see if she's in a class," she said, starting to punch a series of buttons on the telephone.

A glass wall separated the reception area from a big room filled with equipment. There were StairMasters, stationary bikes, weight benches, and an endless number of other gadgets, all occupied by sweating young people of both sexes. If it hadn't been for the abundance of mirrors, the intense illumination, and the music that pumped out of the second floor, it could have been the torture chamber of a medieval castle. While he was waiting, Espinosa glanced from the weight room to the secretary's shirt, cut so low on all sides that it resembled a bib. The girl finally got lucky with one of the buttons.

"Albinha, there's someone here to see you." After several seconds of listening, she said: "Mr. Espinhosa."

"Espinosa."

"Mr. Espinosa," she repeated. "He says it's personal."

"Tell her Júlio gave me her address," he interrupted.

She repeated it, moved her gum around in her mouth a few times, stuck her finger through a hole in her shirt and, after a couple of "uh-huh"s, hung up.

"You can take the stairs on the other side of the weight room. Third floor."

Espinosa walked across the weight room like a priest walking through a nudist colony. Even though he was used to walking up three flights of stairs in the building where he lived, the two flights at the gym left him slightly out of breath. He didn't know if it was from the display of muscled youth around him or from the secretary's shirt.

Alba's office was an aquarium of glass in the back of the third floor. It was furnished with a big table with a half dozen chairs around it, two metal filing cabinets, and a kind of built-in closet that occupied one of the side walls. The back wall was plastered with posters of the Olympics. The only feminine touch was the vase of flowers in the middle of the table. Alba was sitting down, filling out forms. She smiled and extended her hand.

"You're a friend of Júlio's?" she asked, still smiling and inviting him to sit down in front of her.

"Not exactly. We met yesterday afternoon and talked for a while at his house." He paused. "I'm Inspector Espinosa, of the First Precinct."

"Police?" asked Alba, wrinkling her nose. "Police inspector? Did something happen to Júlio?"

"No, don't worry."

"I know!" she said. "It's about the husband of that chick Júlio's been going out with."

"Has he gone out with her?" Espinosa pounced, but Alba had already gotten over her surprise and was back on the defensive.

"Are you investigating the death of the businessman?"

"I am."

"And do you by chance suspect Júlio?"

"Do you think I should?"

"Officer, if that's why you've stopped by, I think you're on the wrong track. I don't know anything about his relationship with the executive's wife. But anyway, Júlio would never kill anyone—he can't even fight with me, no way he could kill a man. As far as I understand, someone can kill someone else by accident, or because of an uncontrollable impulse, or after premeditation. From what I read in the papers, it wasn't an accident. Júlio doesn't have uncontrollable impulses—he errs on the side of too much control in everything he does. And premeditation? Out of the question. He doesn't have the nerve. So if Júlio's a suspect, Officer, you better keep looking."

Espinosa felt like clapping. Not only did the girl have a good figure, she also had a good head.

"Dona Alba, I didn't say Professor Júlio was a suspect. Actually, right now I'm not looking for suspects, just trying to clear up some coincidences."

His serious, slow tone calmed Alba down.

"The professor told me that on Thursday he was with you until six o'clock and that at nine you went to a Japanese restaurant."

"Chinese."

"Sure, Chinese. I don't care about the restaurant's nationality, I'm just looking at the times and a few subjective details. For example. How was the professor feeling when you left at six and when you saw him again at nine?"

"We didn't split at six, but at six-thirty. I don't think I left him in a very good mood. I fought a lot with him."

"May I ask why?"

" 'Cause he hadn't shown up for a week. I think he was hanging around that Bia Vasconcelos."

"You think or you're sure?"

"I think. He told me he was only with her on Tuesday, during a meeting at the school."

"Did he mention having been with her in a bar downtown after the conference?"

"No, but that's just like him. Júlio is a seducer, and it's just as natural for him to seduce as it is for a dog to wag his tail. They both do it for the same reason: attention, a little bit of affection. He's not a conqueror, he's just nice and attentive and sweet, and women love that."

"And even though you fought, you went out to eat together just a few hours later?"

"Júlio knows I blow up. I get really mad, but then it passes and I don't hold a grudge; when he called and asked me out for dinner I was already over it."

"And how was he?"

"Fine, calm, like always."

"Thank you very much," said Espinosa, getting up, "you have been a great help. In case you remember anything that could be important, here's my card." And as he was leaving: "Your gym is very nice."

"Júlio designed it," she said with a smile.

On the way out, he said good-bye to the secretary—one more chance to remember what she looked like.

One thing Espinosa had to give Júlio: good taste in women. Even though they were different, Bia and Alba had three things in common: beauty, brains, and independence. While he was driving, he compared the two women. Bia's looks were more aristocratic and her sensuality expressed in small details; Alba's were more wild and her sensuality, like the rest of her, explosive. Culturally, Bia's superiority was unchallenged, but emotionally, Alba seemed richer. Bia was surely more interesting; Alba, in spite of her extreme personality, was more straightforward yet still had a relaxing presence. Without realizing it, Espinosa was tallying up the same characteristics Júlio had on Thursday when he was leaving Ipanema and heading for Jardim Botânico.

He didn't consider Júlio and Bia suspects. Even though he believed that the capacity for killing existed in everyone, in criminals and in saints (maybe even more so in the latter), Espinosa also believed that powerful forces worked to prevent this capacity from materializing into action. There were simply too many obstacles for Bia and Júlio. Both of them were young, good-looking, professionally successful, with no financial problems, emotionally stable, with unblemished pasts and promising futures. It was enough to prevent anyone without an apparent motive from committing a premeditated (at least, so it seemed) murder. Even though he knew that placid housewives could commit hideous crimes, Espinosa couldn't quite accept the hypothesis that either of these two people, or both, had committed the crime.

He tried to imagine Bia leaving the Bar Luiz, making the taxi stop two blocks away, "casually" running into her husband, kissing him warmly, and walking arm in arm to the parking garage, only to kill him once they got in the car. It didn't make sense. He couldn't see Bia as a cool, calculating assassin. And above all: why would she do it? After all, if Ricardo Carvalho wasn't the ideal husband, at least he let her do whatever she wanted. He was so self-centered that he wouldn't even have noticed if she was having an affair. He gave her money and freedom. All she had to do in return was show up and look pretty at the occasional social event.

The same reasoning applied to Júlio. He didn't have any relationship with the dead man; he didn't even know him. His relationship with Bia was far too fresh to inspire such a sweeping, passionate gesture, and one whose final outcome was so uncertain. According to both of them, the only thing that they had shared was a beer. He was inclined to believe what Alba had said: Júlio didn't have the daring or the rashness—or the motive—to commit the crime.

It was time to explore other avenues, so he decided to start with the dead man's firm, Planalto Minerações.

15

He left the car at the station lot and walked to Rua do Ouvidor. He didn't like Planalto Minerações, he didn't like the executives of Planalto Minerações, he didn't like what Planalto Minerações did, but, all the same, there he was. He didn't have to show his badge—the receptionist recognized him as soon as he walked in.

She didn't look surprised when he asked to talk to the president. He sat down as if he had a long-scheduled meeting. The receptionist pressed a key on her phone, announced his name in a low voice, answered a few questions, and turned to Espinosa:

"Dr. Daniel will see you. Just a minute, please."

Like all the rooms, the reception area was done in black, gray, and white. The only colors came from the flowers in the vases and the clothes people wore. The CEO's secretary came to get him herself. She wasn't tall or blond or pretty. She looked more like a mother superior than a secretary; she didn't have a determinate age or gender.

"Hello. Be so good as to follow me."

It wasn't an invitation—it was an order.

After passing through a hall and two rooms, they came to the CEO's office. Except for the size, it didn't look much different from Cláudio Lucena's office: the same absence of colors, the same kind of furniture, the same sterility. There wasn't a single excessive object, not even gracing the big glass-topped table, behind which Daniel Weil was seated. He got up to greet Espinosa.

"Hello, Officer. I hope you've come with some news that will help clear this up." He spoke as if he were opening a directors' meeting.

"I'm afraid, Dr. Weil, that nothing has been cleared up yet. I've come to ask for your help."

Espinosa understood it was a game: this man hadn't gotten to be the CEO of a multinational corporation merely because of his puffed-up speechifying. But he also knew the old man was susceptible to that kind of adulation.

"How can I help you?"

"By talking to me about Dr. Ricardo: what kind of work he did, how he got along with the other directors, and anything that you think might throw some light on the crime."

Daniel Weil spoke for an hour and ten minutes, an oration fit for a parliament. He talked about his rise in the business, his big international deals, his benevolence toward needy communities, his vaccination campaigns in Africa and in war-torn Asian lands, how he provided new technology to people working little pick-and-shovel mines in the Northeast, and the dedication of the company's workers, from the most humble all the way up through Ricardo Carvalho and Cláudio Lucena. Not a single reference to the disappearance of Rose.

Espinosa left reeling. He'd need some time to let the old man's smoke screen blow away. Not only had the figures of Ricardo and Lucena gotten fuzzier, but he could no longer distinguish between Planalto and the Rotary Club. The skill with which the old man obfuscated was impressive. After the interview concluded, Espinosa had asked if he could talk once more to Dr. Cláudio Lucena. The old man had agreed, a little put out, clearly of the opinion that after his speech there would be little else left to say. But he arranged a visit with Lucena nonetheless.

Lucena, although he was smooth and smart, had a weak point: narcissism. Well fed, he could furnish something useful, even when talking to a police officer. Espinosa still found the man's soft, droning voice annoying, but he emerged from his long conversation with a few interesting tidbits.

Planalto Minerações was a subsidiary of a multinational with offices in Brussels, Amsterdam, London, and Rio de Janeiro. Its business was locating and extracting gold in the Third World. It had ample capital and modern technology. Since it wasn't concerned with buying land, only exploiting the subsoil, it made deals with property owners great and small, which often meant familial and political conflict. This was where Ricardo Carvalho had proven such an implacable negotiator. It became clear that this was now Lucena's job. The rest of the conversation was purely rhetorical. Not a single question about Rose. If the workers of that company were dedicated to their bosses, the reverse didn't seem to be true. As they were saying their good-byes, Espinosa asked:

"Could I talk to your secretary for a couple of minutes?"

"Of course, Officer. I'll make sure you have all the time you need."

Dona Carmem was tall and thin, with pronounced bones, and her skin was naturally dark; she was neither pretty nor ugly, with attentive black eyes and a professional smile. Like Rose, she'd been chosen as the result of a competitive process. She'd been working at Planalto Minerações for four years and knew more about Cláudio Lucena than he did himself. She was well paid; in return, she was expected to be competent, dedicated, and discreet. They met in the empty executive conference room. She waited for Espinosa to take the initiative.

"Dona Carmem, we're not only dealing with a murder but with the disappearance of your colleague. I need your help in both cases."

"I don't know how I can help you, Officer."

"First of all, by telling me about Rose."

"I can tell you about her as a coworker, but I don't know much about her personal life. We've worked together ever since I came to Planalto Minerações four years ago, but we never really became personal friends."

"Has Rose been with the company longer than you?"

"Yes. When I was hired she'd already been here almost a year."

"Was she selected the same way you were?"

"Yes. But the final decision was made by Dr. Ricardo, who was going to be her boss."

"Is that how it was with you?"

"That's how it is with all the executive secretaries. The company makes a selection, but the final decision is made by the person you're going to work with. That seems reasonable, since it's a very close, very time-consuming relationship."

"Did you two talk a lot? Did you talk about your problems?"

"Naturally. Our offices are next to each other and, except on special occasions, we keep the door between them open. When the directors are busy with a project or closing a deal, we hardly have time to see each other, but when things calm down, we have time to talk."

"Was she any different on the day or days before Ricardo Carvalho's death?"

"No, except on Thursday afternoon, when she called Dona Bia."

"Did you overhear what she said?"

"No. I just heard her call and say Dr. Ricardo's wife's name; after that she closed the door that separates our offices."

"Do you remember what time she left on the day Dr. Ricardo died?"

"They left almost at the same time. She must have taken the next elevator."

"Did she seem different that day?"

"No. I didn't see her much that day. I remember when she left because she came into my office to return some eyedrops she'd borrowed. She already had her purse when she said good-bye. Dr. Ricardo and Dr. Lucena had just left."

"You said that the relationship between a secretary and her boss is very close and very time-consuming. How close was Rose's relationship with Dr. Ricardo?"

Before the secretary could reply, he added:

"I know it's a delicate question, but your answer could be decisive in helping us find out what happened to your colleague."

"Officer, it's a close relationship, but not an intimate relationship. I plan Dr. Lucena's trips, type his contracts and memos. I know about his doctors' appointments, I send flowers to his wife on certain dates, I know how he's feeling even before he says hello in the morning . . . but I don't sleep with him. I think the same could be said for Rose, although we never talked about it."

"Thank you, Dona Carmem. In case you remember anything that could be important, please give me a call."

Before Espinosa could get up to leave, Carmem put her hand on his arm and asked:

"Officer, do you think Rose is all right?"

For the first time, someone at Planalto Minerações had shown real interest in what had happened to the secretary.

16

After offering Espinosa a drink, Dona Maura ran her finger along the rim of her glass while she told him her story. Her eyes were red from tears new and old; she had the tired voice of someone who'd said everything there was to be said in life. Espinosa had respectfully avoided the plastic-wrapped sofas, destined for more illustrious visits he imagined would never come. The living room was scrupulously clean. The frames above the sideboard were arranged at strict angles to one another, a geometric arrangement with aesthetic pretensions. In a silver frame, standing out from the rest due to its size and central position, was a photograph of Capitán Euclides in uniform. He had been killed by an exploding grenade during military exercises in camp, Espinosa had been told.

When her hands weren't fiddling with her glass, Dona Maura smoothed out her ash-colored print dress or pulled the skirt by the hem, making sure it adequately covered her knees, even though they were covered by the top of the table. The years of voluntary seclusion in the Tijuca apartment had contributed to her general pallor and her premature aging.

She had been as sad as it was possible to be. Or so she thought, until Rose disappeared last week. When her husband died, her daughter was only nine, and since then Dona Maura had only lived for her. The visits of her husband's old friends had with time become more infrequent and finally ceased completely; for a few years now, she hadn't entertained anybody. All her hopes were placed in the tall, thin man with the tired voice sitting in front of her.

No, she hadn't noticed anything special about her daughter, just that she was a little worried after Dr. Ricardo's death, which she thought was natural enough. She hadn't said anything that could provide a clue to her disappearance, and she hadn't mentioned the visit she was going to pay Bia Vasconcelos last Thursday. Rose had always been extremely discreet and didn't talk much about what went on at Planalto Minerações.

She'd had boyfriends, like any girl, and had been thinking about marrying one of them, an army lieutenant, but memories of the endless moves she'd made when her father was alive didn't help her already unenthusiastic love. For the last two years she'd had fewer and fewer boyfriends. Phone calls were rare, and there were practically no male visitors. She seemed to grow increasingly dedicated to the company, even though her mother thought that in places like that men were the only ones who moved up—women could spend their whole lives as secretaries.

In the beginning, Rose talked about Ricardo Carvalho. Dona Maura even noticed a certain enthusiasm, but a couple of years ago, Rose suddenly clammed up. Her mother feared there'd been some falling-out between the director and Rose. For days she wondered how to ask the question, not wanting to meddle in her work, and fearing a response that would confirm her suspicions. At dinner, she danced around the subject before asking. The answer was immediate and accompanied by a wide smile.

"Don't be silly, Mom. I get along wonderfully with Dr. Ricardo."

And she never brought it up again. A new worry, though, took its place in Dona Maura's busy mind. What did "get along wonderfully" mean? Housekeeping and soap operas let her put off the answer for an indeterminable time.

Not once during the conversation with Espinosa did she ask any question or make any comment suggesting that her daughter was dead. She didn't have to; it was clear in the visible fright she displayed every time the phone rang. However innocent the call, it required all of her strength to answer. At one point in the conversation, she offered Espinosa coffee. Out of kindness and because she needed a break. Speaking, even more than thinking, was clearly deeply painful.

Espinosa looked around the room. All the wood was polished. Inside the cabinet, whose front didn't betray a single fingerprint, was the wedding china and crystal, arranged with the same geometric rigor as everything else in the room. It occurred to him that she hadn't invited him to sit on the sofa not because she didn't think he was important enough but because she thought the table was more personal. There, mother and daughter ate breakfast and dinner; there, they talked more than anywhere else in the house. Because he was somehow linked to her daughter, Espinosa was now an intimate. They drank the coffee silently, eyes wandering around the room or fixed on the cups.

"Does your daughter keep a diary?" Espinosa said, careful to keep the verb in the present.

"Not as far as I know," said the lady, surprised by the question.

"You understand, Dona Maura, that we need to get our hands on everything that can provide information about what's happened to Rose, including diaries, letters, notes, phone calls, et cetera. I know that you respect your daughter's privacy, but in these circumstances I've got to examine her room. If you would come with me, you could be of great help."

"Do you think she ran off because she thought she'd be killed too?" the woman asked with teary eyes.

"What makes you think she ran off? Was she being threatened?"

"No, it's not that, it's just that she never left without telling me. . . . Do you think she was kidnapped?" She continued her line of questioning, as if she didn't want to wait for or hear an answer.

"The answer could be in her room, among her personal belongings."

Somewhat reluctantly, Dona Maura led Espinosa into Rose's room. It was extremely neat, which made it easier to examine. The problem was that he didn't know what to look for. He went through closets and drawers, looked under the bed (he always did that), and opened all the suitcases and purses.

"You know her things, ma'am. Is anything missing, any dresses, shoes, underwear? Any suitcases?"

"I already thought of that. No, it doesn't look like anything's missing."

On the shelves were about two hundred books, of reasonable quality. On the shelf closest to the ground, three dark, blank spines attracted Espinosa's eye. They were old daybooks. The ones from the last two years were missing.

Max

Max had tried out a few parking lots in the Zona Sul, where the rich people lived. He didn't really like supermarkets—they were usually frequented by couples or entire families, making action difficult, sometimes even impossible. How was he supposed to hold up a car packed full of little kids who could start bawling at any second? He preferred solitary women—they got scared and handed over everything, hoping to avoid something worse. That's how it had happened the first time. He'd lost his job more than a month earlier and hadn't managed to find another one. Even though he'd graduated from high school, he didn't have any real skills. He'd committed his first robbery out of desperation, but it was so easy—and so lucrative—that he didn't see any reason to go out and look for a job. So that's what he'd been doing for the last year.

He tended to have the most luck in the Menezes Cortes parking garage, in the downtown business district, which was deserted after six. But he was well aware that if he kept hanging out in the same places he'd run a higher risk of getting caught. He never attacked men, especially if they were young and strong—they could fight back, and his plastic revolver wouldn't do him much good then. He wasn't a wimp, but he wasn't ready to come face-to-face with young businessmen who go to the gym and take martial arts. Old guys, though, were fine—they were quick to frighten and never reacted.

He'd already been hidden for more than half an hour behind a column near the emergency exit when he saw a well-dressed businessman carrying a briefcase heading toward a car parked just a few feet away. He was relatively young, tall, strong, with a decisive step—definitely off-limits. He saw him get in his car and roll down the windows. Instead of starting the engine, though, he leaned his head back and lit a cigarette. After a few minutes, he put out the cigarette and rolled the windows back up. Instead of the noise of the engine starting up, Max heard only a muted clap.

He waited a few minutes. No movement inside the car. He looked around to see if anyone was there. Nothing happened. Apparently no one, besides him, had seen or heard anything. He crept toward the car and peered inside. The body wasn't moving. On the front seat, beside the driver, was a briefcase. Next to that was an envelope; on the ground was the revolver the man must have used. He glanced around again to see if there were any witnesses. No one. He opened the driver's door and the inside light went on. He recoiled, startled by the light, and closed the door. Again, he looked around the parking lot. Nothing stirred. He opened the car door once more and slid his hand between the dead man's chest and the steering wheel. The body was pressed against the steering wheel, complicating the search, but he still managed to get his hand on the wallet. He tried to reach the briefcase, sliding his arm behind the dead man, but he couldn't make it. Right when he was about to bail he noticed that the passenger door was unlocked. He closed the door, went around to the other side of the car, and opened the other door. The briefcase was open. Next to it lay an envelope addressed in capital letters: TO THE POLICE. Inside was a wad of bills held together by a rubber band. Hundred-dollar bills. Lots of them. He put the envelope inside the briefcase, next to the revolver, put the briefcase under his left arm, and closed the door. As he was turning around to leave, he thought he saw a woman's silhouette in the doorway to the stairs—but only for an instant; maybe it was just his imagination. He went down the stairs and was soon out on the street.

1

Max was worried about the briefcase. It was too good for someone like him, with gilded, engraved initials—none of which matched his. A little detail, he thought, but little details are what ended up killing people. On the corner of Rua Sete de Setembro, a street vendor was selling big plastic bags. He tried out a few before finding one that covered the whole briefcase. The best fit was white with big red roses, so he took another one, not quite as good, with black and gray squares. The handle was flimsy, so he decided to carry it beneath his arm, gripping it from the bottom. Though he thought he no longer stuck out so obviously, he still decided to get out of the general area as fast as he could. He crossed Avenida Rio Branco and headed for the subway stop in the Largo da Carioca.

In the jam-packed subway car, he kept the bag pressed against his body. In spite of what he had just gone through, he felt, at that moment, like a lowly government clerk heading home after a long day at the office. He thought about the wife who wasn't waiting for him, about the kids he didn't have, and about the house that wasn't his, where, as a favor, he lived in a room far in the back. Suddenly, he was shaken by a fear he'd never had before: What if I get robbed? Obviously no one would ever suspect that he was carrying several thousand dollars, but these days people got held up on the commuter trains, on the buses, in the subway, for no real reason, just to pilfer a little something from the working class.

In the Central do Brasil station he'd have to change trains, but he decided to keep going toward Tijuca—the area around the Central do Brasil was especially sketchy, even more so at rush hour. Besides, he'd found a seat. He thought about moving the revolver, taking it out of the briefcase and putting it in the bag, within reach, so he could fend off any prospective robber. But the operation would surely attract attention—he'd have to open the briefcase, which was inside the bag; take out the revolver; close the briefcase; stick the revolver into the bag, next to the briefcase, which was inside the bag—all in a rush-hour subway car. It was better just to lie low.

How many bills were there in the envelope? A hundred? Two hundred? Were they all hundreds? He calculated: ten thousand, twenty thousand dollars! He'd never seen so much money—and he hadn't even looked in the wallet he'd tossed in the bag. His hands started sweating. Luckily the bag was plastic-coated; otherwise it might get wet and break under the weight of the briefcase. He wiped his hands on his pants—one at a time—so as not to let go of the handle. What else was in the briefcase? He'd seen an envelope. The revolver looked imported—that could be worth something. He started smiling when he realized this was the first time he'd ever robbed a man his own age—and such a risky target, such a strong man. Except, of course, this guy was dead. They must have been about the same age. How idiotic. A young, good-looking, rich guy pumping a shot into his head, just like that. What the hell did he do that for? It couldn't have been for love; rich people didn't kill for love. They killed only for money.

He got out at the Praça Saens Pena. He was far from home, but at least he was also far from downtown, and the area wasn't as dubious. In any event, he couldn't hang out on a bench in the park, like a moron, waiting for some police patrol to ask for his documents. "But of course, Mr. Officer, they're right inside the briefcase, next to the loaded revolver with one burned-out cartridge. Actually, though, sir, I don't have any ID, but my initials are engraved right here." Thank God he was white; he'd run a greater risk of getting approached by the cops if he were black. But even being white, he still had to get a ride to Méier. He also had to get rid of the wallet and the briefcase.

He crossed the plaza and turned onto the first relatively deserted street he found. A few people on the sidewalk, most of them heading home after work. Ahead, a shuttered grocery store with garbage bags piled in front. He chose the one that looked emptiest, dumped the contents onto the curb, and walked to the next block with the empty trash bag held alongside the plastic bag he'd bought. After checking to make sure he wasn't being watched, he removed the contents of the briefcase, making sure to look in every compartment, and did the same with the wallet. He shoved it all in the plastic bag, folded it in the middle. Then he stuck the empty briefcase and wallet into the trash bag, tied it up, and tossed it onto another pile of trash bags in front of an apartment building. Now everything was fine—poor people were always dragging around bundles. His survival strategy was simply to lie low: he was a regular guy, without any particularly distinguishing characteristics. Physically, he was so average that wherever he went nobody noticed him. Socially, he'd been born invisible.

It was almost nine o'clock at night by the time he got off the bus on Rua Dias da Cruz, in Méier. The house, squeezed between two others, was long and narrow. His sister and her two little girls occupied the rooms at the back; in the front one—which took up more than half the house—was the little junk store his sister had opened when her ex-husband left her. There wasn't an inch of empty space. Little pieces of furniture, clothes, shoes, clocks, appliances, dishes, dolls, toys, decorative objects, boxes, cans, bags of every size, a sewing machine, tools, pens, glasses, ashtrays, knickknacks, a wooden airplane propeller hanging from the ceiling. The archeological remains of the working class. In the tiny yard, in the back of the house, the equally tiny room Max occupied had a bathroom whose shower was aimed directly at the top of the toilet seat.

He didn't pay rent—he tossed in a little something whenever he could, when he got lucky at work. He'd changed jobs so many times that no one bothered to ask him anymore exactly what it was he did.

The store was dark; only the bluish light of the TV weakly lit up the hall in front of his sister's room. She responded to his "Hey" without even looking up from the evening soap opera. The girls were asleep. He went through the kitchen, crossed in two steps the little slice of earth they called "the yard," entered his room, turned on the light, slid the bolt across the door, tossed the plastic bag on top of his bed, ripped off his clothes, went right into the bathroom, sat down on the toilet, and had an attack of diarrhea. Conveniently, he didn't have to get off the toilet to take a shower. Without drying off, he put on some shorts and a T-shirt and dumped the contents of the bag onto the bed: the wad of bills he'd taken out of the envelope; the revolver; the money from the wallet, along with a few laminated cards, a photo, some business cards; and the envelope with the handwritten letter. He put all that aside, removed the rubber band from the money, and started counting. He counted too fast, got mixed up, and had to start over again, slower this time. He counted it twice, made sure the bills were all hundreds, and counted one more time. Twenty thousand dollars.

The money from the wallet was by contrast a trifle: one fifty, two tens, and two ones. ID card, driver's license, and a few business cards with phone and fax numbers. No credit cards. The picture was of a woman. Very pretty, Max thought. It could only be the wife. No one walked around with a picture of their mistress in their wallet.

When he picked up the gun, his hands were drenched in sweat. It was a Colt .38 with DETECTIVE SPECIAL inscribed on the barrel. He could probably get about three hundred bucks for it. He removed the bullets, carefully cleaned the whole piece, and hid it inside a suitcase under the bed. Only then did he return his attention to the envelope.

He had to read the letter a few times before it made sense. On the top of the page, in block letters just like the ones on the envelope, was written: TO THE POLICE. Right underneath, also written by hand, was: "The twenty thousand dollars is a payment for disappearing with the gun and this note and filing this case away after not finding the murderer. No one will be compromised. Your conscience will be clear, since you're not stealing anything—I'm giving it to you."

Max couldn't believe his eyes. He turned the paper over again, checked to make sure nothing else was in the envelope, and reread the letter again. Still clutching it in his hand, he let himself lie down on the bed, staring at the ceiling. The guy was completely crazy, he thought. Who shoots himself in the head and then leaves twenty thousand dollars behind for the cops to take off with the gun? It's putting too much trust in corruption. And what if he hadn't died? With all that cash, the police would have finished the job. But why'd he want to hide the suicide?

One thing did make sense to Max: he hadn't stolen the money, he'd just gotten paid for a service. He wrapped up the money and the note in several plastic bags, one around the other, and hid it all in the tank of the toilet. He'd seen that in a movie once. He managed to fall asleep only as day was breaking.

He got up three hours later, surprised by the morning noises. He sprang out of bed, went into the bathroom, sat on the toilet, stuck his hand into the tank, and felt the weight of the floating plastic bags. He got off the toilet and looked at himself in the mirror above the sink. He didn't see a new man; he just saw a worried man. He shaved, got dressed, and decided to get some coffee at the corner bar. He needed to think about what to do, and he could think more clearly in the street than at home. The money he had in his pocket, plus what he'd taken from the wallet, would last him for a few days. He didn't want to go around exchanging dollars left and right—no one would ever believe that he'd received them as legitimate payment. He needed some money now, before he decided what to do with the dollars. He made up his mind to sell the revolver. You could get rid of a gun without creating problems, whereas dollars could raise suspicions of more dollars at home.

He decided to try out the Portuguese guy who owned the bar.

Not interested. "I don't need guns. I've got my fists."

He tried, without success, a few of the shopkeepers he knew. On the bench where the local underground lottery players hung out, they all agreed that he should leave the gun so they could show it to interested parties. They'd report back the next day. He went back home, dug out a box from his sister's store, wrapped the gun in some newspaper, put it in the box, and tied it with string. It had never occurred to him to keep it—he knew that was a one-way street. He had no problems sticking up rich people in the Zona Sul; he knew they'd only lose the money they had on them and maybe a watch or a piece of jewelry—and the world would take it upon itself to replace whatever they'd lost. Killing was another story. That's why he always robbed people with a plastic gun: even in a critical situation he couldn't imagine shooting anyone. He'd never committed any crime in his own neighborhood—he worked only in the Zona Sul and downtown, and he never planned anything. And he worked only when he was running out of money. He was very much aware that the more robberies he committed, the greater his chance of getting caught.

He walked around the neighborhood until lunchtime. He ate lunch with his sister and then went to his room to ponder his next move. No thought of buying a car or fancy clothes. He'd give some money to his sister and the girls, saying he'd won it at the races (even though he'd never been to the races in his life). He could spend a week in Saquarema or Cabo Frio—with a woman, of course. He liked to fuck, he just didn't know how to talk to women.

A week in a hotel—by the first day they'd already have said everything they needed to. They could spend the other six fucking, even though to do that he didn't need to take a trip. He remembered once he'd gone out on a date with a girl to get pizza. He'd spent the whole time staring at his glass of beer and the other tables without saying a word while the girl hummed the first line of an old carnival samba under her breath. Maybe it was better to travel by himself; he wouldn't have any trouble finding women in those places, especially with so much cash in hand. Now he was wondering if he should go to the beach or to the mountains. He'd grown up in Méier, far from the beach, so he wasn't really attached to the sea—maybe it was better to go to Caxambu or Cambuquira. He fell asleep. At four in the afternoon, he woke up, smiled, and dressed to go out.

He walked down Rua Dias da Cruz until he reached the Méier subway stop. He liked the action on the street—it was a relief to be safely anonymous in a big mass of unknown people. He stopped in a bar to have a coffee and the waiter didn't even look at him. In the store windows, nothing really turned him on: he was a survivor, not a consumer. He got home in time to see the evening news. The death of the executive director of Planalto Minerações was one of the lead stories. The police had already started looking for the murderer. "Don't bother," Max thought. "He's already been caught and sentenced to life."

2

He sold the gun for half what it was worth. He didn't care: he had enough money at home. He decided to exchange the dollars little by little, one bill at a time, always in different exchange houses. He burned the dead guy's documents, hanging on to only the picture of the wife and one of the business cards, which he stuck in with the dollars inside the toilet tank. He didn't know why he kept the picture and the card; he didn't have any intention of contacting the widow—he wasn't crazy.

Twenty thousand dollars. If he spent four hundred a month, which was a lot, he could live four years without doing a thing. Stretched out on his bed, hands folded behind his head, he looked around the whole of the little room with a tiny movement of his eyes. He felt a slight discomfort, almost pain. Four years doing nothing—doing what? Locked up in this little fucking cubicle? He'd decided that stickups and robberies were out of the question—he couldn't run the risk of getting caught with all that cash in his house. So what was he supposed to do for four years? Go out every day, pretending he was heading to work, and just hang out, roaming the streets? Sit on park benches in the afternoon, like some old fart?

He'd been locked in his room for a day and a half, thinking. He'd tried to help his sister in the junk store, but he couldn't manage to concentrate on the simplest of tasks. When a customer asked a question, it took him a while to figure out what they were saying—and even longer to try to answer. He decided he'd do better to stay in his room. So that was it: he'd earned his retirement and didn't know what to do with the rest of his life. If he simply hung out and didn't do anything, he wouldn't have anything to spend the money on, and could live on two hundred dollars a month. In that case, the four years would stretch to eight.

He'd always lived by daring, never by planning. And now here he was, stretched out in bed, planning a stupid, miserly future, fearful of being robbed. It wasn't what he'd had in mind for the rest of his days. The key word was "daring." What difference did it make if he were stuck in prison or in that shitty little room in an ugly neighborhood? What most intrigued him was not that the guy had killed himself—lots of people did that for lots of different reasons; what he didn't get was the cash and the note. Why kill yourself and then leave twenty thousand dollars for the police to run off with the gun? The first answer, obvious to Max, was that he didn't want it to look like suicide. And if he wanted it to look like murder, he'd probably want someone else to be blamed for it. But no one kills themselves just to blame someone else. It doesn't make sense. One thing was for sure: the guy really did want to kill himself. He'd done everything so calmly and deliberately. He'd even smoked a cigarette first. It looked like he was listening to music, waiting for his girlfriend. Maybe the guy was Catholic—he knew the Church thought anyone who killed themselves died in a state of sin. But the guy wasn't going to fucking fool *God.*

Suddenly, Max jumped out of bed and stood up, looking at the wall. Of course, damn it! The insurance! The guy had a shitload of life insurance that wouldn't be good if he killed himself! He started to pace around the room—two steps toward the bathroom, two steps toward the door. In one of his trips toward the bathroom he kept going, sat down on the toilet seat, and removed the plastic sack from the tank. He took the card and the picture and replaced the cash. He needed to see if he was right. It was two in the afternoon. For an hour he practiced what to say and do. He got dressed, threw the card and the photo into his bag, bought two phone cards in a kiosk, and went looking for a pay phone sheltered from the noise of the street. He dialed and cleared his throat. When he heard a voice on the other end pick up, his heart started beating faster.

"Hello."

"I would like to speak with Mrs. Ricardo Fonseca de Carvalho, please."

"Speaking."

"Good afternoon, ma'am. I'm calling from the insurance company. I'd like to speak with you about your husband's life-insurance policy."

Silence on the other end. Three or four seconds that, for Max, seemed like hours.

Finally: "I'm very sorry, I'm just not ready to talk about that yet . . . besides, I don't know anything about my husband's life insurance. You should get in touch with his secretary at Planalto Minerações. She takes care of all of his papers."

"Of course. Could you give me her name, please, ma'am?"

"Rose."

"Thank you."

When he hung up, it felt to Max as if his whole plan had just collapsed. That's why he didn't like to plan anything—something always got fucked up, and nothing ever happened the way it was supposed to. He decided to have a coffee at the bar while he thought about what to do next. Maybe it was better that way. The widow could have taken issue with his proposal and he wouldn't have had any way to twist her arm—maybe she didn't care about the insurance money; maybe she'd call the cops. He decided to call the secretary—it was better to deal with her than with the widow. He went back to the phone booth and called Planalto Minerações. The receptionist transferred him to the extension.

"Hello."

"Rose?"

"Yes, who's that?"

"It doesn't matter, honey. Just listen carefully. Your ex-boss wasn't murdered—he killed himself. He set the thing up so it looked like he was murdered. That means he must have had a huge life-insurance policy he didn't want to lose. It so happens that I can prove that it wasn't a murder, he—"

"Who is this?" Rose interrupted. "You're totally insane."

"Don't interrupt, just hear me out," Max went on. "I've got a letter he wrote by hand. If you're a good secretary, you'll know that his briefcase is brown leather with the initials R.F.C. in gold letters on the front. If you still don't believe me, I can give you the number of his ID card and his driver's license. Oh, and his wife is really pretty, if the picture in his wallet is of his wife."

Rose heard everything, petrified. There was no doubt this guy had Ricardo's things. She didn't know what to do—if she hung up, she could lose the contact. She was still completely confused when Max started talking again.

"Listen up. I not only have the handwritten letter—and you can see if it's real or not, because I was in the garage when he killed himself—but I've also got the gun."

Rose couldn't manage a single word.

"So listen closely. If he has an insurance policy, it must be for a lot of money. I could make it worthless—all I've got to do is send a copy of the letter to the insurance company, which would be too bad, because then no one would get anything. So I'm proposing that we divide it up by three, if you manage to talk the widow into it. It's four o'clock. I'll give you an hour to dig out the policies. You must know where they are. You can see how much they're worth and think it over. I'll call back at five on the dot."

He hung up.

He knew that the next hour would be decisive. Not only in determining if he was right about the insurance but also regarding the secretary's values. Maybe she needed a little nudge, a little pressure, a threat; maybe she just wanted to be sure he was telling the truth. He walked around for close to an hour, thinking about the possible ways she could respond. At five, he called back.

"Rose?"

"Y . . . yes."

"Well? Did you find it?"

"Yes."

"Great! I knew you wouldn't let me down. So how much is it?"

"Almost a million dollars."

Max almost collapsed. He completely lost it. He cleared his throat, coughed, and repeated, voice cracking:

"A million dollars?"

He couldn't imagine how much money a million dollars was. It was beyond the realm of the thinkable.

"About," the girl responded crisply, almost professionally. "Depending on the value of the dollar on the day it's redeemed."

She went on:

"How am I supposed to know you're telling the truth? How can you guarantee that you didn't kill Ricardo Carvalho and are just playing around now?" The secretary's voice had changed markedly.

"Honey, because if I'd killed your boss I wouldn't be taking the risk that you'd turn me in."

"But you stole his things."

"A misdemeanor, baby."

"Don't call me 'baby.'"

"All right, honey. Now listen up. We should make a date and I'll show you the letter—you must know his handwriting better than anyone. And I'll tell you how I found it—I'm sure you'll believe me. Anyway, it'd be impossible not to believe me. Before we meet, though, this is what you need to do—"

"I didn't say I was going to do anything."

"I know, honey, calm down and listen. We don't know if the widow is going to be cool with our proposition—"

"Your proposition," said Rose sharply. "I'm not doing any proposition and I think you're nuts."

"Fine, but let me finish. Like I was saying, she could be loaded and not think a million dollars is a big deal, or she could have really strict principles and hate the idea—the same could go for you. Tell her I'm threatening you, that if she doesn't accept the proposal I'll send the letter to the police, and I'll send it to certain people, people who are going to want to pull this deal off themselves—people who aren't very nice. It's a choice: either the three of us make some good money or nobody gets anything. Call her and make a date for tonight around seven. I'm sure you'll be able to talk her into it. After you leave her house, meet me in the Largo da Carioca subway station. Bring some flowers, so I can recognize you. I'll bring the letter."

He hung up before she could say a word.

He was using the same technique he used during robberies: don't give the victim time to think. Secretaries were obedient, disciplined people—she would obey. Rose had had two chances to hang up on him and hadn't—proof that she was interested. Besides, a chance at three hundred thousand dollars doesn't come up twice in the life of a secretary.

As for the widow, she didn't look like a fool: the husband was dead, so why should she refuse his offer? She really didn't have the right to a penny, and here he was, offering her three hundred thousand dollars.

3

Rose waited a few minutes before reaching a decision. She was sure the caller was the man she'd glimpsed in the parking garage. The question wasn't who he was but what to do about him.

Ricardo's personal documents were in a separate file, which she herself had organized. Inside the life-insurance-company envelope there was another one containing the actual policy. The payout was about a million dollars and the beneficiary was Bia Vasconcelos. A million dollars was a lot of money for anyone, but Rose thought the widow could give it a pass. She had a good job and was the only daughter of a rich man: sooner or later she'd have her million.

Which wasn't her own case. It was embarrassing to be a secretary. Her mother had been right when she'd said that only men move up in business—women were secretaries until they died. And as for an inheritance from Ricardo, she thought she had more right to it than Bia Vasconcelos, who didn't even use her husband's name.

The second phone call removed all her doubts about the unknown caller. It wasn't the scheme of a murderer—it was the scheme of an opportunist. An unscrupulous opportunist, to be sure. No one who spies on a suicide and then takes advantage of it to rob the dead person is worthy of respect. She started wondering what he was like. Middle-aged, occasional criminal, impulsive, not much in the way of critical-thinking skills. He couldn't be completely brainless, because he'd figured out the insurance thing. He didn't seem dangerous, but she shouldn't make it easier for him.

The proposition was the first thing. Clever, the idea of threatening Bia Vasconcelos with sending the letter to the police. The *really* good idea was something else, but he hadn't come up with it. He had suggested that he would send the letter to the insurance company out of revenge, in the event Bia didn't comply. He hadn't thought of negotiating directly with the company.

She knew enough about Bia Vasconcelos to know that she'd never let herself be blackmailed. She was too proud—she'd rather let the insurance money go. There would be no dealing with her. It hadn't even occurred to the police that Ricardo hadn't been murdered, and the insurance company would have to fork over a million dollars to the widow. If the letter didn't leave any room for doubt, it would be a perfect negotiating tool: the letter in exchange for five hundred thousand dollars. For the company, it was better to pay half a million than a million, and Rose had enough experience in the business world to know they'd do it. But there were two problems. First, she didn't have the letter. Second, once the proposal was made to the insurance company, they'd try to prove it was a suicide in order not to have to pay anything to anyone.

She'd have to meet the guy who called and convince him to hand over the letter. That problem, depending on who he was, could most likely be solved. The second was more complicated. Obviously, the cops hadn't checked out the crime scene very well. There was so much murder evidence that they hadn't considered suicide—and, given their assumption that he'd been shot by someone else, hadn't looked for powder residue on the dead man's hand. If she tried to negotiate with the insurance company, they could have the body exhumed for another, less routine forensic exam.

These were questions Rose couldn't answer now. The best thing was to get her hands on the letter and delay exhumation as long as possible. Meanwhile, she'd have to find a way to get the guy off the case. She spent the next forty-five minutes cooking up an emergency plan; she could put the finishing touches on later.

The first step was to call Bia Vasconcelos in an anguished voice, making a date . . . and then not showing up. After that she'd have to go home, talk to her mom, pick up some things, find a hotel near downtown, and show up at the Largo da Carioca subway station at nine. Not forgetting the bouquet. That detail summed up, for her, the kind of guy she was dealing with.

It wasn't hard to sell the story to her mother. She was sincerely worked up, and it helped that a lot of the story was true.

"Please, Mom, listen and try not to interrupt me. I know that a while back you thought I was sleeping with Ricardo—now I can tell you that you were right. It started on a trip to the Northeast. Afterward we got together regularly, on the days when he claimed he had to leave the office early to go play tennis. He would wait for me in his car, in the Menezes Cortes parking garage, and then we'd go off to a hotel. This Tuesday I left the office a minute after him. Right when I got to the top of the stairs on the second floor, when I was still in the doorway, I saw a man firing at Ricardo. He saw me, but I ran down the stairs. I was scared and didn't know what to do—I couldn't say why I was there—so I got in the subway and came home. The man must have followed me and found out our address—he called to say he'd kill me if I said anything to the cops—and now he insists on meeting. I don't know what he wants. Maybe he wants to kill me. I'm going to disappear for a while. Maybe he'll lay off or get arrested. You can't tell anyone that I was here today or tell anyone this story. My life depends on your keeping the secret. It's better for you not to know where I am—don't worry, I'll be safe. As soon as things calm down, I'll be in touch."

The old lady wanted to ask questions but couldn't utter a single word. She couldn't make sense of anything she'd just heard. She couldn't speak. She stood mute in the middle of the living room, staring at the china cabinet. Rose took advantage of her momentary paralysis to go to her room and get a few things—just a few, so they wouldn't be noticeable if anyone searched the room. She was about to leave when she remembered her diaries from the past two years. She put them in a little suitcase with the other things. Then she gave her mother a few pointers on what to say if anyone asked, promised she'd be well and safe, and took a taxi to Flamengo.

The Hotel Novo Mundo was accustomed to receiving businesswomen traveling alone. She checked in as a professor from the Federal University of Espírito Santo. She left her suitcase in the room, made sure her clothes would do for the meeting, and had them call another taxi. At nine she was in front of the ticket window in the Largo da Carioca station with a ridiculous bouquet of flowers in her hand.

A few minutes later, a little kid handed her a piece of paper: "Buy a ticket, go to the platform, get on the first train, stay there a few seconds, and then jump out as soon as departure is announced." She did what the note ordered and got out at the precise moment when the car's doors were closing, still carrying the bouquet. The guy was exactly as she'd pictured—a little better looking, maybe.

4

Max walked up to her with a smile on his face. The girl was much as he'd pictured her: obedient, shy, and scared—but he hadn't expected her to be so pretty.

"Sorry about making you get in and out of the train, but I needed to make sure you were by yourself."

"And who'd you think I'd be with?"

"Who knows? You could have talked with the police," Max said a little awkwardly. "But it's fine: what's important is that you showed. Let's go somewhere we can talk." Taking the flowers from her, he steered her toward the exit; he dropped the bouquet on the turnstile as they were leaving.

"Let's go to Cinelândia—we can have a beer there while we talk."

During the walk—neither of them spoke—Rose noticed he was tense, but she suspected it had more to do with his inability to start a conversation than with the situation they'd found themselves in. She finally broke the ice.

"I still don't know your name."

"Max," he said. "Short for Maximiliano."

He was wearing jeans and a jean jacket and a T-shirt with the words I LOVE RIO—with red hearts in place of both of the *o*'s. Rose was wearing the most discreet dress she owned and minimal makeup. No jewelry, and hair up in a bun. Max was charmed by her discretion and tidiness. They got to the restaurant and sat down at a table outside. He ordered a beer and she got a Coke with ice and lemon.

"So," he began. "Did you talk to the widow?"

"I did, but it wasn't easy. At first she was furious—she wanted to call her father, her friends, the cops, but I finally managed to calm her down. But even then she wouldn't believe the story of the suicide. She said that you're crazy, that you killed and robbed her husband and are just trying to take advantage of her."

"And what do you think?"

"I don't know. I'm confused. It's hard to believe that Dr. Ricardo killed himself."

"Well, it was the most obvious and most intentional suicide I've ever seen."

"Dona Bia said you made that up so you wouldn't get accused of murder."

"Honey, nobody saw anything. No one could ever connect your boss's death to me. I didn't need to protect myself from anything. Why would I raise any suspicions about myself if I wasn't totally clean?"

"I believe you," Rose said shyly. "That's why I'm here."

And she went on:

"It's just hard to believe that Dr. Ricardo would kill himself."

"Well, believe it, babe. The proof is right here in my pocket."

And, in a deliberately slow and dramatic gesture, Max drew an envelope covered in blue plastic from his jacket pocket. He carefully unfolded the plastic, removed the letter from inside the envelope, and slid it across the table.

Rose read it a few times, without touching the paper. There was no doubt about it. The letter was from Ricardo; she knew that handwriting better than her own. What made her reread it several times was the content. She knew how sly Ricardo was, but she never thought he'd be capable of pulling off a stunt like this. Negotiating with the police, even after he was dead, sure of coming out a winner: she couldn't help feeling a certain pride.

"And what about the twenty thousand dollars?" she asked.

"It's all true. I've got the money," Max answered, and then went on: "Do you understand what's happening? We're not doing anything wrong. The money was for whoever made off with the gun. It just so happens that I showed up before the police got there. I did exactly what he wanted. I have a right to that money."

"Yeah, but the money was to hide the suicide, and now you want it plus the insurance money. If we do that, we're betraying Dr. Ricardo."

"Honey, we're not going to publicize the suicide. We're just gonna cut a deal with the widow. Besides us, no one is going to know anything, unless the wife doesn't come around."

"I don't think she will if she can't see the letter," Rose said.

"Fine. We'll make a copy and show it to her."

Rose knew her next steps would be decisive. She asked him to put the letter back in the envelope and sat for a few seconds staring at her glass, thoughtful. Finally, she whispered, looking into his eyes:

"Max, I believe you. I believed you when you called and I believe you even more now. I've never done anything like this and I don't feel like I'm doing anything wrong. I don't want to spend the rest of my life as a secretary in that company. With that money I could buy myself an apartment. I live with my mother in a rental. I could open a business, a little shop . . . but only if Dona Bia agrees. I can see her letting go of all that money, just so she doesn't have to share it with us."

"But she can't be that stupid," said Max, outraged.

"It's not stupidity, it's pride. You don't know her. Money's not a problem for her. She's the only child of a rich father. As incredible as it may seem, a million dollars is going to make her richer, but it's not going to change her life. I think the only thing that could bring her around is if she was convinced that her husband killed himself. Every woman is responsive to that. We just don't know how she'll react. She could get mad or feel guilty, and both could work in our favor."

Max was intoxicated. It was like the words were perfumed. Finally, he'd found a partner. Pretty, smart, obedient, and needy. There was no reason not to trust her. He was thinking what a lucky guy he was when Rose spoke up.

"We need to make a copy of the letter—we can't take the chance of handing over the original to Dona Beatriz."

"I could do that in the morning," answered Max.

"Yeah, but there's one thing that worries me. The clerk in the copy shop makes the copy, and they usually glance at the document to make sure it can be copied. On this letter, the capital letters to the police at the top of the page would definitely attract their attention. We can't take that risk."

Max's look suggested he was out of his depth.

"If you want," Rose went on, "I have my own copier in my office at Planalto Minerações. I'm the only one who uses it, and no one will see anything. But you'll have to leave the letter with me at least until my lunch hour tomorrow. You know where I work and I can give you my address, which you can verify right now by calling my house. My mother can't sleep until I come home."

"I don't doubt you," said Max.

"But you should. You just met me, you don't know who I am or what I might do."

"I don't need to know anything else." There was a touch of pride in Max's voice. "In my line of work, I have to know immediately what kind of person I'm dealing with—a wimp, a bully, someone who's going to shut up or someone who's going to run screaming down the street. And I've never once been wrong. You aren't a swindler. Besides, as you yourself said, I know where you work—"

"And where I live," she added, taking a napkin and jotting down her address and phone number on it.

Max folded the paper and put it in his jacket pocket without reading it. He was much more interested in the real woman sitting in front of him than in addresses, references, or guarantees. Things were going a lot better than he had planned or even imagined. The starry night, the perfect temperature, the Biblioteca Nacional and the Teatro Municipal all lit up—everything made Cinelândia the ideal setting for a tale that, in Max's mind, was only just beginning. A new life.

Rose was afraid everything was moving too fast. The guy shouldn't be so trusting—his excessive optimism and trust could turn on her in a matter of seconds. She tried to change the subject; it wouldn't do to look too interested in the letter. She asked about Max himself—what was his story?

Max thought everything was going along just fine until she decided to ask about his life. What the hell did that have to do with anything? What did she want to know? That he lived in the maid's room in his sister's house in Méier? That his main occupation was holding up women in parking lots? That he was such a pussy that if any woman ever screamed he'd bail the fuck out of there as fast as he could? What did she want to know? Why did women always want to know everyone's life story? He winced.

Rose saw it. Better keep the conversation strictly business—no personal questions except what she absolutely had to know. On the other hand, she couldn't ignore his obvious interest in her, plan or no plan. The trick was to mix the two ingredients in exact proportions. She didn't have the whole night, either, unless Max was thinking they'd end up in bed together, which would be rushing things, a tactical error. She didn't know anything about him. He must be between thirty-five and thirty-eight—no older. Good-looking, good body, but an attentive eye could tell that life hadn't dealt him a very good hand. His clothes were tacky, his hands were delicate but badly cared for, and his slightly low-class accent got worse when he was irritated. The only thing he kept contained were his gestures. What was he doing in the parking garage if he didn't have a car? Rose tried to paint herself as complete a picture as possible with the few things she knew about him. It was puzzling: even with Max right in front of her, she couldn't get a take on him. He was a strange mixture of good looks and bad form.

He soon forgot his irritation with her personal questions. Max was studying Rose's face as if it were a beautiful inanimate object—until he noticed that he himself was being studied by that same face. He was surprised. While he was looking, he'd lost himself completely in the act; he'd melted away. Rose's attention gave him back his own body and self. He felt good, without knowing why. He took the envelope out of his pocket and handed it over to her.

"I'll wait for you tomorrow, at your lunch hour, on the corner of Rua do Ouvidor and Avenida Rio Branco."

He gestured to the waiter, paid the bill, got up, waited for Rose to put the envelope in the bottom of her purse, and, taking her arm, said:

"We can get the subway right here—I'll take you home."

They rode home in silence. To make up for the awkwardness and distract him from thinking about the letter, Rose let their bodies touch a little when the train shifted. At ten-thirty, she walked into her building. They said good night in the lobby. Then she got in the elevator, pushed a button at random, waited for the automatic light in the corridor to go off, went up, went back down, and waited awhile in the dark, until she was sure that Max had really gone away. Just after eleven-thirty a taxi dropped her off at the Hotel Novo Mundo.

5

Max got to the corner of Rua do Ouvidor and Avenida Rio Branco before noon. He'd forgotten to ask Rose what time she ate lunch, and he'd also forgotten to ask which of the four corners they were going to meet at: the intersection was one of downtown's busiest. He chose the corner closest to the Planalto Minerações building. In spite of the hour, the temperature was pleasant; the sky was cloudy but it wasn't raining.

Max turned his eyes in the direction of Planalto Minerações. Every woman who surfaced on his visual horizon held a promise of Rose. Surely she'd talked the widow into it. She'd have to be an idiot not to accept—nobody throws away a third of a million dollars. If she put up much resistance, he'd naturally agree to give her half and divide the other half between himself and Rose. He was reasonable. After all, she was the beneficiary. Meanwhile he'd better keep an eye on the other corners—Rose could be coming from a different direction. He was, though, pretty visible: she wouldn't have a hard time finding him. He decided to relax and look at the newspapers and magazines in the corner kiosk. There was a big open map of the city. Twelve-thirty. He was early.

It was one of the busiest hours of the day for cars and pedestrians. Every time the light changed, a terrifying quantity of people accumulated on the curb, waiting to cross the street. Max disappeared, swallowed up by the crowd. At times like that, Rose could miss him. Better back off the corner a little bit. They should have planned to meet at the entrance of her building: they would risk being spotted but couldn't miss each other. She'd probably decided to wait for everyone else to go to lunch so she could make a copy without being seen. One-ten. Maybe something had happened. And what if the police had decided to interview her right then? Better to call and make sure everything was okay; but to do that he'd have to move from the meeting place. No reason to worry—one-twenty—lunch went till two.

He thought about the events following the scene in the parking garage. Everything had been completely unexpected: the suicide, the twenty thousand dollars, the note, the dead man's certainty that his request would be honored, the value of the policy, Rose. Most impressive was the note. Everything led him to believe that the businessman had no doubt that he'd be taken care of. True, he'd been wrong about who would take care of it, but the result was the same. The note was the key that opened the insurance company's vault.

It was only as he was considering these facts that it occurred to Max that they could negotiate directly with the insurance company. If he and Rose had to give up the widow's part, why not deal directly with the insurance people? He and Rose would get the same amount, with the advantage of not having to count on the widow. The company could keep her 50 percent and they would get the other 50 percent, without getting her involved. Fantastic. He needed to talk to Rose right away.

Quarter to two. Something must have happened. On the corner diagonally across from his was a phone. He could call without abandoning his post. He'd copied the Planalto Minerações phone and fax numbers onto a piece of paper; it wasn't such a good idea to walk around with Ricardo Carvalho's card on him. He decided to wait till two. During the last fifteen minutes he mistook several women for Rose. He realized that he'd only been with her once, that women can change their appearance completely from one day to the next: all she'd have to do was change her hair, her clothes, her makeup, add sunglasses, and—a new woman. But there was no reason Rose would do that. Or was there? He crossed Avenida Rio Branco diagonally, before the cars had completely stopped. On the curb, a kid was selling phone cards. When he got the piece of paper out of his pocket, his hand was sweating.

"Good afternoon, Planalto Minerações."

"I'd like to speak to Rose, Dr. Ricardo's secretary."

"Rose didn't come in today, could I take a message?"

". . ."

"Hello, are you there? Would you like to leave a message, sir?"

". . ."

Max's vision grew blurred and he felt the blood drain from his head. He wasn't afraid of fainting: his legs were firm and the hand holding on to the telephone was as strong as pincers. The emptiness he felt was not a lack of blood but a lack of ideas. He couldn't think. All he could do was hang up the phone.

She could have gotten sick! Of course! That was it. He took the phone off the hook again and turned over the piece of paper; there he'd written Rose's home number. The voice on the other end was weak and trembling but answered on the first ring.

"I'd like to speak with Rose, please."

"Who's calling?"

"A friend. Please, it's urgent. Is she sick?"

"Rose didn't come home last night. . . . I don't know what happened to her," the lady responded, obviously shaking. "Who are you?" she repeated.

"I'm a friend," he said without much conviction. "I dropped her off last night, I saw her go in."

"I've never heard your voice. You can't be telling the truth. Rose went to work yesterday morning and hasn't come back home since."

Max couldn't believe his ears. He now wasn't sure if Rose was Rose or, at least, if he and the lady were talking about the same Rose. He checked the address. It was the same place he'd dropped her off. Well, what if the woman he'd met had taken Rose's name, address, and phone number, but wasn't Rose? The thought seemed absurd. Hadn't he called Planalto Minerações first and asked for Rose? And hadn't she answered? And what if the other secretary, when she heard a man's voice, had decided to play around and when push came to shove couldn't take it back? Because of what was at stake, some people could even have killed Rose to temporarily take her place. It was a fact: the woman he'd been with the night before had taken the dead man's note, the only possible key to the million-dollar vault. He was still holding the phone in his hand, a little bit out of it, but not enough to avoid hearing the woman's voice on the line. He hung up.

He stood in front of the phone, gaping like an idiot, staring fixedly inside the phone booth. A voice behind him asked:

"Are you done?"

He realized that it had started to drizzle; his face was wet. He had completely lost his sense of direction. He felt his head empty again and thought he was about to faint. He leaned on a pole and waited for the feeling to pass. Even without seeing himself, he knew he was as white as a sheet. As soon as he felt better, he went into the Empregados do Comércio shopping center. In the middle was a good café. He ordered a big cup of coffee and ended up drinking another as well.

The café restored him to his normal state of agitation. He went back to Avenida Rio Branco and started walking toward Flamengo Beach. He was totally disoriented and didn't care where he was going. He walked without noticing people, without looking out for cars, without worrying about the soft rain that was still falling. As he walked through Cinelândia, he glanced at the bar where, the night before, he had sat with Rose, making plans and dreaming about the future. What made him feel like a total imbecile was the fact that he had included in that future the young woman he'd found so docile, meek, obedient. "Imbecile! Moron! Retard!" he said out loud. At the end of the avenue, he found the easiest place to cross over the several lanes of traffic and got to the Monumento aos Pracinhas in Flamengo Park. He didn't want to go anywhere; he just wanted to walk. He walked around the monument, crossed the paths in the park, and came to the stone wall of the Glória Yacht Club. He walked along the wall, a few feet from the boats anchored there. Many had foreign names; on some of them he couldn't tell if they were names of places or people. *Maria Candelária, Vagabond, Bruma Seca, Rosa do Prado* (this one discomfited him a little), *Casablanca* (sounded like a movie), *Tokay* (suggestive of the Orient), *Dona Dinorá*. Why would anyone name a sailboat *Dona Dinorá*? Maybe it was the name of the beloved, but then it'd be just *Dinorá;* or it could be someone close, a mother, grandmother, girlfriend . . . and then it'd still be *Dinorá*. *Dona Dinorá* sounded like the name of the boss's wife. He continued walking alongside the wall, past the club, and ended up on Flamengo Beach, deserted on a rainy afternoon.

He walked across the stretch of sand and wandered almost a mile along the water's edge. Finally, he sat in the sand in front of the Sugarloaf. Until this point, he'd just been letting his ideas flow, but now he needed to figure some things out. One thing was for sure: the secretary had pulled a fast one. With that nice-girl face, she'd set up the whole thing and dropped him. She'd had everything in place by the time she'd met him. And the moron had acted like such a genius. It was clear to him that after his second phone call to Planalto Minerações she had been in charge. Max went over every moment of the conversation they'd had the night before, remembering Rose's every gesture, her meek gaze, more interested in him than in the money. He started to sob convulsively, more out of anger than sadness. He cried until he was exhausted. He was less than two hundred meters from the Hotel Novo Mundo.

6

A whole week had passed uneventfully. No sign of Rose. No indication whether she was dead or alive. The suspects in the murder of the businessman weren't really suspects, for the simple fact that none of them had any motive. A kidnapping attempt was a very remote possibility. And any robbery, if there'd been one, was nothing more than sheer opportunism. It was Monday morning in the Praça Mauá station, and Espinosa's soul was not very radiant.

"Espinosa, phone," shouted someone who didn't feel much better than he did.

"Inspector Espinosa?"

"Dona Bia, how have you been?" he answered, immediately recognizing the voice.

"You've got a good ear, Inspector."

"And you have a lovely voice."

"Thanks. . . . Inspector, there are a couple of things I thought I should tell you—I don't know if they're important, but they seem interesting."

"Would you like me to come over?" he asked hopefully.

"No, don't bother. It's not much and I can tell you over the phone, unless you're really busy now."

"No, no, take your time."

"The first thing happened on Thursday, and I only really thought about it two days ago. I was home, around two-thirty or three, when a man called me, saying he was from the insurance company and wanted to talk about Ricardo's life-insurance policy. I didn't know there was a policy—Ricardo had never mentioned it. I told him to get in touch with Rose. It was only this weekend that I connected the call with her disappearance. I could be imagining things, but I thought I'd better tell you."

"Indeed, thank you. And what else? You said there were a couple of things."

"The other thing is that when I was cleaning out Ricardo's things, I found a gun case . . ."

"Yes?"

"That was empty."

There was a moment of silence, long enough for both to consider that the other had hung up or that they'd been cut off—but each knew the other was still there.

"Couldn't he have taken it out of the case and put it somewhere else where it would be handier? In the bedside table, maybe, or in his dresser drawers, or in a briefcase?"

"No, Officer, those were the drawers I was cleaning out. And as for the briefcase . . . Ricardo only had one, and he always had it with him. You already asked me about it."

"Thank you, Dona Bia. If you find the gun, please let me know. I'll be in touch with you later. Again, thanks for calling."

After he hung up, he decided that life wasn't as bad as he'd thought a few minutes ago.

Monday morning boasted a weekly event: all the drag queens, pickpockets, and drunks they'd locked up during the weekend were sprung loose. The station looked like an open-air market.

"Welber!" cried Espinosa, without much hope of being heard. But he was.

"Welber, go to Planalto Minerações and deploy all your charm on Cláudio Lucena's secretary. Get her to help you search Ricardo Carvalho's office."

"What am I looking for?"

"A life-insurance policy and a revolver. Try to find out if the company has any standard life-insurance policy. If not, ask what insurance company they usually use. If Ricardo Carvalho had one,

Cláudio Lucena might have one too—they were good friends. As for the gun, check out every square inch of that office. Go on ahead—I'll call Dr. Weil and Dr. Lucena to ask them to help you out. I'll leave the secretary to you. First, though, go by Bia Vasconcelos's apartment and get the gun case she found in her husband's closet."

"Inspector, you mentioned an insurance policy, and I remembered—last week your friend the investigator came by twice."

Welber's voice had gone down an octave. Espinosa was all ears. "Which one?"

"That huge ex-cop with the gray hair."

"Aurélio."

The ex-officer was free, so they decided to have lunch at the Bar Monteiro, near the corner of Rua do Ouvidor, one block from Planalto Minerações. The choice had nothing to do with the location and everything to do with the good beer and pork sandwiches. When Espinosa got to the bar he didn't have to look very hard; Aurélio took up most of the available space. He was even taller than Espinosa and weighed about three hundred pounds, all muscle. Next to him, the little bar table looked like a board standing on its side. Despite his size, he rose briskly to greet his friend.

"I'm sorry we didn't run into each other last week, Aurélio, but I was all caught up in the case of the executive murdered in the parking garage."

"That's exactly why I was looking for you."

The waiter appeared to take their order.

"Two pork sandwiches and two beers."

"Was he insured by your company?"

"He was—the beneficiary was his wife."

"And . . . ?"

"That would be it, if he hadn't been insured for a million dollars."

"A million dollars?" asked Espinosa, practically leaping out of his chair.

"More or less, depending on the value of the dollar."

"When did he take out the policy?"

"A little over two years ago. Normally we'd investigate, but with this amount at stake, and taken out such a short time ago, we've got to really dig."

"Did anyone else at Planalto Minerações have a policy with you?"

"Cláudio Lucena, but not taken out at the same time or for the same amount."

"Who did it first?"

"Lucena."

"In that case, Ricardo Carvalho, when he was deciding to take out a policy, could have asked his friend, which would mean that, besides Ricardo, Cláudio and their secretaries must have known about the policy."

"One more thing," added Aurélio. "At the same time Carvalho took out the policy he traveled to New York several times. From what I understand, Planalto Minerações deals more with London and Amsterdam than with New York. It would be worth finding out if any of their business would have taken him to New York around then. He could have gone to have tests done, consult a specialist. . . . Just after that to take out a million-dollar policy is a pretty big coincidence."

"Fine, but the coincidence is between the trips and the policy, not an illness and the policy. There's no sign Ricardo was sick—in fact, he was a picture of health. Besides, be careful not to put the cart in front of the horse. Ricardo Carvalho wasn't killed because he had a life-insurance policy; he was killed, and then the question of the insurance comes up."

"I agree that people don't get killed because of insurance policies; if that were the case, no one would take them out . . . except for the beneficiaries."

"Aurélio, like you said yourself, the only beneficiary is the widow. Do you think Bia Vasconcelos shot her husband in the head to get the money?"

"I don't know much about her. I've never seen her myself, but she looks very pretty in the photo. From what I've heard, Ricardo fucked everything in sight, and the wife could have been angry enough to blow his brains out. As far as we can tell, she's financially independent—she probably wouldn't kill for money. But on the other hand, since she's the only beneficiary . . . no one would suspect her. Too obvious. She wouldn't kill for money but because she was sick of being betrayed."

"How old-fashioned."

And, after that comment:

"Tell me something, Aurélio. Were you the one who called the widow on Thursday afternoon?"

"No, I didn't even know they'd called."

"Someone called, and the widow, not wanting to talk about it then, suggested that the guy get in touch with the husband's secretary."

"And did they call?" the investigator asked.

"I don't know. The secretary disappeared on Thursday, after a mysterious phone call to the widow. We still don't have any idea where she ended up. Another detail that could be interesting is that Carvalho had a revolver that disappeared. I still don't have any details about the weapon, but as soon as I do I'll let you know."

Espinosa finished the story by telling him about Bia's meeting with Júlio on the afternoon of the murder. The sandwiches and beers came. For a few minutes, they were respectfully silent. Before he'd finished the first half of his sandwich, Aurélio ordered another one. Espinosa knew Aurélio wasn't hiding anything, just as the investigator knew Espinosa wasn't holding back. The fact was, though, that neither of them knew much. They could always go out for more beer and sandwiches when they found out something new. They talked about their old times in the police force and about their salaries. Everyone understood the unwritten law that you didn't talk about wives and kids. When they were finished, they said good-bye, promising to keep each other up-to-date.

Espinosa didn't go back to the station by the shortest route; he went by the used-book store on Rua do Carmo first. He found a nice translation of *The Life and Adventures of Nicholas Nickleby*, by Dickens, in two volumes printed on coated paper, for less than the cost of the sandwiches and beers. He strode into the station carrying it like a trophy under his arm. Welber arrived later.

"So, how was it?" asked Espinosa.

"That secretary's a tough one, but she ended up helping. His papers and documents are all in a personal file, very well organized. We looked at every page. No sign of a life-insurance policy. But I did find this."

In a package, wrapped in a handkerchief, was a box of .38 caliber bullets.

"They were in Ricardo Carvalho's desk drawer. I went to Bia Vasconcelos's apartment and got the gun case. It was for a Colt .38."

The ammo was imported; the box was missing about twenty bullets. They were identical to the bullet that had been removed from the executive's head. Why was Ricardo Carvalho armed? What was he scared of, or who was threatening him? It looked as if he had taken the gun to work on that day, or the day before. What for? The gun wasn't in the office, it wasn't at home, and it wasn't with him when he was killed. The possibility that someone had stolen the gun from the car was remote. When the police got there, there were several witnesses—anyone who had tried to take the gun would have been seen, even a cop.

Another idea was that Ricardo hadn't been the one who'd left with the gun, and that the box of bullets could have been put in his drawer by someone else. Rose? Cláudio Lucena? Both had left about the same time Ricardo had. Even Lucena, who'd run into him in the elevator lobby, could have been waiting for him, dashed quickly into his office, planted the box of bullets in his drawer, and still gotten back in time to bump into him before the elevator got there—especially when everyone was going home and the elevators were moving slower than usual. Rose could have done the same thing. Either one of them could have followed him into the parking garage and shot him. One thing seemed clear: whoever killed Ricardo Carvalho had stolen his briefcase.

Espinosa summed up his conversation with Aurélio for Welber. He couldn't resist telling him the story of the million-dollar life-insurance policy.

Only on Wednesday, over a week after the death of Ricardo Carvalho, did Espinosa start shaking down his informers. In fact, he'd already started the process, but not with the required emphasis. A few threats here and there encouraged the first information to start trickling in. There weren't any new lowlifes around, there was no news of any hired guns, no sign of a briefcase with embossed initials. He squeezed a little harder—a few threats of interrogations, a few hints of enforcing the law—and the first real information reached his ears: an underground lottery in the Zona Norte had been given a gun to sell, a foreign weapon that matched Espinosa's description.

7

Max's depression waned as his anger waxed. He couldn't let anyone know about the twenty thousand dollars. And he'd even given the bitch that possibility. He had only two options now: first, be satisfied with the twenty thousand dollars and shut up. On the other hand, he knew where she lived, and she'd left her mother all alone. Someday she'd have to come home.

He'd already been locked in his room for almost a week, leaving only once a day to eat. When his sister finally knocked and called his name, he tried to put her off but was surprised to see two men there, a surprise that soon changed to shock when one of them flashed a badge and mumbled something Max didn't hear, or didn't want to hear. His sister's wide-eyed stare was all questions.

"Get dressed," said the younger officer.

In the car, it was once again the younger one who ordered him to cross his legs, handcuffing his right wrist to his left ankle. On the drive from Méier to the Praça Mauá, they didn't speak to him once. When the older one finally broke the silence, they were already inside the interrogation room.

"So, Max, let's put aside the formalities. We know your name, address, and occupation, so we can get straight to the point."

Max wondered what occupation they had attributed to him, but decided not to ask. The older one opened a big dark envelope, from which emerged the Colt .38 Detective Special. Max's eyes almost popped out of his head, and his blood seemed to drain from his veins.

"Well? How long have you been walking around shooting people?"

Espinosa's voice was calm and collected, as if he had all the time in the world.

"I . . . I didn't shoot anyone, sir."

"I understand. So your gun went off all by itself?"

"It . . . the gun . . . it's not mine, Officer."

"Well, if it's not yours, whose is it?"

"I'm not exactly sure."

"You're not exactly sure?"

Espinosa stroked his incipient beard and looked at Max patiently.

"And, without knowing *exactly*, who could the gun belong to? Because if it's not yours and you don't know whose it is, then you sold a stolen gun. We know you don't use a gun at your job, so how do you end up wandering the streets trying to sell this gun to anybody who wants it?"

Again, Max was curious to know what exactly it was they were talking about: his "job." He still didn't ask. He was even more interested in knowing how they'd located the gun, and there was no doubt that it was the same gun.

"Officer, if I tell you, you won't believe me."

"Try me. You never know."

"I got the gun out of a garbage bag."

"And how did you know it was in the bag?"

"Because I saw when they put it in."

"And who put it in?" asked Espinosa, as if he were talking with a child.

"It was a woman."

"A woman?" It was Espinosa's turn to be surprised. "Why don't you take it from the beginning."

"Last Tuesday, I was on the corner of Rua da Quitanda and Rua São José a little after six, when along comes a woman walking real fast, almost running, who bumped into me and kept walking, fast, looking behind her, like she was being followed. Close to where we were, there were a bunch of garbage bags. She stopped, looked around, took something out of a briefcase, and shoved it into one of the bags. As soon as she was gone, I opened the bag and there was the gun right on top. I tore off a piece of plastic, wrapped it up, and took it home. When I saw it was imported, I thought I could get a good price for it. I offered it to some shopkeepers until the lottery guy took it to see if anyone was interested. That's the whole story."

Max's vendetta had begun.

"No, it's not, Max. That's only part of the story. I want to know a lot more. Unless you want to be accused of the murder."

"What are you talking about, Officer? I never killed anyone."

"But this gun did, and I want to know who was holding it when it was fired."

"Then I guess it must have been the girl."

"What did she look like?"

Max described her as best he could.

"Welber, get the photo we took from the house, mix it in with some others and bring it over here."

A few minutes later, Welber brought over five pictures and spread them out on the table.

"Which of these is the woman you saw?" asked Espinosa.

"This one here, doctor. That's her," said Max excitedly.

"What did the briefcase she was carrying look like?"

"It was brown leather."

Espinosa looked at Welber and they both left the room. The story made sense—he wouldn't have been able to make it up. At least, he couldn't have made up Rose, and he couldn't have guessed the exact day and hour of the crime. And there was the detail of the briefcase. Everything made perfect sense. The only thing that didn't make sense was Max himself.

After letting Max wait for an hour, they came back in.

"We're going to release you," said the older one, "but you are prohibited from leaving the city or going to any unknown place. We found you the first time and we can find you again. If you try to play around and hide out, Detective Welber here will make sure you never dream of fleeing for the rest of your life. Stay at your sister's house, where we can find you. You can go."

Espinosa knew that Max would be more useful loose than in jail. Besides, he had a feeling Max hadn't killed the businessman. He didn't have the face of a killer.

Max walked out of the station dumbfounded. He would rather have been knocked around and threatened in the usual way. The idea that they'd believed him and treated him well! Unheard of, from what he knew of the police. That inspector was different, but it still didn't make sense. They must have worked like hell to find that gun, and he still couldn't understand how they'd done it. They'd come straight to him without even searching his room, taken him to the station, after which he'd made up a story, they'd believed it (or pretended to believe it), and then they'd let him go. He didn't understand a damn thing.

"They treated me like a king. The only thing they forgot was to ask for my lawyer."

Two hours later, Max already had started remembering it like that.

"Don't be an idiot, Bro, no one's going to pry you out of that shithole in the slums and think you're a king. Those cops are getting ready to jump you. And what'd you do anyway?"

"I didn't do anything, Sis. They made a mistake."

"Max, *we're* a mistake. No one makes mistakes with people like us—everything they say is right just because they say it."

Max thought for a few seconds about what his sister said and started thinking again about what had happened at the station. How did they know about him? The allusions to his "job," his "occupation": what did they really know? And if they knew, why did they let him go? The only reason he could imagine why he was at home and not behind bars was that they thought he could lead them to the secretary, but that was exactly what he hoped for from them. It was obvious that they didn't know about the twenty thousand dollars—and certainly not about the note. Even though they'd found the gun, they were still convinced it was a murder and not a suicide. He laughed, not about that, but about the fact that only a few days earlier he'd been screwed and couldn't go to the police—and now the cops were coming to him. Maybe he could count on their help in finding Rose. He was over the sadness but had kept a little bit of his anger—essential if he was going to look for her himself. Luckily he hadn't sold any of his dollars; they could trace his hidden fortune just like they'd traced the gun. The best thing he could do was hide the money somewhere else. If they found Rose, she could tattle and the whole police force would come after him; he'd have to take the precaution because of the secretary. In the event that they found her, she'd be faced with the story he made up, and the least she would do in return was spill the beans about the suicide, the note, and the dollars. On the other hand, without the police, the chances of getting the note back were remote. There was still another side of the question he had to think about. Now that the gun had led the cops to him, the note was the only alibi he had to protect himself against the murder charge.

Spring had begun a week ago. For Rio de Janeiro, that meant that any and all residues of cold had been banished; for Méier, that meant that summer had begun. The little low-roofed room with a window you could barely get a breath through wasn't the best place to ponder the situation. In spite of the pain he was in, he had liked walking in Flamengo Park the week before. It was far. But he had felt good. The sand, under the rain, had made a moist, slightly hardened cushion, and the part underneath had still been dry. It reminded him of himself: dry and empty on the inside.

8

When he decided to call, it was already eleven at night, but Aurélio answered on the second ring.

"How 'bout another round of beer and sandwiches? I've got a few little pieces to add to the puzzle."

"Espinosa, I've been thinking about you." Aurélio's voice was happy, though he sounded a little tired.

"What about tomorrow at one—same place?"

"Fine, but unless you want me to stay up all night worrying, give me something to chew on till tomorrow."

Espinosa explained that the crime weapon had been found, but omitted any reference to Max or the story he'd told about Rose. They agreed it would be better to talk about the details the next day.

He wasn't tired; he was hungry. The icebox didn't offer much besides some old freezer-burned vegetables, little pieces of cheese accumulated throughout the last decade, three slices of bread of unknown age, and a few bottles of beer. He decided to grab a beer and order a pizza.

What concerned him the most was that Max's story made perfect sense and that he wasn't giving it the importance it deserved. The secretary is seen fleeing the crime scene and hiding the gun in a pile of trash, the ballistics tests confirm that the bullet that killed Ricardo Carvalho was fired from that gun, the secretary's mother suggests that something was going on between her daughter and the businessman. It was enough to mix those ingredients and come up with a crime of passion. The fact that Max was there at exactly the right place at exactly the right time was a coincidence. It was just tough to believe in that kind of coincidence.

He went to bed late and got up late. When he arrived at the Praça Mauá it was ten-thirty in the morning. He passed the time until his meeting with Aurélio writing reports, filling out forms, and answering the phone. The day was nice, even seen from a window in the Praça Mauá. At a quarter to one, he headed toward Rua da Quitanda.

He arrived at the same time as Aurélio. Much of what Espinosa knew he'd learned from him, and he didn't feel right about hiding information from his old colleague. So as soon as they sat down he got to the point.

"Aurélio, I didn't tell you everything last night."

"I know—that's why we're here."

Espinosa told him what he knew about the death of Ricardo Carvalho. Locating the weapon thanks to his informers in the underground lottery, Max selling the gun, who Max was, Rose's disappearance, the conversation with her mother, the possible affair between the secretary and the executive, and, finally, Max's story about how he'd found the gun. Aurélio heard him out without a word. At certain points he suspended his sandwich in the air, gaping and waiting; it looked like the scene had been frozen.

"What do you think about this Max?" he asked when Espinosa had finished the story.

"I don't think he committed the crime," Espinosa replied. "He's not a known criminal. He's probably carried out his share of misdemeanors, but I haven't heard that he's ever threatened anyone's life. According to the lottery people, there are rumors that he sticks people up in parking lots with a toy gun. I think he's relatively harmless."

"Espinosa, nobody who robs people is harmless. Even with a toy gun."

"He's a small-time thief, Aurélio. He's never hurt anybody and has never taken more than some unsuspecting shopper's pocket money."

"And that doesn't seem like much to you?"

"Compared to murder?"

"I'd like to see him, to make up my own mind."

"I can take care of that easily," said Espinosa.

"And what about his story?" asked Aurélio.

"That's the point. I don't believe a word he said. And that makes him a suspect—I'm just not sure of what crime."

"Do you think he could have been the secretary's accomplice?"

"I don't think so. He's not qualified. He's never shot a gun, and there's no sign that he knew her, but I don't discount the possibility that they met after the murder."

Aurélio picked at his teeth and put the broken toothpicks on the plate.

"Tell me something, Espinosa. Did anyone check to see if there was any powder residue on the executive's hand?"

The question was asked without emphasis. Espinosa would have said that the emphasis came from not being emphasized. It jolted him, maybe because he'd been asking himself the same question for a while, without stating it so clearly.

"Suicide? You're not saying that because it's a convenient answer for the insurance company? After all, it's your daily bread."

"Maybe," said Aurélio. "But I wouldn't eliminate the possibility."

"Aurélio, nobody kills himself and then runs off with the gun . . ." He kept looking at his friend as he completed his sentence: "Unless someone else did that for him. As for examining his hands," he went on, "of course they didn't, because it didn't occur to anyone that it was a suicide. It was an obvious murder scene—at most, a robbery and a murder."

"It still is," Aurélio said. "I'm just tossing in a few more ingredients."

Espinosa was convinced that Rose was the solution to the puzzle. As long as she didn't turn up, Max's flimsy story was all they had to go on. The idea of suicide was supported by very tenuous evidence and posed almost insurmountable problems. In any case, whereas last week they were at square one, now, at least, they had a few leads. With a little luck, they could figure it all out in another week. His conversation with Aurélio, as always, had been highly useful. For both sides, he figured. They said good-bye around three.

Since he'd been transferred to the Praça Mauá station, he'd fallen into the habit of going downtown to a bookstore every Friday afternoon. Since he was only a block away, he decided to stop by the used-book store on Rua do Carmo. He was taken with an old illustrated edition of *Moby-Dick*. It wasn't anything rare or expensive, but it struck his fancy.

Another Saturday was upon him, and he had once again resolved to organize the books in his apartment. He was looking forward to a rainy day. Nothing better than a rainy Saturday to inspire him to arrange his books. The biggest problem was that he had a lot of books and no bookshelves. Friday ended without any more news.

He liked Saturday mornings. While he ate breakfast and read the literary supplement of the paper, he decided to continue organizing his books into a kind of "living bookcase." The section he'd done the Saturday before was still standing, which encouraged him to keep going as high as he could reach. At lunchtime he figured he hadn't made much progress—the first chapter of *Nicholas Nickleby* being responsible for the delay. At four, when the phone rang, his progress was virtually nil. It was Welber.

"Inspector, they found Rose's mother dead. Murdered. The experts already went over. I'll come by and get you."

The ride to Tijuca was quick, but long enough for Welber to convey what little he knew. The old lady had been killed by hanging, but a preliminary investigation hinted at something more. It had happened at lunchtime. The doorman saw her come back from the market around eleven in the morning. A little before three, he rang the bell—he'd promised to fix the flusher on the toilet. He waited a few minutes and rang again. Since no one answered, he used the key to the service door Dona Maura had left with him. The body was seated and tied to one of the dining room chairs; one of her arms dangled free. She was gagged with a scarf. The cause of death was determined as strangulation, by means of the nylon rope removed from the clothesline.

Before he even entered the room, Espinosa smelled blood mixed with ammonia. There was blood on the table, on the woman's body, and on the floor. The detectives shuddered when they saw the dangling arm. Three fingers had been cut off with the meat shears now lying on the table along with a little bottle of ammonia . . . and the fingers. The bottle of ammonia added an extra note of perversity to the horrific scene.

"It's exactly what you're thinking," said the investigator, who was watching Espinosa examine the scene. "It was used to wake her up every time she passed out."

She'd surely been tortured to reveal something she didn't know. They didn't need to cut off three fingers to figure that out.

9

When they sealed the door it was already dark. In spite of their fatigue, neither wanted to eat. Before heading back to the station, they looked for a place nearby to have a beer. They couldn't get rid of the image of the fingers on top of the table.

It took them a few beers to calm down. During the first one, they didn't talk; during the second, they made a few comments about the bar, whose tables had invaded the narrow sidewalk; when the waiter brought over the third, Espinosa addressed his colleague.

"How are you feeling?"

"About the number of beers or about the lady's fingers?"

"About the beers—about her fingers I don't need to ask."

"I feel okay—as well as can be expected."

During his twenty years on the police force Espinosa had seen a lot—almost everything, he thought—but it was impossible not to be shocked by the sight of a lady whose fingers had been cut off with shears before she was hung. When they'd walked into the living room, as he was still trying to pull himself together, he had seen Welber run toward the bathroom. The idea that this was the work of a fellow human being was as repulsive as the scene itself.

"I'm okay," Welber said again.

"So drop me off at home. I don't think you want to spend Saturday night drinking in a bar with a policeman."

Welber looked as though he was considering doing just that, if Espinosa was inclined to a personal conversation—which would be extraordinary—but the inspector didn't follow up. Not that Espinosa had secrets anyone would eagerly discover—he couldn't imagine anything of interest to his coworkers—but, as far as he was concerned, he was happy for his personal life to stay that way. Right now a serious conversation and a little attention might be good for Welber, but Espinosa didn't feel up to the role of shepherd of souls. Before the beer could become a pretext for confidences, he asked for the check and got up from the table. On the way back to Copacabana, the conversation never strayed to personal matters.

Espinosa had been a policeman for almost as long as Welber had been alive. He'd lost a lot of his old preconceived notions. He hadn't arrived at any visible truth and was constantly enlarging the part of his mind where he stored doubts.

He reached home wondering if he had one history or several. Depending on the response, he could be one or several different people. Before he turned on the lamp in the living room, he decided it was a stupid question, even though he dragged a little uncertainty with him into the bathroom.

His married life was so far in the past, so far removed from his present life, that it seemed to belong to someone else, in the same way the present man had little to do with the boy in Fátima. His own son, because of the time he'd spent abroad, seemed like someone else's.

His relationship with his first wife had gotten sticky even before they were married. They met when they were law students, when she was a freshman and he was an upperclassman, and fell madly in love. The little announcement on the school bulletin board announcing a test for admission to the civil police was like a poster advertising a movie with a happy ending. He could work as a night watchman, finish law school, and still intern at a law firm. Green light for marriage. She pointed out at least a dozen reasons why he shouldn't join the police. Notwithstanding her objections, he took the test and got in. They got married. A year later, their son was born. The marriage lasted until she finished law school. Four years.

While he was reminiscing, he turned on all the lights in the apartment, for no apparent reason other than to shed some literal light on himself. Then he did the same in reverse—turning them all off one by one, leaving on only the lamp in the living room. He took a long bath, unwrapped a sandwich that was sitting in the refrigerator, opened a beer, stretched out on the sofa, and started thinking about death—not about the abstract idea of death but about specifically how much time he had left. Aged forty-two, on a Saturday night, in a bachelor pad in Copacabana. He decided he was already dead. He went to bed.

PART II

October

1

I opened my eyes, in no hurry to wake up. The memory that started off my Sunday was Dona Maura's fingers on the table. I closed my eyes and tried to go back to sleep. It didn't work. It was after eleven and I'd slept enough. The light that worked its way through the venetian blinds was weak, almost nonexistent, and was accompanied by the sound of rain, which I wasn't sure if I really heard or just imagined. After a few minutes struggling with reality, I decided to get up and make coffee. While I was waiting for my morning gurgle I picked up the newspaper at the door and went to brush my teeth. The vision that greeted me in the mirror was of a man whose hair and general demeanor recalled one of the Marx brothers. The recollection was more disturbing than amusing. I decided to go downstairs to the kiosk and pick up *O Dia*, probably the only paper that would cover the story. In the *Jornal do Brasil* there was nothing about the murder. They hadn't filled the press in on the severed fingers, which certainly would have made the story stand out; without that detail, the death of an old lady in an apartment in the Zona Norte didn't really deserve to be noticed by a newspaper of the upper-middle class. On the way back, walking up the stairs, I found the little item on an inside page of *O Dia*. The coffee was ready. It smelled good, but my mouth held a bitter taste.

Minutes earlier, when I was preparing to get up, even before I'd opened my eyes, an image had tried to force its way out of the confusion of sleep, but was chased off by the gray light of the day and the sound of the rain. While I was brushing my teeth, it tried to insinuate itself again, but was cut off by the melancholy vision of Harpo Marx. Now it erupted with greater force: Bia Vasconcelos seated by my side for breakfast, walking through the living room, picking up a book at random, choosing a song. The vision only lasted a few seconds. Bia disappeared, and in her place came Júlio, my ex-wife, Alba, Rose (although I'd only seen her in a picture). I tried to recall the image of Bia, but in vain. Maybe the problem was the living room. The difference between our apartments was striking. The clean sophistication of the designer and the baroque heaps of the book-buying cop. I got up from the table and went to look at myself again in the mirror, then returned to the living room. The colonial table, the sofa, and the armchairs with their stray cushions (inherited from my parents and retaining the original upholstery), the pictures, and the so-called decorative objects, together with the image in the mirror, suggested that Bia and I inhabited completely different universes.

My living room has a little balcony about a foot wide and six feet long. The advantage of this little detail is that, instead of a window, the living room has glass doors and venetian blinds facing the street. I opened the blinds and the doors, at the risk of letting rain in on the carpet, to see if my spirits would be lifted by the fresh air. All that resulted was an encounter between the day outside and my own inside, both gray. I got another cup of coffee in the kitchen. I'd quit smoking a while ago, but now was the moment I missed it the most. According to Bia's testimony, her husband had also stopped smoking a few months earlier. But there had been a cigarette in the ashtray and an open pack in the glove compartment. Some people still keep a pack around even after quitting. Obviously, the murderer wouldn't be smoking while he was shooting the businessman—and he'd be even less worried about putting the butt out in the ashtray. The person who smoked that cigarette was someone Ricardo knew or Ricardo Carvalho himself. In that case, either he'd decided to start smoking again, or he no longer needed to worry about the bad effects of smoking.

The books piled up against the wall bore witness to my efforts to cooperate with the cleaning lady. There was probably some charm in the mess of the apartment: the disorder did not simply reflect the lack of order; it distorted normal ideas of order. But even though such ideas reassured me, I felt absolutely sure that Bia Vasconcelos would never live in a place like this, which meant that we weren't compatible. I still had the strong desire to smoke; I served myself a third cup of coffee.

Who could have cut off the poor lady's fingers? The violence of the mutilation was even more shocking than the murder itself. It was obvious that the two crimes were connected, just as it was obvious that the disappearance of Rose had involuntarily provoked the death of her mother. If the same person had killed Dona Maura and Ricardo Carvalho, I could eliminate some suspects, especially Rose. I couldn't see her torturing and killing her own mother. Bia and Júlio had already been taken off the first list of suspects, now even more reasonably. Cláudio Lucena could have given the order, but couldn't have carried out the crimes, especially the second. Of the known suspects, Max was the only one left. There wasn't any reason to go look for an "evil son of a bitch who tortures and kills little old ladies." That wasn't the crime of an evil son of a bitch but of a cold-blooded psycho. And everyone and anyone could be the psycho.

After I opened the balcony door, I went back to the table to continue reading the paper. The gray sky was the same color as the building across the way. The rain was falling harder, and a wind from the southeast started spraying it into the room. I rose again and closed the glass door, leaving the blinds open. I walked around the apartment. A fourth cup of coffee was out of the question. The papers didn't have anything else to say for themselves, and the only phone call that would have mattered that Sunday morning hadn't come. Bia wouldn't have liked my shelfless bookshelf. What put Bia so far out of my league? Because she was rich and educated in Europe? Or because she was an artist and I was a cop? Ever since I'd met her, I'd been asking this question at least once a day. I didn't have any illusions about people's purity—I knew very well that a nun can be even more violent than a policeman, and that a workaday husband and father can be capable of unimaginable perversity. I didn't think I was any different. I'd ended up being a cop in the same way you might end up teaching high school. How I viewed myself and my profession was different from how most people regarded "cops," and Bia Vasconcelos didn't seem to be any different from the rest on this account. Cops play a role in society only when they're investigating something. The phone rang. Welber.

"Inspector, I'm sorry to bother you on a Sunday morning, but Max has disappeared."

"What do you mean? He's not at his sister's house? He didn't go out to take a walk? It's a Sunday," I added, even though I knew that that didn't make any difference for a lowlife like Max.

"He's gone, Inspector. Since last night, nobody's seen him anywhere."

"Keep looking. If that guy disappears, we'll look like fools—we had him in our hands."

Max's disappearing right after the murder of Rose's mother was a suspicious coincidence—especially as the only thing he had going for him was that he didn't look like a murderer. Max couldn't have known about the old lady's death, unless he was the murderer himself or was again "just passing by," since the only news of the murder had appeared in today's *O Dia* and he'd been gone since the night before.

The amount of time the chief had given me to take care of the case and write up a minimally helpful report was running out. And even though the original dossier had grown by one more murder and one more disappearance and by the discovery of the murder weapon, I didn't think we'd made significant progress on the Ricardo Carvalho case. Max was an ideal candidate. A marginal, petty thief, with no criminal record, who'd sold the murder weapon to the illegal lottery in the Zona Norte. Not even his mother would believe the story about how he was walking by the crime scene at the exact moment when the alleged murderer was getting rid of it. And yet, for reasons I couldn't quite describe, I didn't think that he'd killed the executive. The other possibility—if you believed Max's story—was to put it together with a few things Dona Maura had said and charge Rose. That is, if anyone could locate her . . . and if she was still alive. Excepting these two possibilities—not even hypotheses, just mere possibilities that might lend the case some coherence—I didn't have anything else. The idea that it was a crime of passion committed by Júlio, with or without Bia's help, was ridiculous. Attributing the crime to an occasional murderer, with no link to the victim, who'd meant only to rob him, didn't make sense either. Ricardo had been killed with his own gun, which left two possibilities. Someone had gotten his gun, at or before the moment of the crime, to shoot the executive. Or Ricardo Carvalho had committed suicide. The second possibility was complicated by two factors. The first was that the weapon hadn't been found inside the car. The second was that this version didn't account for the disappearance of the secretary or the murder of her mother.

The rain had slowed down a little, so I opened the balcony window again. I looked in the icebox and found two frozen items: pasta with red sauce and pasta with red sauce. I chose the first and left the second for dinner. This Sunday was turning out to be as electrifying as every other.

After I ate the first serving of pasta without even bothering to take it out of the packaging, I dedicated the next three hours to reading the *Nicholas Nickleby* I'd bought at the used-book store. Just after five, the phone rang for the second time.

"Inspector Espinosa?"

"Yes?"

"I'm sorry to be calling on a Sunday, but you said if I remembered anything. . . . It's Alba Antunes."

"Don't worry, ma'am, nothing could make my day any worse. You saved the day."

"Please don't call me ma'am."

"Okay, Alba. What have you remembered?"

"I didn't remember anything, but something happened I thought I'd better tell you about."

"Yes?"

"It could be nothing or just my imagination, but . . . the last few times I've gone out with Júlio, someone followed us in a car."

"Tell me more."

"Well, once we went to the movies and then out to eat. As I was driving, I noticed that there was a car behind us the whole time, on our way to the theater and then to the restaurant afterward. The next day, Júlio came by the gym to pick me up. This time he was driving, but I looked around and saw a car behind us. It was the same one as the night before and I'm sure he was following us. I couldn't see the face of the driver—both times it was dark and I couldn't even tell if it was a man or a woman."

"Did he try anything? To force your car over or threaten you in any way?"

"No. He didn't bother us at all, even though it's not that much fun to be followed. But there's another detail, Inspector. I didn't say anything to Júlio."

"Why not?"

"He's really paranoid. Every little ache and pain makes him think he's terminally ill. Once, he freaked out and decided that he had mercury poisoning. If I tell him we're being followed, he's as good as dead. What worries me is that when I'm alone, nobody follows me, which makes me think the stalker is after Júlio. And Júlio can't defend himself at all, Inspector."

"Even if that's true, couldn't the impression that you're being followed come from the same paranoia? I mean, it's not unheard of for one car to be behind another during a long drive."

"And sit and wait for us while we eat, watch a movie, and fuck?"

". . ."

"The only thing I can say," she continued, "is that if he had wanted to do something to us, he already would have done it—there were plenty of opportunities. Unless he's waiting to get Júlio by himself. I can't ask him if he's being followed without freaking him out."

"And you think he's really so vulnerable?"

"I don't think so, I know so. When we fight, I have to control myself so I don't scare him too much. My anger is a little . . . exuberant. When I get a grip, I see he's terrified, looking for the nearest exit."

"Alba, there's not a lot I can do for you. If this goes on and becomes a stalking, I can ask for protection. For now, be careful, avoid deserted places, and keep your eyes open. If you're sure you're being followed, it's better to tell Júlio so he can watch out."

"Fine. I'm more intrigued than scared."

"If they keep following you or try anything, call me immediately."

The strength of the feminine maternal instinct perplexed me. All a man has to do is look unprotected and show the look of a cow lost in a field for a woman to rain down on him instantly. Júlio was obviously a fool, but still, two marvelous women were ready to help him decide between strawberry and chocolate ice cream. That Alba wasn't stupid. If she said they were being followed, they were. Now they needed to find out why and by whom, and at this point the police couldn't make it any easier—we already had two disappearances and two murders. Which made finding Max right away even more crucial.

I don't like October and I don't like Sunday. October was starting on a Sunday. The only thing worse would be if Monday fell on a Sunday. The rain started up again, and the best thing to do was wait around until I could eat the second serving of pasta.

2

"I would prefer not to," Bartleby the scrivener repeated calmly and peacefully to his boss and protector. Me neither: I would prefer not to. I'd prefer, on Monday morning, not have to go to the station, not have to attend the release of all the rowdy drunks, transvestites, pickpockets, tough guys, hookers, and junkies. I'd rather not have to fill out useless forms or write reports as an expression of police incompetence. I'd rather, when I meet a pretty woman, not have to start out with the ominous line: "I'm Inspector Espinosa from the First Precinct."

It so happens that my boss will never hear the sentence "I would prefer not to," especially not from my mouth. In high spirits I headed to work on Monday morning. The rain from the day before was still coming down, mistier and more insistent, dampening the soul more than the body.

Welber filled me in on the details involving his frustrated attempts to find Max. He had disappeared with all his belongings. There was nothing left in the room in Méier. His sister didn't even know that he wasn't home. Max had vanished without leaving any clue as to where he was going. Nothing he'd said to his sister suggested that he'd disappear like that. I was starting to believe it had been idiotic to leave him alone. Either I'd completely misjudged him or something had happened between the day he was released and Saturday that made him break the deal I'd made with him. Bums don't usually break deals with the police—they know they won't have a second chance.

I didn't believe that both crimes had been committed by the same person, even though I was sure they were related. In fact, they had only one detail in common: there were no fingerprints besides those of the victims themselves. If my suspicions were correct, we were dealing not with one but with two murderers—which didn't help brighten my Monday morning.

It would have been hard for Max to go to a different city. He was a rat in the mazes of Rio de Janeiro; he wouldn't feel right in a different environment. He was hidden somewhere in the city, and eventually he'd have to stick his neck out. The fact was that Max hadn't seemed inclined to flee, and, in that case, someone—I didn't have any idea who—was killing and disappearing people.

The morning passed without event. Before people started cracking jokes about how we'd released the principal suspect, I put Welber in charge of activating our webs of informants to help find Max. He was probably holed up in some fleabag hotel. I ordered a Big Mac and a milkshake from the McDonald's on the other side of the plaza and sat around waiting for some kind of inspiration that would change the direction of the investigation. "Change the direction" was a euphemism. We weren't going anywhere. Cops in American movies didn't have to feel so helpless. The medical experts practically solved it for the detective, who just had to wander the streets of New York, San Francisco, or Los Angeles. If the medical people couldn't figure it out, there was always the possibility of sending a hair to the FBI. The next day we'd even know what soccer team the criminal rooted for. Here, in the fabulous Third World, we're lucky if the medical report tells us whether the victim died from a gunshot or poison.

Welber was holding an envelope.

"Inspector, we've gotten the ballistics results."

Freire had been good enough to send them over. The results were detailed and exhaustive. The gun Max had sold was the same one that had killed the executive and the same one whose case Bia Vasconcelos had found. What we'd concluded in our investigation was now technically confirmed: Ricardo Carvalho had been killed with his own gun. This gun would have been tossed into the garbage by Rose, his secretary, picked up by Max, and sold to the gamblers. Obviously, Max had accused the secretary to protect himself. There was a detail, though, that I bumped up against now, reviewing the case. For him to have blamed the secretary, he had to know that she had vanished. Otherwise she could unmask him. How could he have known that? The same held true for the second murder. If his disappearance was linked to the death of Rose's mother, how could he have known about that? Max knew way too much.

This week would be the last the boss had given me to investigate the case. If I couldn't make at least some minimal sense of it, I couldn't justify working on it full-time. And I'd have to go back to regular duty—which would make progress unlikely. It was true that we didn't know very much, but that was exactly why we needed more time. I'd have to wait and see if the chief would agree.

I needed to check something out. I called Aurélio. He wasn't there. I left a message. We managed to catch up at the end of the day.

"Hey, Espinosa. Another beer?"

"I'd love to, but first I need some information. Are you by any chance following the professor and his girlfriend?"

"What professor, Espinosa? . . . In any case, I'm not following the professor and his girlfriend. Who are they?"

"People linked to the case of the executive. They're not important. Thanks anyway, though. I didn't think it was you, just because you wouldn't have been noticed. But I needed to make sure. Let's get a beer tomorrow, if you have time."

I hung up with the feeling that something was about to happen—and that it wasn't something good.

Whoever was following Júlio and Alba wasn't too worried about being seen. That could mean two things: it was either an incompetent amateur or someone who didn't care if they were noticed and even made sure that they were. I had to find out if they were just trying to scare Júlio and Alba or if they meant to do something more meaningful. I called the gym. The receptionist with the perfect body answered. I said my name, which she didn't take for Espinhosa, and asked for Alba.

"Inspector, what a pleasure. How are you, sir?"

"If I'm going to call you by your name, it's not fair if you call me sir."

"All right," she said, a little embarrassed, "it's just that your name is so fancy. Wasn't Espinosa the name of a philosopher?"

"True."

"Well then! There's no difference between calling you sir and calling you by the name of a philosopher."

I decided not to go into it, as the issue wasn't my name or what she should call me but her own safety. Júlio's too, true, but for the time being I was more worried about her.

"Any news?" I asked her.

"Why are you asking? Because of what I told you? Are you worried about me?"

I said yes to the last, thereby answering all three questions. "Are you going home by yourself?"

"Is that an offer?"

"It's a concern, but it could be an offer."

"No one's coming with me. I'll take you up on it. I should be getting out of here around eight."

"Don't leave before I get there."

It was ten to six. I thought it was best to leave before I got caught in rush-hour traffic. On the way I fantasized about things I can't confess to. I got to Ipanema an hour early, so I went into a bookstore I like. Forty minutes later I emerged with a Joseph Conrad under my arm. At ten to eight I arrived at the gym and was disappointed to see that the receptionist had already gone home. Since I knew the way, I went in and up the stairs behind the weight room. One of Alba's partners met me and invited me to wait in the aquarium-office. Alba was in the shower. She emerged a few minutes later, smelling of soap, her smooth wet hair hanging over her shoulders. She took my arm and said good night to her friend. We went down the stairs; she looked like a schoolgirl. As for me, ever since the receptionist had looked at me as if I were some kind of prehistoric animal, I had no idea what they thought of me in that gym. When we got to the sidewalk she asked:

"Are you really worried about me or are you just hitting on me?"

In fact, I was a prehistoric animal. I didn't know what to say. Also, if the answer to the first part of the question was "yes," the second was probably "maybe."

"I'm worried about you," I said a little awkwardly.

"That's it? Too bad."

"Where's your car?" I asked.

"I didn't drive. I really only do when it's raining. I like to walk, and I live pretty close by so I walk whenever I can."

"Then let's take mine—it's on the other side of the street."

"Why don't we walk? It's a nice night and we can chat. We'll be there in twenty minutes max."

"It would be safer if we drove."

"You are really worried about me," she said, clearly frightened.

"Alba, two people have been murdered and two are missing—and within just over a week. I don't want to make it any easier for them, but if you want, we can walk."

We were in front of the gym. The lights were on and it felt safe. The same couldn't be said of the street. The trees cut off some of the light and there weren't a lot of people around—the street was almost exclusively residential. I left the book in my car and went back to the door of the gym, where Alba took my arm again as we headed toward her house. As soon as we started walking, I heard an ignition being turned on. Since we were facing the oncoming traffic on a one-way street, I wasn't worried. I looked behind us and saw a metallic gray car turning the corner. It was too dark to see what kind of car it was.

"What did the car that followed you look like?"

"I'm not sure about the year or the make, but it was metallic gray—that I did notice."

We walked awhile in silence. This, despite her usual chattiness; I was thinking about the pistol I had under my left arm, practically useless because Alba was holding my right arm. I'd already made sure no one was following us. There was no reason to worry, except for the silver-gray car that had left the same time we did. I moved Alba to the other side to free up my right arm and gave her my left. She was quick—she realized what it meant and asked if I wanted to go back and get the car. I calmed her by telling her that there was no problem, we could keep walking. We'd gone a block and the tension had been considerably alleviated when I noticed the silver car turning the corner one block ahead of us; it was headed our way. I told Alba to stand behind a tree and not to move, while I walked down the middle of the street to intercept the car. It was already halfway down the block when the driver saw me. He accelerated and stuck his arm out; I only had time to jump back and grab my gun. He fired one shot. His aim wasn't very good: he was firing with his left hand, the car was moving, and the street was dark. When he passed us I already had my gun out and shot three times: one of the shots shattered the rear window. None of them seemed to have hit the driver.

Alba was glued to the tree, terrified. People came out of the buildings to see if we needed any help.

"No, thanks. Everything is fine. Give me a minute to dig this bullet out of the tree. No, no one was hurt—the only casualty was the tree, but nothing serious."

While some people tried to help out, others stood around and pontificated on how violent Rio had become.

"Let's get out of here," I said. "We'd better go get the car."

Alba let me lead her without a word.

We retraced our steps, retrieved my car from in front of the gym, and went to her apartment. The trip was made in near silence; I spoke only once, to ask how she was feeling. I accompanied her to the apartment, and as soon as we got there, she asked me to check every room. I called the station to log in a quick report of what had happened, providing a description of the car and the license number. I couldn't give any details of the attacker. The only thing I saw clearly was the barrel of the gun pointed straight toward me.

"Can I get you a whiskey, vodka, or beer?" Alba asked, breaking her silence. "I'm having a whiskey. Double."

"Thanks. I'll have the same, but it doesn't need to be a double."

"Espinosa, the son of a bitch wanted to kill us."

"I'm not so sure. If he'd wanted to, he already would have."

"Why do you think that?"

"Nobody goes to all that trouble just to shoot a tree. I think it was more staging than a real attempt. Of course he could have killed us, just like he could have been killed, but I think it was a calculated risk."

"If all he wanted to do was scare us, we can call him right now and tell him I'm scared shitless. He doesn't need to do anything else."

She said this with a loud voice while she was looking for ice in the kitchen. She served two drinks of the same size and sat next to me on the sofa. She got up to turn on the stereo. To my surprise, she put on the *Peer Gynt Suite*, by Grieg. She came back and sat down next to me again, propped up on the arm of the sofa, with her feet, in socks, on top of the cushions.

"Espinosa, who do you think that guy is? Who did he want to kill? You? Me? Both of us? And why? What did I do to make someone want to kill me?"

"I can't answer any of those questions. The only thing I know is that it's got something to do with the murder of Bia Vasconcelos's husband and the secretary's mother."

"What secretary's mother? Shit, they killed the secretary's mother too? What's going on?"

"The mother of Rose, Ricardo Carvalho's secretary. Rose disappeared the day after the murder and the mother was found at home the following Saturday, also murdered."

No reason to mention the severed fingers.

"And you think the attack today has something to do with those murders?"

"I've got to; otherwise I'd have to admit that they're random events, which is contradicted by the fact that you two were stalked a few days ago. Maybe they thought I was Júlio, since the other times you were with him. When they saw me more clearly, I was walking toward the middle of the street, reaching into my coat—obviously getting out my gun—and the driver got scared and shot first. It could be that wasn't what he originally meant to do. I'm very sorry. But this whole thing still isn't very clear to me."

"You could have been killed," she said, as if only then did she realize the danger I'd been in.

"I don't think he'll try again. It's much easier to kill someone than people think—especially if you're not worried about the consequences. He already got what he wanted, at least from you. I'm just not sure if he thought I was Júlio. It's not likely that you were targeted. I suspect he wanted to get to Júlio and only in the last second, when he saw me getting out my gun, did he realize that he'd gotten it wrong. The only thing he could do then was shoot; if he didn't, I would have shot him."

"I'm still just as surprised. Why would anyone want to shoot at Júlio?"

"Good question. Maybe he knows the answer."

It was ten till nine. Less than half an hour ago someone had tried to kill us. The whiskey helped take the edge off, but it couldn't erase the memory of what had just transpired. We hadn't eaten, and I didn't want to keep drinking on an empty stomach; I didn't know how much tolerance Alba had, but my own was minimal, and I didn't know where that would lead.

"You don't eat dinner?" I suggested more than inquired.

"I'm not hungry, but if you want I've got some things in the fridge, or we could order a pizza. I just don't want to go outside."

We decided to order a pizza, which I ended up eating almost entirely by myself, substituting beer for the whiskey. At ten-thirty, with the conversation taking a decidedly personal turn, I thought it was time for me to go.

"You're going to leave me all by myself?"

"The danger's past. He won't try anything else, at least today, and something tells me you're safer without me or Júlio around. Anyway, keep the phone nearby, and if you get suspicious, or someone threatens you, call me immediately."

"Okay, but I'd feel calmer if you were here."

Not me, I thought as she finished the sentence. I got out of there fast, before I changed my mind. It was still Monday, and something told me that the week would be long and eventful.

I didn't go straight home. First I stopped by Júlio's house. It was more than obvious that I wouldn't find a silver car there with a broken rear window and, perhaps, a bullet hole in the upholstery. I didn't know exactly what led me to sneak around his house at eleven at night. His car, which wasn't gray or silver, was parked in front of his house, and the hood was cold. There was a light on in the front room that served as his office. In spite of the noise from the neighbor's TV, I could hear music on inside the house. I drove off, feeling like a complete idiot.

The three flights of stairs left me lightly panting. On the answering machine, two messages: Aurélio, asking me to confirm our lunch the next day, and Bia, asking me to call her if I didn't get home too late. I didn't know when "too late" was. I assumed that eleven-fifteen at night wasn't yet the early morning. I took off my blazer, removed the holster, opened a beer, and called her. She answered on the first ring.

"Sorry to call so late, but I wasn't sure what you meant by 'not too late.'"

"Thank you for calling, Inspector. It's fine, I never go to sleep before one."

"Has something happened?"

"I don't know, I'm not sure—it's more of a feeling."

"Go on, please."

"I think I'm being followed—that is, I'm sure I'm being followed, but nothing else has happened."

"How are you being followed?"

"In a car. No more than one person."

"A silver-gray car?"

"How did you know that?" And, after a few seconds: "Are the police following me?"

"No."

"Then how do you know what color the car is?"

"Because I fired three shots at it."

"Huh?"

"I fired three shots at it tonight."

"What's going on? How could you fire at the car when you're just finding out now that it's following me? And why? Not because it was following me."

I figured Bia must be completely shocked and thought she deserved some clarification. I told her everything that had happened, without telling her the name of the girl I was with, unsure how much she knew about Júlio and Alba.

"Are you all right? You weren't wounded?"

"I'm fine. Neither I nor, apparently, our stalker was hit."

"Fortunately."

"Can you describe what the person looks like who's following you?"

"Unfortunately not. I noticed the car—always the same one—but I couldn't make out the driver."

"I don't think they're planning to harm you, but in any case if you notice you're being followed again, see if you can manage to call me. Do you have a cell phone?"

"I do."

"Don't leave home without it. If you're being followed, call me from the car, preferably without the stalker noticing. And remember, they won't be in a silver-gray car next time."

I was sure that the car would be found the next day, abandoned.

I was already starting to admire the efficiency of the stalker. Whoever it was had made it more than obvious that they were following, but no one had ever managed to see their face. And I was also convinced that, when they shot at me, it wasn't to hit but to distract.

I put off talking to Aurélio until the next morning. I wanted to shower and go to sleep. I managed to do the first, but the second wasn't so easy.

3

Everyone at the station had already heard about the shooting. The car had been abandoned in a street in Botafogo. It was stolen. Two of the three bullets had hit it. There were no bloodstains. I had only hit metal and glass. So much the better. Welber came over to ask if everything was okay, if I had seen the gunman, wondering how he knew I'd be at that place at that time.

"I didn't see who fired—just an arm holding the gun."

"And how did he know that you'd be there?"

"He didn't. It was dark and he mixed me up with Júlio Azevedo. He's been following the couple for days. Last night Bia called saying she's being followed too, and she described the same car."

"What does he want?"

"I suspect he's trying to scare people. After my reaction, he'll probably come up with a new strategy. Any news of Max?"

"None. The sister seems really worried. He's never left before with all his things. He had a suitcase under the bed that's no longer there."

"Welber, nobody disappears without a trace. What we have to find are the traces Max and Rose left. Go back to the house in Méier and comb every inch of that room. In the meantime, I'm going to Rose's apartment."

I called Aurélio. He wasn't there. I called back and left a message rescheduling our lunch for the next day. I got a Big Mac and a milkshake to go and headed toward Tijuca.

The apartment still bore signs of what had happened. It would never again be as clean as it was when Dona Maura was alive. I started with the photographs. Surely the lady had a box of them, or even an album. It wasn't hard to find the box—it was in the wardrobe, a shoebox tied up with string. There were hundreds of color and black-and-white pictures. The older color ones were faded, but the black-and-white ones were in pretty good shape. I spent two hours looking through them, trying to identify people and places. Almost every one of the pictures was from the time when the husband was still alive. In the ones with Rose, she was still little. Just like Dona Maura's life, they ended with his death. They revealed nothing about where Rose might be.

After eating lunch, I dedicated the rest of the afternoon to Rose's room. Wardrobe, dresser, shelves, suitcases, purses, boxes, notebooks, books—I didn't skip anything. Every book was removed and examined: they could have some paper, photograph, love letter, dried flower—anything that might provide a clue. The only thing I found was nothing. There was nothing to indicate that she worked at Planalto Minerações and was Ricardo Carvalho's secretary. It couldn't be by accident. No one can erase every trace of their professional life (and perhaps love life) unless the erasure is intentional. And, in this case, she'd done it very skillfully. The only hole was the two missing daybooks. It was unlikely that they were at Planalto Minerações.

The apartment had two bathrooms, one for the mother and one for her. Her toiletries were all there, including her toothbrush. Perfumes, creams, combs, brushes, pads: nothing was missing, which confirmed the report that Rose had vanished after leaving Planalto Minerações, around six o'clock on the Tuesday afternoon of Ricardo Carvalho's murder.

The only problem with that scenario was that it was too cut-and-dried. If things had happened that way, why would someone have to torture and kill her mother? She wouldn't have anything to reveal. If she'd been tortured, it was because the torturer believed that she knew something.

It was dark when I left the apartment. The doorman avoided speaking to me, poor people's natural defense against the police. I went straight home. The answering machine indicated I'd missed several calls. The first two were from Aurélio, one saying he'd gotten my first message and the second confirming the rescheduling to Wednesday, same time, same place. The third message was from Welber, urgently asking me to call; something was happening with Bia Vasconcelos. The following messages were from Bia: "Inspector, it's Bia Vasconcelos. I'm being followed again and I think by the same guy. It's not the same car, now it's a little black truck, I don't know what kind. I'm on Avenida Atlântica heading toward Ipanema." Next call: "Inspector, it's me again, I called the station but no one knew what I was talking about. I'm still on my cell phone, traffic is slow and he's slightly touching my bumper. It's not easy to call without his noticing. He's very close. I'm talking without putting the phone against my ear so he won't see. I already tried to get up on the curb but he's still on my tail. I'm going to go to the first gas station I see." Then: "I'm going into a gas station on the corner of Ipanema Beach and the Jardim de Alá. He came in behind me. He can see me talking. . . . I'm going . . ." Next message: "Inspector, I'm at a friend's house in Ipanema. Please, call as soon as possible." She left the number and address. I called the number. The phone was picked up on the first ring.

"Where are you speaking from?" I asked the feminine voice that answered.

"Who do you want to talk to?" she asked nervously.

"I'm Inspector Espinosa, I'd like to speak with Dona Bia Vasconcelos."

Bia came on the line immediately.

"Inspector, thank God, come get me, please. I dumped the car at the gas station and fled."

"And the stalker?"

"I don't know, I lost him. I got a cab, we turned onto Rua Visconde de Pirajá, and I didn't see him after that. I think he got mixed up when I left the car at the gas station."

"Very good. Stay where you are—I'm on my way over. I should be there in ten minutes. Until then, don't answer the intercom, don't open the door for anyone. When I get there, I'll ring three times. Who's there with you?"

"Just my friend and the maid."

"Tell her not to leave. Nobody leaves till I get there."

"Fine. Please come soon."

It took me fifteen minutes to get from Copacabana to Ipanema, even with light traffic. I found Bia and her friend very tense. I didn't see the maid. After the introductions, I asked her to tell me everything in detail, including whether she would be able to recognize her stalker.

Bia told me what there was to tell. She thought she wouldn't be able to identify the person—he was wearing glasses and a hat or cap. She hadn't thought to remember the license number; she was too scared and nervous. When she went into the gas station, he came in too. At that moment, she saw a taxi that had just filled up; her car was blocking the stalker's. She quickly opened the door and got in the cab. After making sure she wasn't being followed, she remembered the friend who lived nearby. While she was telling the story, Bia looked at the friend for confirmation, as if the friend had been there, and the friend nodded her head as if she'd in fact participated.

"Fine. The first thing is to go get your car. Wait here while I go. Can I have the keys?"

"I left them in the car. Keys, papers, phone, everything."

"Don't worry about it. I'll be right back."

The manager of the station had parked the car. After identifying myself and making sure everything was all right, I asked the attendant who'd waited on Bia when she ran off if he'd seen a big black car, like a pickup truck, that had arrived the same time she had. The kid didn't remember—it was a busy time and he didn't notice every car, and besides, he was dealing with the car whose owner had disappeared. I thanked them for taking care of the car and went back to Bia's friend's apartment, which was only a few blocks from the gas station. There was no suspicious truck.

I went up to the apartment, where the women were waiting. The maid had joined them.

"There's nothing more to worry about—at least for today."

The phrase, meant to calm, came out like a threat.

"What do you mean 'for today'?" asked Bia's friend. "Do you think he's going to be back tomorrow?"

"I don't know about tomorrow, but he'll probably be back."

"But what does he want?" Bia asked.

"I don't know yet—he's not trying to hurt you physically, that's for sure. I think he's just trying to prove that he can show up anywhere at any time."

"For what?"

"Persuasion."

"Persuasion of what?"

"He hasn't said yet."

"Inspector, what are you trying to say? I don't get it."

"They're just suppositions. I think he wants something from you, and not only from you but from the other people he's doing the same thing to, but he hasn't decided to reveal what it is yet. Maybe he thinks the time isn't right, or maybe he doesn't know exactly what it is he wants. When he finds out and when it's the right time, he'll already have created an atmosphere in which he can intervene more directly. But, as I said, these are only ideas, and very vague ones at that."

"What should I do? What do you think I can do?"

"Change your routine a little and stay away from places where there aren't a lot of people around when you're by yourself. At the first sign of anything suspicious, let me know immediately. Always keep your phone in your purse."

"Do you think this has anything to do with my husband's death?"

"I do. Now I think it's time I took you home. You go in your car and I'll follow in mine."

I followed her to her building, looking at all the many trucks we passed. We arrived without incident. While the doorman put her car in the garage, we stood talking in the lobby. We could have gone up—there was no reason to wait for him. But she didn't extend the invitation directly or even insinuate that I should come up. We said good-bye there on the pavement and I headed home.

Bia's presence continued to disturb me. Alba disturbed me too. Different disturbances. Both were intense, but the one Bia provoked was, besides intense, extensive; it affected a bigger part of me. And it lasted longer. I took a hot shower, which for me is better than Valium, and behind the ice trays I found one last frozen dinner, which at first glance looked like pasta with red sauce or lasagna with red sauce. I opened a beer and waited for the three beeps from the microwave.

4

As soon as I walked into the station, Welber came to meet me. He wanted to know if I'd found anything in the old lady's apartment. I said I'd only found some empty spaces, but that we shouldn't let that get us down because things often show up in empty spaces. He hadn't had much more luck in Max's room. He had noticed two things, though. The first was that the cover of the toilet tank was slightly out of place—besides the fact that the tank, which hadn't been cleaned in a while, had water stains on the outside, as if someone had stuck their hand in the water and dripped on the tank a little as they removed it. The other item of note was a piece of blue plastic tossed into the garbage can that still had marks on it, indicating that it had been folded. We concluded that Max had hidden something in the tank. It couldn't have been too many things: jewels, money, drugs. Considering that there was no sign that Max was mixed up with drugs, it could probably only be jewelry or money. Probably something he'd picked up in grocery-store parking lots. There was another possibility: the plastic could have been used to wrap up the gun, I thought silently, not saying anything to Welber. I needed to sort my ideas out. The scene was setting itself up effortlessly in my head. Rose getting to the parking garage with the gun from Ricardo's drawer hidden in her purse. They meet, as usual. She gets into the car and, before he turns the key, she fires on her lover and leaves, running, and meets Max with the gun in her hand. She tosses the gun to the ground and runs away. Max grabs the gun and follows her. He tries to blackmail her. Rose flees, afraid of being turned in. The scene made sense, but I knew that there were two facts it didn't explain: Ricardo Carvalho's life-insurance policy and the murder of Rose's mother.

I called Aurélio to confirm our lunch. I still hadn't decided if I should confide in him about my latest fantasy scene—I hadn't even told Welber. I kept thinking about the possibility that Rose, upon being blackmailed by Max, seduced and then killed him, hiding the body afterward. But that would require cold blood and didn't jibe with the picture of the nervous girl throwing the gun down in the parking lot. Unless she didn't throw it away . . . and Max forcibly disarmed her. Even so, the insurance and the death of the old lady still wouldn't fit. I let my head fantasize freely, effortlessly.

I got to the restaurant before Aurélio. It wasn't a good time to find an empty table, but I didn't have to wait more than ten minutes. When Aurélio finally showed up, I was already working on my first beer. He threaded his three hundred pounds through the tables with the smoothness of a cat, something that always fascinated me.

"The advantage of being late is that your friend's already scored a table," he said with his big smile.

He arranged his huge body as best he could in the space we had been allotted, fixed a familiar eye on me, and said:

"So you want to tell me about the little birdie you let fly away?"

He said it without malice, irony, or judgment. As I understood him, he meant to say: "Watch it, buddy. They could get you."

"The little birdie isn't going to get out of the yard. He could be less benign than I thought, but I don't think he's a murderer. He's too shy. He doesn't have the fearlessness of a killer."

"Espinosa, it's not for nothing that you've got the name of a philosopher. Who's ever heard of calling a robber shy? He holds up women and old couples in parking lots and you come tell me he's shy, that he's too scared. Damn, Espinosa, you're the shy one. This guy gets picked up with the crime weapon, tells a story not even he believes, but he comes across a sainted policeman who believes him. You're that guy's lucky number, Espinosa."

Aurélio's voice was as big as his body, and he knew it; he talked as if squeezing the hand brake of his car. You could smell the burning rubber.

"I'm not a saint, Aurélio; it so happens that sometimes I let intuition take the place of reason. That doesn't mean that I'm his get-out-of-jail card; if he's guilty, I'll get him."

"I just don't want you to hurt yourself, pal, or for anyone to get you because of your saintly soul. After all, was Espinosa a philosopher or a saint? I'll tell you what I think. This Max went, as always, to rob somebody in the parking lot. When he saw the guy get into his car, he thought he could count on the surprise factor and threatened him. He wasn't counting on Ricardo being armed and turning the whole thing upside down. Through a stroke of luck, Max managed to get the gun out of Ricardo's hand and fire it. Nothing would have happened if the moron hadn't tried to sell the gun. After that, the only thing he could do was come up with the story of the secretary."

"Aurélio, you know as well as I do that that story is only good for sending that poor guy to jail, that it's got nothing to do with what really happened. And how do you account for the disappearance of the secretary, her mother's death, or Ricardo's life-insurance policy—which, if I may say so, was discovered by you? Just to find a quick culprit you're going to toss all that out? I know you're a good cop, so I can't accept what you're saying."

"Okay, the story isn't very well put together, but it so happens that there are people trying to get rid of you."

"In fact, Monday they almost managed to."

"How?"

"A guy in a car shot a tree a few inches above my head."

"Damn it, and you're still trying to protect this lowlife?"

"Aurélio, you never saw this Max. I'll turn in my badge if this guy was driving a car in Ipanema, shooting with one hand while with the other he was weaving his way through all the parked cars and dodging the bullets I fired at him. No way. That's a job for a professional, not a loser pickpocket who lives in his sister's house."

"In that case," said Aurélio, "someone new has come on the scene, since none of the known players fit that description. Unless you believe that guy Lucena, Ricardo's partner, is going around firing at cops."

"That guy wouldn't kill anybody—he'd hire someone."

"So, my friend, you're back at square one."

"Unfortunately, at square one I had one body. Now I've got two bodies and two disappearances. I'm worse than at square one. What about your investigations?"

"Nothing to report. The idea of requesting an exhumation was shelved—there's nothing to justify it. I'm as lost as you are."

From what I knew of Aurélio, he was hiding something. I also knew that what he was hiding wasn't anything he'd share; there was no sign that he would trade me his information for some tidbit of my own. Or, perhaps, I could no longer decipher my friend's language.

Aurélio drank beer as if it were *guaraná*. Not me—three beers could hold me for the rest of my afternoon. We said our good-byes when I was on my third or fourth, Aurélio having put back a dozen.

On the way to the Praça Mauá, I resisted going into Carlos Ribeiro's used-book store. The old bookseller could wait for another day. I always tried to take different routes back to the station. There weren't many possibilities, but there were a few variations. On that day I stopped by an old office supply on Rua da Quitanda instead because I'd seen a bottle—maybe up to a liter—of Parker Quink ink in the window. I had a Parker Vacumatic that dated back to the war—the second, naturally—and I couldn't resist the box: dusty, but the printing on it was perfectly clear. Even if I were possessed with a writing fever, I couldn't ever manage to use all that ink. It was a common bottle in the schools back when people used fountain pens, the seller informed me. As I left the store, I fantasized about the prisoner in his cell, with only paper and pen. I thought about my Parker Vacumatic and the washable royal blue ink. It was enough to write my own memoirs and every other prisoner's. I remembered that I was a policeman and not a prisoner. I'd have to come up with some other fantasy, which for me was never a problem. What was tough was keeping myself on a level of reality compatible with my profession.

"Inspector, no sign of Max. We put everyone on it—gamblers, hookers, night watchmen, doormen, besides the sister's whole neighborhood—and we couldn't get any sort of line on where he might be."

"Look in the hospitals and morgues—there's no more obvious clue as to where someone ended up than their own body."

I realized the sentence was meaningless and pompous, but it had already left my lips. Until that moment I hadn't considered that Max might be dead, but given the death of Dona Maura, it was a very real possibility. If he wasn't the murderer, and I didn't think he was, chances were high that he would be the next victim.

"Look for unidentifiable bodies, especially burned and mutilated ones."

It was just after four. The station was hot and full of people. They talked loudly, the telephones were all ringing at once without anyone answering, and from some indistinct place came the ear-splitting sound of a battery-operated radio. I stuck the bottle of ink in my desk and went down to the plaza. After less than fifteen minutes, it started to drizzle and I came back to the station. The rest of the day didn't add a single comma to the story of my life.

5

Thursday morning. It had been sixteen days since Ricardo Carvalho's death, and I hadn't given the chief anything to justify sticking with the case. Before I was sent back to regular duty, I thought I'd pay Max's sister a visit. I parked the car on a cross street. Before knocking on her door, I walked one block to the left and one block to the right, looking for the lottery players. There they were, just across the street on the same block. I came back and found the door open. I entered without ringing the doorbell. The woman recognized me immediately. Without visibly moving, her body shrank back like an oyster. From the silence of the house, I figured the girls were at school. I asked if we could talk and suggested we close the door to avoid interruptions. She was still young and might have been pretty, had she taken even the least bit of care of herself. In spite of her slenderness, her body weighed on her and her spirit was bitter.

"I want to help you—I know your brother's not a bad person."

"You're the detective who was here with the other guy and took my brother to the station."

She said this without anger or emphasis, just naming the game, not the rules. She seemed to realize that I would establish them.

"I'm Inspector Espinosa. I was here with my colleague Detective Welber."

She nodded her head, agreeing with something she herself had said. Then she sat in the only chair there was in the room while I settled onto an old wooden trunk that leaned against the wall. I interpreted this as a sign that she was ready to start talking.

"You haven't helped much and we need to find your brother. I think he's in danger."

"He's always been in danger. Ever since we were left alone, he's been in danger."

"But he's managed to survive. I think this time the threat is greater. What I mean is that now his life is in danger."

"Inspector, for us, our lives are always in danger."

"So you know what I'm talking about."

"Max said you treated him well," she said, changing the tone of the conversation.

"There was no reason not to."

"What do you want from me?"

"I'd like you to help find your brother . . . while there's still time."

"I've never known anything about his life. Sometimes he'd disappear for weeks on end. When he got back he threw in some money and didn't say a word."

"He never said where he was going, he never mentioned anyone's name or talked about any place?"

"Nothing. I don't even know when he left. I just know that someone called him, a man, and I answered, but I don't know what they talked about. Max hardly said anything, he just agreed."

"When was this?"

"Friday afternoon. I don't know if he stayed here on Friday night."

"Did he give you anything to keep for him?"

"No."

"Please, don't hide anything from me. His life could depend on your answer."

"Max wouldn't give me anything illegal to hold on to. I never touch anything that could get me into trouble."

"I never said that it was illegal." I said this as if I were pointing out a flaw in her defense, but the woman simply ignored my observation.

"Did the man who called leave a name?" I asked. "How did he sound?"

"He didn't say his name. The voice was rough, someone used to giving orders."

"He only called once? Had you ever heard that voice before?"

"I'd never heard that voice before, I'm sure of it."

"Your brother hid something inside the toilet tank. Do you have any idea what it might have been?"

"No, I didn't even know he'd hidden anything, especially not in the toilet."

In spite of her defensiveness and her obvious discomfort talking to the police, her attitude wasn't humble or submissive. There was a pride in the woman that rendered her immune to all my efforts to intimidate her.

"I'm going to leave my phone number and Detective Welber's. If you hear any news or if you remember anything that might help us find your brother, call—but don't say anything to anyone else, even the police."

We said good-bye with a handshake, wordlessly. From her house, I went straight to the nearest gambling post, which was little more than an improvised table underneath a marquee. A man with gray hair, seated on one of the benches, kept track of the game, while two others hovered around him. I waited until there was no betting, approached the table, and sat on the bench next to the dealer, discreetly showing him my badge. The gray-haired man didn't flinch. He looked at me questioningly, while the other two moved closer.

"What do you know about Max, the guy who sold the revolver?"

The three looked at one another, looked at me. One of them cleared his throat and lit a cigarette.

"I don't want to make trouble for you. I just want to know if anyone's seen him or knows anything about where he is."

Silence. Then the guy with the gray hair spoke.

"We haven't seen him since last week."

"He must have come out of his house carrying a bag or a suitcase. He could have been with another man. Try to find out if anyone saw or knows anything. Call this number. Don't talk to anybody but me."

I left thinking about the paradox: I trusted the information I could get from lowlife street gamblers but was wary of that same information in the hands of my fellow policemen. The worst was that I didn't even know exactly how much I distrusted them, but one of the things I'd learned from a life on the force was not to confide in other officers.

Back at the Praça Mauá, I decided to eat a Big Mac at the McDonald's on the corner of Avenida Rio Branco. I was thinking about the relation between fast food and the fast life when Welber appeared.

"Espinosa, we've found something."

When Welber called me by my name, it meant he thought the news was important.

"They've found a burned body, by the side of a backstreet, in the Baixada."

The night before, we'd put out a notice asking for news of any bodies found, especially those mutilated to hide their identity. Just before noon we had gotten the information Welber was now passing on.

"The body is charred, impossible to identify. All we know is that it's a white man about as tall as Max."

From McDonald's we went straight to the Forensic Institute.

When the expert showed us the body, the first thing I noticed was its similarity to the meat in my hamburger. The second was the severed hands. The body looked as if it had been grilled in a barbecue until every single inch was burned. If this had been an American movie, the identification could have been done with dental records. But it so happens that almost nobody in Brazil has dental records, especially poor people, who usually don't even have a dentist and, if they did, wouldn't have any records. The carbonized body bore no traces of clothing, shoes, or adornments, but even before the examination I was sure it would turn out to be Max. If any exam could verify with certainty the identification of the body, which I doubted. A gallon of gasoline would had been enough to cause that damage. The experts wouldn't have much trouble determining the cause of death. Maybe a bullet. The severed hands and the fire came afterward. The identity of the dead man, however, could be established only with a DNA test, for which the police weren't equipped and which was expensive—which meant it wouldn't be done. I added another body to the count. Now we had three dead people and one disappeared.

6

As we were leaving the Forensic Institute, I told Welber I suspected it was Max's body. Size, sex, color, and body type. As for the severed hands, someone who could cut off an old lady's fingers with meat shears was perfectly capable of feeding Max's hands through a meat grinder and giving them to the first stray dog they came across. We decided not to discuss our suspicions with anyone else. We walked to the car in silence.

"Welber, we have to find the secretary. Something tells me she's the missing link in this whole scheme. Although 'scheme' is maybe a strong word; what we've got is nothing more than confusion. We have to find Rose to see if we can make the leap from confusion to a scheme. Even if for no other reason than that there are enough corpses to stand in a little line in our conscience."

"Inspector, we don't even know if she knows about her mother's death. The only report of it was published on a page deep inside a paper she probably doesn't read. Besides, we don't know whether she's still in Rio or went to another state. All we know is that if she went anywhere she didn't fly, unless she used a fake ID, which wouldn't say much except that she didn't want to be found. Trying to find someone in the bus station who might have seen her is practically impossible. A hundred thousand people come through there every day, and it's already been two weeks since she vanished. All we can guess is that if she left Rio, she certainly didn't know about her mother's death."

"So we'll make sure she finds out."

"How?"

"Even though it's been five days, I think if we provide the

ingredients for a sensationalist story, there's a chance Dona Maura's murder could make it onto the national news."

Welber was driving. He slowed down.

"It's pretty damn cruel . . . finding out about your mother's death like that. . . . They'll talk about the torture . . ."

"I know it's cruel, but there's no other way. If she's alive, chances are she'll be the next victim. We have to find her before the murderer does, or make her come find us."

The rest of the afternoon and the next morning were used to plant the story. The fingers were the passport to the national networks and newspapers in other states, eager for juicy stories about violence in Rio de Janeiro. We hadn't expected that the news would acquire such exaggerated dimensions, though. Before the end of the week, one network had brought together a round table of psychologists, psychoanalysts, and psychiatrists to talk about perversion, psychopathy, and psychosis, trying to formulate a psychological portrait of the mutilating monster. But if the message was practically guaranteed to get to the addressee, it didn't win us any friends at the station. The chief almost cut off our fingers.

The weekend would be dedicated to waiting. At the end of Friday, I called Bia and Alba to see if anyone had bothered them. There was a clear difference in the way they responded. Bia, without saying anything explicitly, made it clear that I was a policeman. She was nice, but even in her friendliest moments she insisted on calling me "Officer." I decided it was almost impossible for us to get closer one day, not because she was rich but because I was a cop. For some people, any barrier can be ignored—racial, religious, economic—but a cop is a cop. And I think they're right.

Alba's reaction was much different. From the outset she had abandoned the ceremonial phrases, while also eliminating the physical distance. When we were walking down the street the night we were shot at, she had taken my arm with both hands—this even before we were attacked. Bia and I had never touched, except for the handshake when we'd met. Bia made me feel like a foreigner. Alba made me feel like a friend.

The first call had been to Bia. She wasn't home, so I called her studio. The phone rang before the machine answered. I said my name, and before I could finish the message, she picked up.

"Inspector Espinosa, so good to hear your voice."

I wasn't convinced of the truthfulness behind those words.

"How are you, Dona Bia? Have they left you alone for the last three days?"

"Fortunately, Officer. I think the stalker's given up."

"In any case, keep doing what we talked about. Try not to go out alone. If you have to, avoid deserted places, never go out without your phone, and, if you suspect anything, call me."

"Don't worry, Inspector, I understand. Thank you for your concern."

I don't know why, when she hung up, I found myself thinking about the movie *sex, lies and videotape.*

Next I called Júlio. Same thing. Polite, formal, nice: "No, Inspector, no one's bothered me. Thanks for your concern."

Damn, they were meant for each other.

I called Alba at the gym. I got transferred a few times before she picked up.

"Hey, Espinosa, you must have thought I'm really dangerous. After all, the first time we went out together they shot at you!"

Surely a different kind of reception.

"How's it going, Alba? I'm just calling to see if they're leaving you alone."

"Espinosa, do you think I work out all day so they'll leave me alone? The day that happens it'll be 'cause I'm dead."

"I'm not talking about that kind of stalking," I said, trying not to smile.

"Oh, no. I think you sent him running. Speaking of running, you don't want to run a little here at the gym? Not that you need to—you're real trim—but the other day when you walked up the stairs you were out of breath. That's from not exercising."

Was she slightly mocking me or was that just my impression?

"Alba, just looking at those guys took my breath away."

"Espinosa, the girls took your breath away. Our receptionist is still waiting for someone else to look at her the way you did."

"Touché."

"Huh?"

"You're absolutely right. Can I see you home again today? If I leave here now, I can be there by seven-thirty."

"Okay, I need to leave around eight. But there's just one thing . . ."

Perhaps Júlio was going to be there too.

"What is it?" I asked.

"At seven-thirty, Adriane will already be gone."

"Adriane? Who's Adriane?"

"The receptionist!" she said laughing.

"But you'll still be there, that's the important thing."

I hung up, surprised at myself. Friday night had begun.

We weren't meeting professionally; that was clear, but it also wasn't clearly a date. It was hampered by the previous dates, which had been strictly professional, although the last one had ended with an unambiguously affectionate tone. My juvenile fantasies had always included finding myself with a woman in a dangerous situation: I heroically protect her with my own body, and from that closeness bursts forth a devastating passion. The danger was quickly and efficiently mastered, and we had a green light to love. The scene with Alba reproduced the fantasy perfectly—except for the devastating passion. Perhaps, given my congenital incompetence for romance, I'd let the moment pass. I wasn't sure, but as far as I could tell, all signs seemed to point to a second chance.

The truth was that at a certain time in my life I realized I no longer spoke the language of dating. When I was a kid, at parties, just dancing with a girl or squeezing her hand when taking it were unmistakable signs of flirtation. If a woman stared at me a millisecond longer than normal, it was obvious that I could try more; if an introductory handshake lasted that same extra fraction of a second, it meant there was a possibility; a wink of the eye could mean the start of a love affair. We were minimalists without realizing it. Now when a woman like Alba grabbed my arm with both hands as we walked; when, on the sofa, she asked if I was going to leave her all by herself but in the same breath referred to Júlio as her boyfriend, I didn't have any idea what was going on. I had lost my old dictionary and hadn't yet found a new one. The effects of marriage.

I got there at a quarter to eight. I went right to the staircase behind the weight room. Alba saw me arrive, came down, and we met halfway, on the second floor. She was happy, smiling, and fragrant. The last item especially perturbed me. We kissed on the cheek and went down, she one step behind me, both hands on my shoulders. She was dressed all in black: her shoes, socks, shorts, and long-sleeved shirt; on her back she wore a leather mini-backpack. The color in her face compensated for the lack of color in her clothes. When we were already on the sidewalk, she asked if I'd brought my car.

"I did, but if you want we can walk." She looked at me curiously, so I added, "Don't worry, there won't be another shootout."

And we started to walk along the path we'd taken the first time. Once again, she held on to my arm with both hands. Impossible to avoid rubbing bodies.

More out of habit than necessity, as if I were lost, I looked around. A quick glance seemed to indicate we were safe. Nevertheless, at the first corner, instead of going down the same street, we turned right and went to Rua Visconde de Pirajá. The pedestrian and automotive traffic was intense. The temperature was pleasant, most of the shops were still open, and the sky was partly cloudy without threatening rain. We talked like lovers who, for whatever reason, had gone different ways and were just now running into each other. We celebrated the reunion back at the apartment, ordering a gigantic pizza and opening a bottle of wine.

We realized how intense and extensive the reunion had been the next day, our bodies wrapped up together, sheets knotted; light entered through the blinds we hadn't found time to close. My mouth, parched from all the wine, woke me begging for water. The kitchen clock read seven-fifteen. I turned on the coffeemaker. Alba, completely nude, came up behind me and kissed my back. She got a carton of orange juice out of the fridge. We took the coffee and the orange juice to bed. When we got up again it was past noon. Body and soul were smiling.

The Purloined Letter

1

Saturday, one in the afternoon. After calling Welber from Alba's apartment, I retraced my steps from last night back to my car. I was still parked in front of the gym. On the way home, I tried to piece together some of the facts I'd gleaned from Welber. The preliminary examination of the cadaver seemed to confirm my suspicions: the body found in the Baixada Fluminense conformed with the description we'd provided, from memory, of Max. Before being burned, he'd been shot in the head, between the eyes. Professional. I had the feeling we were getting further and further from Ricardo Carvalho, the starting point of the investigation. His murder was losing focus in a foggy succession of events, every one of which, in its turn, seemed to give way to another. Not that the deaths we already knew about didn't seem real: far from it. I was nervous; the center, which had been Ricardo Carvalho's death, no longer held. I felt as if we didn't have a center—rather, we didn't have a set of facts with Ricardo Carvalho's death at the center. I was more inclined to think in terms of several different universes, not a single course of events with a moving center. But these considerations were only truly helpful in disguising the one thing I knew for sure: I was lost; my compass was broken.

Some people, when they get home, are welcomed by their wife, their kids, or by a happy dog wagging his tail. I'm greeted by the answering machine. I'm almost positive that it senses my arrival, hears my footsteps on the stairs, recognizes the noise of the keys, and, since it doesn't have a tail to wag, starts blinking frenetically. And judging by how it was blinking that Saturday afternoon, it seemed like the world had finally discovered me.

Of all the calls, one stood out: a woman's voice I did not recognize who cut off the message before she finished the first sentence or identified herself. There was also a message from Max's sister. After I took a shower, shaved, and made some coffee, I called her. "Some woman called here really early this morning and asked for Max. She got scared when I started to ask if she knew anything about him. She said she had some information about Max. I explained to her that he'd disappeared and that the police were working on it. She asked who was dealing with the case and I gave her your number." Max's sister hadn't recognized the woman's voice. Since the woman had my number and I didn't have hers, all I could do was wait.

Yet another Saturday afternoon: books to arrange, little things to deal with in the apartment, promises to organize the unorganizable. There was a difference now, though: the night before. My awkwardness beside Alba's spontaneity was almost scandalous. While I was always looking for guidelines, Alba simply let herself be. Pure and simple: she let herself be. In bed, she didn't try to be the best lover in the world; in conversation, she didn't try to be smarter or more persuasive; walking around the apartment naked, she didn't try to show off her (beautiful) body, just as she didn't breathe to show that she was alive. Alba was, spontaneously. I was, artificially. Bia was, affectedly. I didn't know if that cleared anything up, but at the very least it underscored the differences. And differences made a difference. If Bia came to my apartment, I was sure I'd waste part of the time trying to explain myself. I kept the furniture because it belonged to my parents; the books were piled up because I hadn't had time to have someone build shelves; I hadn't changed the carpet because I hadn't decided if I would get new furniture. If Alba was there, I'd feel the same embarrassment, but wouldn't feel the need to justify myself.

Seated in the living room, with the door to the balcony wide open, I found my gaze wandering from my foot, which was stretched out on the coffee table, to the building across the way, to a distant hill. Neither my foot nor the hill held any special interest.

I pored over the details of the night before: phrases, stray words, her body, parts of her body, smells, textures, movements, breaths, sweat, gazes, sounds, forms, intensities. What made Alba so accessible while Bia was still out of reach? Was Alba a member of an inferior female subspecies for whom cops weren't considered a problem? Perhaps it could be put this way: cops could be romantically involved only with low-class women. They were an inferior race of males, and the lower classes associated with one another. It wasn't so much a class struggle as a class agreement.

I couldn't deny a certain curiosity about Júlio Azevedo. What made him superior? Granted, he was good-looking, had a nice voice, was an architect and a professor and had an answering machine that responded in three languages. Curiosity was a kind of attraction. And yet I didn't like him. Frightened, hesitant, romantically ambivalent, professionally ambiguous, a careless seducer . . . the picture was strangely familiar . . . but curiosity gave way to indignation, even though I wasn't sure what I was indignant about. It could have been Júlio or it could have been me. I was getting confused. Unbelievable how much I could manage to confuse myself.

Whenever I was by myself at home on weekends—which was almost always—I would set into motion my plan for total organization. The apartment should be as nice as if I were expecting some important guest. The plan didn't entail just surface cleanliness but also my books, CDs, and everything else. Secretly, I believed that once my stuff was arranged, romance would automatically fall into place as well. Because of the scale of the project, however, I needed to decide where to begin. I could start with the books (as I'd already tried) or with personal stuff, clothes, or furniture, with the appliances awaiting repair or with the furniture awaiting the upholsterer. Such tough choices, particularly because

2

Júlio called on Sunday around noon. Bia called in the middle of the afternoon. Both wanted to meet, but preferred to do it somewhere besides the station. When I suggested arranging it that night, rather than waiting for Monday, both seemed relieved. We agreed to meet at one of those bars on Avenida Atlântica with sidewalk tables that seem to attract more tourists than locals. Except for the siege of shoeshine boys, puppet sellers, artists offering to draw a portrait of the lovely lady, flower vendors, and lottery-ticket salesmen, it was an ideal place for a private conversation.

I got there first, just before Bia and Júlio arrived in separate cars. They'd obviously coordinated the calls and the meeting, which didn't affect the meeting but did suggest they were still seeing each other. Bia was dressed in the most discreet way possible and looked lovely. The more she tried to hide herself, the more she shone. Júlio merely confirmed my impression that he physically resembled me; I hoped that was all we had in common. I'd chosen a central table to put some distance between us and the street vendors. It was enchanting to watch Bia sinuously weaving herself through the other tables to get to me. The conversation was a little all over the place until the waiter brought the beers and French fries. As soon as he left, Júlio and Bia simultaneously brought up the reason for the meeting.

"We're being threatened," they said, and, because I didn't look surprised, added, "by the police."

I looked surprised.

"That's why we didn't want to meet at the station."

I asked them to explain.

"As soon as the car chases stopped, the phone calls started," Bia said. "The first was a little incoherent—nothing specific was said. There was a veiled reference to Ricardo's death, but nothing very clear. No requests, no instructions, nothing to throw light on the caller's intentions."

"Was it a man's or a woman's voice?"

"A man's," they answered at the same time. "The second call was more revealing," Bia went on. "As soon as he started to talk, I threatened to call the police. 'No need to call, madam, you are already talking to the police.' I hung up, frightened. I didn't know where to turn. If the guy was telling the truth, I was being threatened by the police force itself. So I decided to call Júlio. I got even more scared when he said they were threatening him too. On the third or fourth call, I'm not sure which, it became clear that the caller was trying to blackmail me, but I was completely confused."

"How many calls were there, in total?" I asked.

"Five or six; I'm not exactly sure," she said.

"Same for me. I think he called us both at the same time, as if he knew when we'd be home."

"Why the past tense? Do you think that just because you're telling me this the calls are going to stop, as if I know who was making them?" I asked, somewhat disagreeably.

"Of course not, Inspector; if we didn't trust you we wouldn't be here."

I also didn't like the plural "if we didn't" and "we wouldn't." I wasn't talking to both of them—why include Bia in the question? It was her turn to talk.

"Inspector, we know it's hard for an honest police officer to hear from two people who are being blackmailed by the police force itself, but if we called you it's because we trust you completely. Besides, we haven't told you everything."

"What are you waiting for?"

Júlio continued:

"In spite of what we've just said, we don't have any proof that the blackmailer is actually a policeman. I got the impression that he had some information, but that he didn't know how to fit it together and was hoping to figure it out through intimidating us. Since it turned out that we didn't have anything to add to what he already knew, the threat wasn't really articulated. It was obvious that he was casting around for some piece of information. He said he knew that Bia and I are lovers—which isn't true but which he doesn't know—and that we killed Ricardo Carvalho for the insurance money—and that we didn't have a convincing alibi—and that it was a shame that two young, good-looking people would end up in a repulsive prison, targets of all kinds of aggression. He didn't ask for anything. He concluded by saying that he'd call back to negotiate the price of our freedom."

My discomfort must have been apparent, since I was the only person in the police who had been in touch with them. I couldn't tell them that besides me only Welber, Aurélio, and the chief knew the details of the case; that would only panic them more. They knew as well as I did that a million dollars was enough to cause most cops' scruples to disappear—even those few who'd had any in the first place.

It's true that, nineteen days after the death of Ricardo Carvalho, many people had access to information, however fragmented—not just at the police station but at the insurance company and at Planalto Minerações as well. I was more inclined to suspect that the caller was someone without any direct tie to the murders and disappearances, someone who was trying to take advantage of the situation. I knew I could count on Welber's honesty, but I wasn't so sure I could count on his keeping his mouth shut. A little commentary, no harm intended—a little carelessness with a piece of paper—a slip of the tongue that raised an eyebrow . . . a million-dollar prize could make corrupt cops fiercer than animals.

"I'm going to ask you to do two things. The first is not to mention these calls to anyone. The second is to keep answering and try to play along with the game. He's going to want to get his hands on the insurance money in exchange for leaving you out of the whole thing. Play along, stretch out the negotiations as long as you can, and let me know absolutely every detail, no matter how insignificant it seems. And don't worry; I won't let you get yourselves into any danger."

I didn't know how I could protect them without getting more people to help. It would have to be just Welber and me—and even that only after I could have a little talk with him.

The idea of prolonging the meeting by changing the subject and relaxing by watching the moonlight over Copacabana Beach was out of the question for now. I had my doubts about whether we could ever do this—at least not the three of us. One of us would have to leave, and it wouldn't be Bia. We said good-bye; she hadn't taken a single swallow of her beer. Maybe she drank only wine or champagne. Beer on Avenida Atlântica was for hicks and tourists. After they left, I sat for a while thinking about what they'd told me. Truth be told, I was thinking more about how Bia had relayed it than about what she'd actually said. It's amazing how I could let images invade the world of words. I should have been a filmmaker. Or photographer. Or painter.

A little boy who couldn't have been more than ten appeared in the space between the tables and chairs. He had a wooden box under his arm.

"Shine, doctor?"

"No, thanks. They're clean."

"It's to help me out."

"They're suede—you can't put polish on them."

"I'll use a rough brush. They'll be brand-new."

"All right, get to work."

And I sat thinking about Bia weaving her way through the chairs, with a graceful movement granted only to those favored by the gods.

3

The next day, I was awakened by the phone. Par for the course on Monday morning.

"Inspector Espinosa?"

It was the same voice from Saturday's cut-off message.

"Yes."

"This is Rose. I used to be Dr. Ricardo Carvalho's secretary at Planalto Minerações."

My mouth was sticky; my eyes tried to adjust to the light coming through the window I'd just opened. My neurons were trying to set up the necessary connections so that my voice wouldn't sound too groggy. I knew it was an important call and tried to rouse myself.

"I was waiting for your call, Dona Rose. I'm terribly sorry about what happened to your mother."

Her voice exploded in a mixture of pain and anger.

"Who was the animal who did that, Inspector?"

"I still don't know, but I hope that, with your help, we'll be able to catch him."

And before she hung up, as she'd done on Saturday, I asked her:

"Where are you?"

"I think I'll be safer if no one knows where I am."

"But I need to know where you are, so that I can protect you."

"Like you protected my mother?"

"Dona Rose, I was with your mother just days before her death and there wasn't the least sign that she was being threatened. It was your own disappearance that led me to her, not any threat she'd complained of."

"Excuse me, but I'm still in shock."

"You don't want to tell me where I can meet you?"

"For now I prefer not to say; I'll call you when the time is right."

"Your life could be in danger."

"I know, which is why I don't want to say where I am. When you want to talk to me, leave a message on my answering machine." And once again she hung up.

If I'd at least eaten breakfast, perhaps I could have been more persuasive. Six-twenty in the morning. The girl got up early. No way I could go back to sleep. So I tried to eat breakfast. I gathered together all the pieces of cheese in the fridge—Brie, Camembert, Emmenthal, and a dry, hard provolone, remains of some ancient party—found some imported jam, prepared an extra portion of toast, and turned on the coffeemaker. It wasn't brunch at the Plaza, but it would do. The fact was, I'd already let Max slip through my fingers and didn't want to do the same with Rose. On the way downtown I thought about how to prevent her from escaping. She wouldn't try to go to the apartment; she was smart enough to know that someone could be watching the building. She could check her messages over the phone, and if she needed money she could always use ATMs. It could be a long time before she showed up.

I got to the station before eight. At ten to nine, Aurélio called. The insurance company was pressuring him to dig deeper into the Ricardo Carvalho case. Forty-two is pretty young to die, especially for someone with a million-dollar policy. They didn't believe that his death was unrelated to the life insurance. The directors were looking for someone to crucify, and Aurélio was the best candidate. He was crying for help.

"Espinosa, I've got to show the company some usefulness. They keep bringing up suicide. They've even suggested that he paid someone to kill him. They think it's impossible for someone with a policy like that *not* to die of old age. For them, life insurance has to be followed to the letter. For a million, you don't die before things start falling off: your hair, your teeth, everything."

"Aurélio, this time I can't help you. I'm in the same situation. My time limit's run out, and the only thing I've got to show for it are more murders and disappearances."

"Why don't we have lunch and analyze everything we've got?" he asked. It wasn't his style; he never forced a situation. He must be truly desperate. I agreed to the lunch, even though I wasn't inclined to give him any more than I already had. I didn't plan to tell anyone about Rose's call. We scheduled the lunch for one, a little against my will; but I didn't feel right denying information to a friend.

Aurélio was really worried. He'd taken early retirement from the force and his pension was substantially fattened by his salary from the insurance company. But to keep that up he had to prove his use to them. This was the kind of case that, if he resolved it in their favor, could result in a healthy raise. He must be under enormous pressure to uncover what the board considered an obvious case of fraud.

We parted with the promise that I'd help him however I could, and I meant it.

As I walked back to the station, I wandered for a while through downtown, on a sort of automatic pilot. I don't like to turn myself off for too long—there's always the risk that I'll get used to it. I think everyone's born on automatic pilot: only a few people eventually take over the controls. Just now I had low visibility. I steered myself through the pedestrians with difficulty; I had a hard time keeping my thoughts coherent. But I managed to get back to the station safe and sound. The week was only just beginning.

It was day twenty. The facts were still pretty hard to link up, and my reports were inconclusive. The two things that seemed indisputable were that the disappearance of Rose was linked to the death of Ricardo Carvalho, and that the death of Dona Maura was linked to the disappearance of Rose but not directly to the death of the executive. It was possible that the disappearance of Max was directly related to all the other events, but I didn't think it was likely. For twenty days on the case that wasn't a whole lot to show. The president of Planalto Minerações had called one more time to find out about the "progress of the investigation."

Monday was coming to an end, but I wasn't going home. The time I'd been allotted to solve the executive's death was up, and this was my first day of routine duty at the station. From that moment on, the investigation of the Ricardo Carvalho case would be lumped together with all the other unsolved cases. The newspapers and television were no longer interested. The media attention allotted to the torture and murder of Rose's mother was due to the brutality of the thing itself, not to its possible link to the executive's murder. The press hadn't established any connection between the two.

4

I had no idea what to expect or how to act with Alba. Only two days ago we'd slept together, but I still felt uptight in the face of her disconcerting spontaneity. There was no doubt she liked me, but I wondered what her liking me meant. It could just mean "I liked sleeping with you" or it could mean "I'm madly in love, you're the man of my life." She still hadn't dismissed Júlio as her boyfriend (maybe "lover" was a better word). Or maybe she just slept around. I was uncomfortable with myself just for posing these questions. I felt as old-fashioned as a tail-finned Cadillac.

I didn't think asking someone else what Alba's actions meant would get me anywhere. If part of her looked like a stereotypical gym bunny, another part of her could hold an intelligent conversation. She had control over her ideas and her voice and listened to Grieg and Vivaldi at home. Someone who didn't know her would judge her on her appearance alone, which (even though it was great) didn't give an accurate indication of her personality.

I called the gym. It was five-thirty. The pretext: dinner the next day. Her voice was happy and fresh.

"Hey, babe, miss me?"

"I thought we could have dinner tomorrow . . . tonight I'm on duty. I could come pick you up—"

"I'd love to, but I can't. I'm supposed to meet Júlio after I get off work."

"Oh, I'm sorry, I didn't know . . ."

"Don't worry about it, babe, I've got to straighten some things out with him. But on Wednesday, if you're around, I'll be ready for another round of cops and robbers," she said.

It was a quiet night. I read a little more of the Conrad, which

I'd luckily left in the trunk of the car and which was a pleasant companion. My reading was interrupted by the occasional police business and by elaborate fantasies involving Bia and Alba—not both of them together; one at a time was already too much for me. At six-fifteen in the morning, the phone rang. It was Rose. She wanted to schedule a time to meet. It was the second time she'd caught me half-asleep. I doubted it could be on purpose—that would be pretty sophisticated for an amateur. She said she'd called my apartment and then, since no one had answered, left a message and remembered to call the station. We decided to meet at six that night in the Largo do Machado subway station. I was supposed to have my left hand wrapped up in a bandage. An amateur.

There was enough time to rest. I went home thinking about Rose. Why did she want to meet me? Unless she was a fool, which didn't seem to be the case, she would know that she risked being accused of Max's murder. Unless she didn't know about it . . . or unless the burned body wasn't his. As soon as I got home, I noticed something different. It took me a few seconds to notice what it was: the answering machine wasn't blinking even though I'd been away for twenty-four hours. It was like being abandoned by your dog. I took a bath, stretched out, and set the alarm clock for five in the afternoon.

The subway station was packed. It was five to six and I was applying the gauze with some tape. I walked all through the station showing my left hand. Two trains came and went without my being approached by any girl who looked like a secretary. I looked around for my hidden friend, but any and every decent-looking girl there was a candidate. Six-fifteen, nothing. At six-thirty, everyone who had been there had been replaced by someone else; only I remained the same. She now knew what I looked like, while I only knew her from pictures.

On the way out of the station I looked for a trash can so that I could rid myself of the bandage, which I did with a certain degree of embarrassment, certain that people were staring at me. Which in fact they were. The voice came from close by and scared me.

"Inspector Espinosa?"

It was a young woman, pretty, wearing jeans, a T-shirt, and tennis shoes, with a purse slung across her chest. Before I could say anything, she said:

"I'm sorry I made you wait so long, but I needed to make sure you were alone."

"And why would I bring someone else to meet you? You don't look so dangerous."

I tried to joke with her, but she was serious in spite of the attempt.

"I'm not talking about a colleague of yours but someone who might know we were going to meet. Let's get out of here?"

We walked to the car silently, surreptitiously checking each other out, a preliminary investigation. As soon as we got in the car, I said, "So, did I pass the test?"

"Sorry about all this, Inspector, but it's just that I'm scared. After what they did to my mother . . ."

"Let's go somewhere we can talk and I can focus on what you're saying."

"Okay, but please, let's go somewhere busy. I'll feel safer."

We went to the Restaurante Lamas, two blocks away. At that hour there still weren't as many people there as she would have liked, but it was a perfect place to talk without being overheard by the next table. It was an in-between time, late for lunch and early for dinner. After we distractedly glanced at the menu, we decided on lunch. I'd just gotten up, so it was too early to have a drink.

"Inspector, I heard about my mother's death on television and I still haven't talked about it with anyone. Why did they do that?"

"Because they wanted information they thought she had, and killed her so she couldn't identify them afterward."

"What information?"

"The first thing was your whereabouts; the second they planned to get out of you personally, I think."

"So my mother died to protect me . . ."

"I'm not sure about that. I think she died because she didn't know where you were."

"They didn't need to . . ."

Her voice was sad and there was a true sadness in her face, but her eyes were as dry as a bone.

"Why are they after you? Who is after you?"

"I don't know."

"What don't you know? Who's after you or what they want? Or both?"

"Both."

"In that case, we'd better get out of here and you can stop calling me at six in the morning just to make me listen to you lie."

"What li . . . lies? What do you know about all this?"

"Certainly less than you do, but enough to know you're lying. For example, what happened with Max?"

The question got her right where I wanted. But she recovered with the classic reply:

"What Max?"

"The guy who said he saw you running out of the Menezes Cortes parking garage after shooting Ricardo Carvalho, and then dumping the gun into a pile of garbage bags on Rua da Quitanda."

"Son of a bitch, he said that?"

"So you do know him?"

"He found out I was Dr. Ricardo Carvalho's secretary and called the company trying to get me to help get money out of the wife."

"How?"

"I never found out exactly. I think it was something about the life insurance money she was going to get. He wanted me to be the intermediary. He called twice the day after Dr. Ricardo's funeral, but then didn't call back."

"From the way you reacted, I got the impression you two had met."

"He wanted to meet up, but I didn't. We never saw each other."

"So then why would he make up the revolver story? Seems to me the story would only make sense if he knew you couldn't refute it."

"Are you implying that he's telling the truth?"

"I'm open to all the possibilities—after all, you haven't denied it. And there are some other things I'd like to know. For example, on the night Ricardo Carvalho was murdered, you left right after he did. Where did you go? I've got a few ideas. First. You two were lovers and got together on days when he was going to play tennis, and the meeting place was the parking garage. I checked out his gym and found out that he only showed up sporadically on Tuesdays and Wednesdays. Instead of tennis, you went to a motel. He got tired of you and you killed him. Second possibility. You went to meet him in the parking garage, as usual. When you got there you found him dead and saw the murderer leaving the scene. Unfortunately for you, the murderer saw you too. You fled for your life. Third idea. Like the second. But with the final variation that you tried to blackmail the murderer. When he threatened your life you took off. Fourth. You were the accomplice—"

"Stop," she interrupted heatedly. "That's all ridiculous."

"So how about telling the truth? You could start by telling me why you scheduled this meeting with me."

"I told you, it's because I'm scared."

"Scared of what?"

"That they'll fucking kill me, like they killed my mom."

"Let's start over. What makes you think they want to kill you?"

"I saw the murderer and he saw me."

"Did you know him?"

"No, but he followed me, found out where I lived, and threatened me over the phone. He said his name was Max."

"Listen, little girl. We've got plenty of reasons to arrest you, but the biggest right now is that you called this meeting just to dump a bunch of lies on me. Some cops are idiots but not all. You expect me to believe that you witnessed a murder, that the murderer followed you home and called you, giving his name and address and that, scared of being killed, you ran off and left your mother for the murderer? Either you're an idiot or you think I'm one. When you're ready to tell me the truth, call me. And don't bother with that ridiculous show in the subway."

I left some money on the table, got up, and left. Before I'd finished opening the car door, she was already pulling on my sleeve.

"I'm sorry. I don't think you're an idiot. Let's talk, I'm ready to tell you the truth. Do you live alone? Can we go to your house? I'm terrified of public places."

5

"He's waking up, don't touch him, we don't know what happened. We should call an ambulance."

The voices were weak but distinct. There was some dirt in my mouth and I felt a strong throbbing in the back of my head. I tried to get up quickly, but my legs wouldn't obey entirely and I was a little shaky. Two boys helped me. I asked one of them what had happened.

"I don't know. You were passed out on the ground when we were trying to park the car; it's pretty dark here and we almost drove over you. Luckily, we came in from the front and not the back. What happened? Did you pass out and fall down?"

They were both asking.

"I was assaulted, I was opening the car door . . . I had a girl with me. . . . What happened to her?"

"We didn't see anything—we were parking when we saw you on the ground. Are you okay? Do you want to go to the hospital?"

"No, thanks. I'm fine."

I wasn't fine. My head hurt a lot and I was still wobbly. I was also a little nauseous. My gun was in the holster and my wallet and money were in my pocket. The only things missing were the car and Rose. I went back to the restaurant to wash up and call Welber. I preferred not to spread this one around the station. While I was waiting, I interrogated the security guard, the doormen, the owner of the kiosk. Nothing. No one had seen anything.

When Welber got there, forty minutes later, I was drinking a beer at a table near the entrance. He looked worried. Before he sat down, he walked around me to examine me.

"Espinosa, the hair in the back of your head is matted with blood. Let's go to the hospital."

I remembered being a kid and hearing my mother say, "If blood comes out it's okay—it's only bad when you bleed internally." While I finished my beer, I gave him a short report of what had happened. We kept looking for someone who'd seen something, but in vain. The place where we'd parked was far from the restaurant's entrance, the stores were already closed, there was no bus stop nearby, it was dinnertime, and it wasn't a busy street at night.

Welber drove me home. On the way, I kept asking him how anyone could have known that I'd be at that place at that time with that person. Okay, so I was followed the whole time. But how did the stalker know I'd be there at that exact moment? Could he have been following me every day, every moment? Unlikely. Tapped my phone? Didn't seem there was any reason to. Just then I was sure that the blow to my head hadn't damaged my brain.

"The answering machine!" I cried.

Welber reflexively hit the breaks and looked at me, frightened.

"The answering machine," I said again.

"What about it? What answering machine?"

"Mine, Welber. It wasn't blinking when I got back home today."

My colleague was increasingly sure that the blow had produced serious damage. Even so, he politely invited me to explain just what exactly I was talking about.

"Here's the deal," I said as if I were talking to a child. "There is not a single day," I began, "when I get home and I don't see the light blinking on my answering machine, telling me I have messages. Today I got back after twenty-four hours on duty and it wasn't blinking. It's impossible that the phone didn't ring all day. Do you know why it wasn't blinking, Welber? Because someone broke into my house and listened to the messages. That's how they knew Rose had called me."

My friend was obviously upset that I hadn't told him anything about Rose. How long had I known about her? Where was she hiding? Why had she fled? I told him about the phone calls and the meeting.

"Nobody could know about it, Welber; you're the first person I'm telling about the girl. Unless she told someone, which I highly doubt given how scared she is."

We got home. The first thing I did was listen to the old messages on the machine. The first message was from Rose. She didn't say who it was, but anyone who knew what was going on could tell. I asked Welber to pour himself a drink and wait while I took a shower. The cold water on my head made me feel better. I came back to the living room wearing a robe, only partially dried off.

"My friend, two observations. First. The son of a bitch is competent. Second. I'm not."

Welber tried in vain to console me.

"The fact is, the guy broke into my apartment, listened to my messages, and vanished without a trace. He followed me all afternoon without my noticing, took the girl out of my hands without my even seeing him, and on top of it stole my car without leaving witnesses. Damn, Welber, the guy's a genius and I'm a moron. I should get out of the police and open a bookstore. If I can still read."

I got dressed and we looked around the apartment. Nothing was missing and there was no sign of the intruder's having gone into the other rooms. We weren't dealing with a thief but someone interested in only one thing: whether Rose would get in touch with me. Now he not only knew the answer to that but to lots of other questions as well, and what scared me was the method he'd used to get his answers. It was a matter of utmost urgency to find out who the kidnapper was and where he'd taken Rose. I didn't even know where to start. No use calling in the Anti-Kidnapping Division or anything like that. It wasn't exactly a kidnapping, or at least it wasn't a kidnapping like the ones the media was taking note of. His objective wasn't ransom in exchange for money. Rose didn't have any money, but she had something of interest to someone who didn't hesitate to torture and kill an old lady. Besides, if I wasn't convinced of the competence of the police, I was even less confident of their honesty.

"We can't completely cover up what happened. We have to report at least the assault and . . . let's call it the kidnapping of a witness whose name has to be kept secret during the progress of the investigation. Or during the disintegration of the investigation."

"Espinosa, all this self-criticism isn't going to get you anywhere. Soon you'll be blaming yourself for the death of the businessman. Why don't we go to an emergency room to have them check out your head?"

"Damn it, Welber, the problem's not on the outside."

I retraced my steps that afternoon for Welber. Then we went over the list of names linked to Ricardo Carvalho's death. We were—rather, I was—frightened by the efficiency of someone who'd managed to grab Rose out of my hands as if he were stealing flowers from an old blind lady. We hadn't yet considered the possibility that it was someone she knew. That was the only way he could have taken the risk of getting so close to us. If Rose had seen him before he attacked me, all he would have had to do was smile at her: *Imagine running into you like this!*

"The other possibility," added Welber, "is that they're all mixed up in this and the whole scene was a farce."

My head still hurt. My self-respect even more. It was incredible that people were dying, disappearing, suffering as a result of a death nobody seemed to mourn and whose resolution didn't seem to matter to anyone but us. I let Welber go.

6

I sat trying to picture Alba's meeting with Júlio. The farewell? The falling-out? The renewal of vows? Love: a romantic, Frank Sinatra version of their previous relationship, together forever. Of course, I wasn't at my best, and my head hurt more than it had the night before.

We sent out a general alert for Rose's kidnapping, hoping that by emphasizing that a policeman had been severely wounded we could provoke some class spirit. We didn't have any illusions that the alert would have any effect, but it was all we had.

The next day, I saw the photograph of Rose distributed by fax and computer. She could have been any woman from twenty to forty. My car was found in Humaitá. Obviously without any useful clues. Even the place it was found, near the Rebouças Tunnel, pointed toward the Zona Norte and downtown as much as toward the entire Zona Sul and Barra da Tijuca via Lagoa and Jardim Botânico. It wouldn't have made any difference, in other words, if the kidnapper had dumped the car at his front door.

I called Bia Vasconcelos. Since I didn't really have anywhere to turn, I just decided to take the most pleasant path. No one answered. I called the studio. She answered. Her melodious voice, her polite, nice, correct way of speaking—it all enthralled me. After the usual greetings came the fatal question:

"So, Inspector, to what do I owe the pleasure of this call?"

In a fraction of a second, I imagined the reverse situation. What would I be like if I were an internationally known designer, rich, heir to a respectable fortune, and a cop from the Praça Mauá station started calling me and showing up at my house? Would I go out of my way to be nice and invite him to my house so we could become friends?

"Inspector?"

I said I was sorry for calling at this hour (in fact, it was a perfectly inoffensive time) and asked if anyone had been bothering her again. She said no. I said she didn't need to worry anymore because the stalker appeared to have gotten what he wanted and wouldn't be bothering anyone anymore, we hoped. She thanked me, relieved, and waited politely for me to say good-bye and hang up. End of the romance.

With Alba, I saw there might be the beginning of a romance, although I wasn't sure, but there hadn't been any sign from Bia that she was in the least attracted to me. At most she might think I was an interesting cop, but nothing more.

Thanks to Rose's kidnapping, I was once again liberated from night duty and back to special status. My immediate objective was to find the girl. After what the murderer had done to her mother, it was clear he wouldn't hesitate to do the same to her. But what was he after? If it was money or some object, she could try to buy time by saying she didn't have it with her, but if it was information, it wouldn't take him very long to get it out of her, judging by the techniques he used. I didn't have any doubt that the murderer would eliminate her as soon as he got what he wanted.

It was eleven-thirty in the morning. I'd just left the station, the day was gray, threatening rain, and my favorite bench in the Praça Mauá was empty. I sat down as usual facing the port (the most interesting thing to watch) and, for no specific reason, remembered the face of Max's sister, more of a character than a person, living out a Greek tragedy in the slums. I didn't even know her name, I hadn't gotten to see her daughters, and even her house seemed unreal. She'd lost her parents, husband, beauty; she'd never had any money; she'd lost her faith; she supported her daughters. She'd probably lost her brother. Max was the perfect candidate for the murder of the businessman, the secretary's mother, the assault, Rose's kidnapping . . . as long as he wasn't frozen in a cabinet at the Forensic Institute. And I was almost sure he was.

It started to drizzle. That was a good reason to get up and start thinking about where to eat lunch. I didn't feel like a cheeseburger and a milkshake, but I also didn't want a plate of rice, beans, beef, and French fries. I started walking toward the Bar Monteiro. Maybe a nice sandwich and a beer would help clear my head. And I'd be right by Carmem, Rose's colleague at Planalto Minerações, who might be able to help me. She'd been the only person there who'd shown genuine concern for Rose. If she'd been holding on to something up till then to try to protect her, she might be more cooperative knowing that Rose's life was in danger.

The rain didn't last long. A few drops occasionally fell, but nothing to disturb my walk. On the way, I decided to stop by Planalto Minerações first. It was lunchtime and Carmem had a few minutes. She didn't seem surprised to see me but didn't want to join me at the Monteiro because she'd brought her own lunch to work. I accompanied her to the room the employees used as a lunchroom, decorated in black and white like everything else. We sat down at a table for four. The lunchroom was still empty. She meticulously folded back some waxed paper to expose a sandwich of black bread with a filling of indefinite color. I quickly told her about Rose's reappearance and sudden disappearance. She seemed genuinely frightened.

"I don't think she's got more than twenty-four hours left to live. She has to be found immediately."

"What do you want from me? How can I help you?"

"Rack your brain. Did Rose ever talk about anywhere quiet she liked to go? Or someone she'd turn to in an emergency?"

"I don't think so. Rose isn't a real nature buff. If she was going on vacation she'd go to a big city, not to the country or the beach."

"And was there any big city she especially liked?"

"New York, Paris, London . . ."

"But nothing here in Brazil?"

"Not that I remember."

"What about hotels she stayed in? People tend to go back to places they've already been."

"She went on several business trips with Dr. Ricardo. They often went to the North or Northeast. I can find out where they stayed just by looking in our files."

"And here in Rio, did she ever have to stay in a hotel?"

The question was delicate and risked exposing possible intimacies between boss and secretary. I was sure that Carmem would try to protect them both. I reiterated that any information, even about her private life, could save Rose's life. But the secretary of the only living director of Planalto Minerações didn't know of any hotel her colleague used here in Rio de Janeiro, by herself or with someone else.

The sandwich was finished. I thanked the secretary and was already getting up to leave when she said, wiping her mouth with a paper napkin:

"I don't know if it's important, but I remember her saying that when she first came to Rio with her parents they spent a week at the Hotel Novo Mundo, on Flamengo Beach, while they were waiting for the apartment to be painted and for their furniture to arrive, and that she had such good memories of that hotel. It was when she was still together with both her parents; right afterward her father died."

I couldn't resist giving Carmem a kiss even as I looked around for a phone. She said I could use the one in the reception area. I told Welber to meet me in the lobby of the Hotel Novo Mundo, and to bring a picture of Rose with him. I left without speaking to anyone else, my heart pounding. I ran to Avenida Rio Branco and grabbed the first taxi. It was a quarter to one when I jumped out at the door of the hotel.

The hairs on the manager's neck stood on end when I showed him my badge, but he tried to be as helpful as possible. I told him that the survival of a woman depended on the speed with which we could track her down, and that it was possible that she was or had been a guest of the hotel; her name was Rose Chaves Benevides. Seeing that I wasn't there about a problem with the hotel, the manager became completely cooperative. He looked in the computer and at a handwritten list; he shook his head at both.

"I'm so sorry, Inspector. No Rose, no Benevides, and the only Chaves we have is a man."

"She could have registered under another name. Look at the women; you can eliminate anyone who's not alone. She's young, pretty, between twenty-five and thirty, brown hair."

To my surprise, the hotel had a reasonable number of single women guests. But the description eliminated a lot of them. The manager was considering several possibilities when Welber showed up with the picture.

"Oh, it's the professor!" he exclaimed happily, only to say, with a worried expression: "But she left last night and hasn't come back yet; the key is still in the box."

We almost flew over the desk but managed to maintain our composure. After the usual excuses, the manager showed us to Rose's room. Before we opened the door, we rang the bell twice and knocked loudly to no response.

The room was obsessively neat. It appeared as if its occupant, with nothing else to do, spent her days arranging the clothes and objects. The arrangement reproduced the geometry I'd seen at her mother's house. We went over the room millimetrically.

Everything in the room was new, functional, and strictly necessary, bought after she had fled. On top of the table, some books. Novels. Lined up next to them were two volumes with blank black spines: the two daybooks missing from the shelf in her room in Tijuca.

The discovery of Rose's hideout, even though it came rather late, was of the utmost importance. From that moment on, we were presented with two scenarios, depending on what the kidnapper wanted. If it was information, Rose was probably already dead. He would have tortured her and she would have told him something. Once he'd gotten the information, he would have killed her. But if he was looking for an object or money or something she couldn't carry with her in her memory, she could protest that it was in her hotel room, and in that case they'd both come to get it. All we could do was pray that the second hypothesis was the right one. And wait.

We decided with the manager that we'd wait inside the room. He was to proceed as usual. Whenever she arrived, whether alone or accompanied, he should simply hand over the key without a word. As soon as they got in the elevator he would call the room and let the phone ring once. I asked him for an extra key so we could come and go whenever we needed to. No one from the hotel, not even him, should enter the room under any circumstances. We ordered some sandwiches and sodas and a thermos with coffee. We'd be prepared to wait a day. More than that would indicate that the first hypothesis was correct.

We ate the sandwiches in the bathroom so as not to leave any strong smells in the closed room. Luckily I had quit smoking. Welber had never smoked: he was the picture of health. I thought of the guys at Alba's gym, I thought of Alba, I thought of Alba's body, I thought of our date that night. I turned to Rose's daybooks. We couldn't turn on the overhead lights; we had to read with the light from the bathroom. We took our positions and began our vigil, trusting in the manager's warning and the second hypothesis.

7

The daybooks, in addition to their normal function, served as a kind of diary in which Rose jotted down, intimately but concisely and sometimes in code, notes about her life at Planalto Minerações. The reason the two volumes were special was that they registered her meetings and travels with Ricardo Carvalho. These weren't descriptions of amorous encounters or narratives of trips, but notes sometimes accompanied by short commentary. The affair had started two years ago (the time covered in the two books). It didn't take long to read the two books—it wasn't a complete text, just quick annotations, most of which had nothing to do with the case.

The codes Rose had used to disguise her commentary were such that anyone could figure them out easily; every written secret is meant to be discovered. After a certain point in the last six months references to New York started appearing regularly. The first one was just "Lucena discovered New York!" I noted the exclamation point. The note could have been an innocent reference to the beauties of Manhattan, if it hadn't been for another, more recent note: "Lucena/New York situation intolerable—something needs to be done urgently."

The sound of the elevator made me switch off the bathroom light instantly. The hall carpet muffled completely any footsteps. Someone knocking on a nearby door and then absolute silence. I turned the light back on. Welber was frozen, seated diagonally across from the door. In the shadows, he could have been mistaken for furniture. In the corner opposite him, near the bathroom door, I was rereading parts of the diaries.

I could make out two different trends in Rose's notes, one corresponding to the intensity and frequency of her affair with Ricardo and another, also mounting in intensity but with an obviously depressive character. The most recent notes referred almost exclusively to the trio Lucena/Ricardo/New York, even though it wasn't clear at first whether the Lucena/Ricardo link was positive or negative, if they were friends or enemies.

The contents of the daybooks were too personal and intimate for the phrase "Lucena discovered New York!" to mean that Cláudio Lucena had discovered the wonders of that city. Most likely Lucena had discovered something that had happened or was happening in New York. It could be something relatively innocent, like Rose and Ricardo's romance, or maybe something more sinister, like something illegal Ricardo was doing in that city, with Rose's knowledge.

Welber was so still in his corner that I was afraid he'd start to snore. I thought it would be better to turn off the bathroom light; reading could only distract me. Between the bathroom door and the bed was an armchair. It looked uncomfortable enough for a long wait. I had already been sitting there for fifteen minutes when Welber got up to stretch his legs. The sudden break in his immobility startled me.

At four in the afternoon, I asked him to find a phone outside the room to call the station and let them know how to contact us in case some information about Rose broke. I also asked him to tell the manager that if he wanted to let us know something more he should call and let the phone ring three times—and that he shouldn't budge from the reception desk under any circumstances. Welber was gone long enough to worry me, until I heard the prearranged knocks and he opened the door.

"The Anti-Kidnapping Division says that the kidnapping wasn't arranged by any known group."

How the Anti-Kidnapping Division could make such a statement with such certainty in such a short time was beyond me. The already dark room darkened further while I thought about it. Another hour passed before one of us spoke. It was Welber.

"Inspector?" When he called me inspector it was something serious. "What are you thinking?"

What he meant was, is it worth waiting here while the murderer could be torturing and killing the girl, just like he did her mother? I'd already asked myself that question a few hundred times. And every time I'd convinced myself that there was no other alternative.

"Welber, I think that if anything happens, it'll be after dark. I don't think he'd risk going out with Rose in broad daylight. It's five-twenty; in another half-hour we'll be in the critical period, until ten."

We decided that from then on everything we did would be in absolute silence and darkness. The manager's warning would give us almost a minute's advantage, but I was convinced that we were dealing with someone much more daring and competent that your run-of-the-mill thief. Whoever had grabbed the girl out of my hands in the middle of the street could easily get to that door without giving the manager a chance to warn us.

Welber had a glass of water and took a swallow every once in a while. I drank coffee instead of water. The thermos was almost empty and the bedside table was practically covered with little plastic cups. The water sent Welber to the bathroom a few times; the coffee gave me a stomachache, especially because I hadn't eaten much that day. Impossible to go to the bathroom. Nothing more grotesque or demoralizing for a cop than being surprised by a criminal while sitting on the toilet. After a while my entire being was focused on my intestines. The world had been transformed into a tube. I tried to distract myself with memories of the last few days, but the only memories that came up were of similar situations. When I was a kid, I'd taken a bus trip from Rio to Cabo Frio, and the bus had gone all around Guanabara Bay. After less than half an hour the stomach pains had started. At first it wasn't so bad, but it kept getting worse. It wasn't the first time I'd taken that trip, and I knew that the first stop came after an hour, at a gas station almost at the other end of the bay, the only stop before Cabo Frio. I thought I could survive an hour. Right when I saw the lights of the gas station I started undoing my belt. The bus just drove right on by. It was the closest to death I'd ever come until age eighteen. I didn't want to relive that anguish just then in that hotel room. I whispered to Welber that I was going to the bathroom, and I made my way in the dark. Fear of getting caught inspired me to relieve myself in record time. I went back to the watch.

Around eight o'clock, my jaw was hurting from squeezing it and my whole body started itching. At first I thought it was mosquitoes, but then I realized I hadn't heard any buzzing. I thought about fleas, but it would have to be a lot of them because I was itching all over. I finally realized it was just nerves. Just then, Welber shifted slightly and made an almost inaudible sign with his mouth. Two minutes passed and nothing.

I wasn't sure if Welber had been trying to warn me or was just breathing when I saw shadows in the light under the door. Then the noise of something being stuck into the keyhole. Not a key—probably a lockpicker's tool; but the lock took a while to give way. When the door opened, the form cut out by the light was indistinct. It could have been a big man slightly stooped or two people holding on to each other, one behind the other. The shape took a step into the room to turn on the light before suddenly backing up into the hallway and firing. We couldn't shoot because we didn't know who we were going to hit; he kept firing at the door. The shots tore plaster from the wall and splintered the doorpost. Welber was the first to cross into the hall. He fell back, shot. When I crossed the threshold to protect him there wasn't anyone in the hall. I ran to the stairs. When I got downstairs everything seemed perfectly normal—no sign of the gunman. I shouted for the manager and ran back to help my companion.

8

Welber was operated on in the emergency room. The procedure lasted more than three hours. He had to have his spleen removed, but the initial prognosis was hopeful. Even though he'd lost a lot of blood, youth was in his favor. He left surgery for the ICU of the hospital. Visits were prohibited. I went back to the hotel to talk with the manager; I got there at ten to one. We were both tense and exhausted. The bar was open twenty-four hours. I ordered the biggest sandwich on the menu and a beer.

The manager looked confused and scared. The key to the professor's room was still in its box; no one had ever taken it out. The only explanation he could offer was that they had come in through the service entrance, without passing through the lobby, and had gone up the stairs instead of using the elevator. Because the halls were carpeted and separated from the stairs by a thick fireproof door, no one downstairs had heard the shots. Only the guests on that floor had heard the noise; they had been the first to come to the wounded detective's help.

"Is he going to live?"

It was the manager's biggest worry. A shootout in the hallway was bad enough, but a murder could really ruin the hotel's image. It was more than that too: the manager seemed genuinely concerned about what had happened to my colleague. I thanked him for his get-well wishes and asked him to tell me in as much detail as possible what the "professor" had done from the moment she'd registered at the hotel.

The first thing he did was find the form she'd filled out upon her arrival. In the space designated "name" she'd put "Beatriz de Carvalho"; profession: "Professor at the Federal University of

Espírito Santo"; address: "Rua Loren Reno, no. 23, Vitória." Interesting, that she had chosen to create a name using the executive's wife's first name and his last name.

She had rarely left the room, the manager reported; occasionally she had gone to the supermarket in the neighborhood or had picked up a bunch of books. She hadn't made a single phone call and hadn't received a single visit. She'd paid for the first two weeks in cash. The few times he remembered seeing her leave were in the evening. On one of the few times they'd spoken, she'd told him she was waiting for her military husband to be transferred to Rio; she'd have to wait until next semester to request a transfer to the Federal University of Rio de Janeiro. In the meantime she was taking advantage of the peaceful hotel to read and write. She ate in her room and never came down to the public rooms in the hotel. The manager figured the military husband must be pretty jealous.

Whatever they had come to get in the room was still there. There wasn't much the secretary had brought with her; the field of investigation was limited. It wouldn't take long to go over the whole room. If it was money or something like jewels or diamonds or gold, it wouldn't be hard to find—but if it were a document, letter, receipt, or something like that, it would require a little more effort. I was exhausted: the wound on my head still throbbed, my eyes hurt from my time in the dark staring at the bright line under the door, and the feeling of failure was overwhelming.

The murderer would be back to get whatever he hadn't managed to get the first time. I thought about sealing the door, going home, taking a bath, sleeping, and coming back the next morning to inspect the room as thoroughly as anything had ever been inspected. But just sealing the door wasn't enough. Someone who could take out two watchful policemen wouldn't worry too much about unsealing a door. I could put a guard on duty. But I didn't want any more casualties. I talked to the manager and decided to sleep in Rose's bed, with the double lock on the door and with my gun at hand. It was a disjointed night; noises inside and out woke me up several times, and the next morning I didn't feel like I'd slept at all.

It didn't make much sense to bathe only to have to put on the same clothes I'd worn the day before. I ordered coffee and began the search. First I'd look for money or larger objects. I started with the bathroom and examined every inch of the entire hotel room. After this preliminary search, I was almost certain that there was no money or gold or jewels hidden in the room. The second phase was tougher. It could include things as diverse as letters, notes, receipts, or simply a number or a bank code noted anywhere, which forced me to examine every page of the books and notebooks Rose had accumulated. At noon I gave up. I hadn't found anything that could be of interest to the kidnapper. Even so, I sealed the door and went home, but not before setting up a police guard in the hotel.

The confrontation in the hotel had entirely changed the course of events in at least two ways. First off, the aggressor didn't know if he'd killed Welber but could be very sure that the entire police department would be coming after him, which would force him to redouble his precautions. Second, he no doubt assumed that I had turned the hotel room upside down looking for whatever he wanted, and that, having found it, I wouldn't have just left it there waiting for him, not even as bait. He'd immediately conclude that I had it on me, which transformed me into his prime target. I wasn't too happy about that—especially because of his proven firepower—but, conversely, I was now in charge of the game. From that moment on, he'd have to seek me out.

After emptying my mailbox, I went upstairs to the blinking answering machine. A useless message from the precinct, another from Alba wondering what had happened to me, a third from

Aurélio, as usual asking if I wanted to have lunch, and another from the detective who'd stayed behind at the hospital, reporting that Welber was in stable condition. I went to bathe, but first I called the station to ask if they could ensure that my phone wasn't being tapped. If I was going to be the target of a murderer, I wanted at least to have a clean phone line.

I took a long bath, trying to wash off the day and night spent in the hotel. I tossed something frozen into the microwave without checking to see what it was and started to return my calls. First was Aurélio. Since I hadn't called him back, he'd gone to eat by himself. He was worried about me. He'd called the station and they'd told him all about the shootout the night before. He wanted to know about Welber. I couldn't tell him anything he didn't already know. Then I called Alba. She was in the middle of a class. I asked her to call me as soon as possible. Finally I called the hospital. Nobody knew anything about the policeman in intensive care, nor did they know who the detective on duty was. The microwave beeped three times and I ate a lasagna with some passion-fruit juice that must have been in the fridge for six months.

Alba called at ten to two in the afternoon. I told her I'd call back in the next ten or fifteen minutes, then left the building and called from a pay phone. At first she didn't understand what was going on, but it finally dawned on her and she didn't ask me to fill in the parts I'd deliberately left out. I told her about the shootout and explained that it wasn't safe to go out with me until things calmed down, that she shouldn't call me, and that it would be better if nobody knew we were friends.

"Just friends?" she asked.

"Honey, friends is already pretty dangerous. More than that's even more dangerous. Soon we can be whatever we want—when it's safe for you, I'll give you a call."

I went back home thinking I could have been a little sweeter, that I could have said good-bye with a kiss, but I still wasn't emotionally up to par.

Around five that afternoon, a police technician with various apparatuses and gauges showed up wanting to know where the building's phone box was located. After several trips up and down the stairs, he reported that the phone was clean: "If anyone's listening, it's not on the phone." When he left, I didn't know whether to be relieved or even more worried. What was he insinuating? That they could have planted microphones in my apartment? But that was for spies, not criminals.

There was no reason to hang around at home waiting for a phone call that might or might not come—and if it came, the son of a bitch would know how and where to find me. I went to the hospital to see how Welber was doing. According to the doctor on duty, he would probably be released from the ICU after a couple of days. He was in stable condition; the major risk now was infection. We'd have to wait and see for the next forty-eight hours.

On the way back home, I stopped by a supermarket to restock my frozen dinners and beer. I bought bread, cheese, and ham as possible variations on lasagna and noodles. If I'd had a dog, he certainly would have been surprised to see me coming home with all those new packages.

The chief had freed me up from routine duty on the condition that I keep him completely up-to-date on the progress of the case. The next morning, I'd go to the station—I wanted to find out what parts of the case people knew about. I wasn't aware of what time I went to bed, but when I was awakened in the middle of the night by a phone call, I had a book on my chest (I hadn't managed to finish a single page). The scare made me think of Welber immediately: had he died? I answered groggily, forcing myself to wake up completely, which in fact happened when I registered the voice at the other end of the line.

"Inspector Espinosa, it's Rose. I have to give you a message from the man who's holding me. You have what he wants and he has me. He's proposing a trade. I'll call back to work out how and when." And she hung up.

Very good. Let's work out how and when. Only one detail complicated things: I didn't have any idea *what* to trade for Rose.

PART III

He Would Prefer Not To

1

Rose had no doubt she'd be executed as soon as the kidnapper got his hands on the letter. Insisting the letter was hidden at the Hotel Novo Mundo had seemed her only hope of avoiding torture and staying alive. Now her life insurance was Espinosa or, rather, the kidnapper's conviction that Espinosa had the letter. But she hadn't had the chance to mention the letter to him. In the restaurant, while she was testing his trustworthiness, she hadn't said anything. When she'd finally decided to tell him, the guy had appeared, taken out the inspector, pushed her into the car, tied her hands, gagged her with tape, and forced her to crouch on the floor of the car while he drove away.

They'd been in an empty apartment for two days. The first instructions had been drastic.

"I'm going to take the tape off your mouth, but I want to make it clear that if you try to shout or ask for help I'll slash your throat."

The way he spoke didn't leave any doubt that he would. It didn't occur to her to try to test him.

The building had many apartments on each floor. Through the bathroom window, through the air shaft, she could hear the sounds of different kitchens, countless radios, and human voices, a mixture that merged into an indistinct noise. From the front window, she could hear the intense traffic on the street. Every time the man left, he put the tape back on her mouth, made her sit on the toilet, and tied her hands behind the tank. The first time, he'd made her take off her pants and underwear before sitting down.

"That's in case you feel like doing something."

An hour later he came back with shopping bags full of food, sodas, soap, and toilet paper. He instructed her to get dressed again, allowing her to wash herself. In the living room she had to lie down silently on a cushion. He sat on another cushion, eating French fries, drinking soda, and reading a book that looked like science fiction. He didn't allow any conversation and at no time tried to touch her. In a corner of the room, on the floor, sat a traveling bag with changes of clothes, arms, and ammunition.

She had the impression that the kidnapper didn't care that she was a woman. He looked at her as an object, an instrument of doubtful utility and a burden he'd be happy to get rid of as soon as possible. In fact, he didn't seem to much care that she was a human being. He'd treat her the same way if she were an animal. The only advantage she had was that she could talk—it let her communicate more easily. His orders were always delivered in a low voice entirely devoid of emotion. Even in the most intense moments, like the shooting in the hotel, he hadn't seemed nervous: he was as cold and functional as a robot. She didn't know how he could tell so instantly that there were people inside the hotel room. It could only have been by the smell, or some noise she hadn't heard. While gripping her neck with one of his hands, he had backed up shooting. Whoever was inside the room couldn't get out; whoever tried was shot. Everything happened very quickly; in a minute they were on a side street. They walked about thirty meters, to the car parked near Flamengo Beach. No one followed them.

From what she could see from the floor of the car, she thought they were in Copacabana, probably at the beginning of Rua Barata Ribeiro. They entered the building through the garage and took the service elevator. The only thing she saw was the hall. They were on the eighth floor. The only time they left was in the middle of the night, to call Espinosa. First the man wrote the text that she would read into the pay phone. In the street, he didn't seem worried; they walked with his arm around her neck. In the elevator, he'd uttered a single sentence:

"Remember, any bullshit and I'll kill you like a roach."

He didn't say anything else until they reached the pay phone. What worried her most was the possibility that, during the call, Espinosa would let on that he didn't have what the guy wanted.

Back in the apartment, he put the cushions together, tied her right arm to his left, and made her lie down next to him.

"Don't worry," he said, "I don't roll over in my sleep." Lying on his back, he slept until dawn without moving.

The apartment had been painted recently and there was a new showerhead in the bathroom. The place looked as if it was ready to be rented or sold. There was only one light bulb in the ceiling, uncovered, which lit up the kitchen and the bathroom when the door was open. In any case, the man wouldn't let her close the door. But he wasn't looking at her when she went to the bathroom. His desire was focused on something else.

2

His life hadn't often been put in danger since he'd joined the force. Most of his days were spent writing reports and dealing with the bureaucracy. The degree to which a policeman was exposed to danger depended more on the policeman's style, on his fantasies and his excitability; Espinosa's style leaned more toward hunting good books than hunting criminals. But whenever he had to go into action or carry out an investigation, his efficiency surprised his colleagues. The difference was that once he was done he reverted immediately to his usual reserve, back to being a stranger. He was well aware what he was like; it didn't matter where he was. Maybe that was why he'd never left the police force: he wouldn't have felt any more at home in another profession. He wasn't a stranger just to his colleagues but to everything—he inhabited a different space and time. That, rather than the shootout the previous night, was what really threatened his life. This and the fact that he'd never been corrupted made him different. People tended to isolate anyone who was different. So he tried to befriend younger officers, fresh out of the police academy, who hadn't yet been corrupted. Welber was one of those, but he was at death's door in the ICU.

Espinosa had been transferred to the Praça Mauá as a kind of punitive quarantine. They hoped he'd learn to be like everyone else. If he didn't change, he'd stay in purgatory; keeping quiet, they made it clear, was the only way to avoid being sent to hell.

Friday morning. Before he left home, he called the insurance company, which informed him that Aurélio had gone to Resende but might be back that morning. He was alone. That wasn't anything new; what was new was that he couldn't enjoy his solitude.

He had to act fast. He hadn't heard anything from the hospital since the night before, but he decided to stop back by the hotel before going to the hospital. The manager came with him, saying that he'd given express orders that no one was to touch the door. Just as he'd said, the door was still sealed. Espinosa thanked him and asked that he be allowed to examine the room by himself. He closed the door, took off his coat, opened the curtains and blinds. He stood a minute gazing at Flamengo Beach and the Sugarloaf behind it, lost, not looking at anything in particular, his thoughts turned to the interior of the room. The scene of Welber going through the doorway and getting hit was more real in his mind than the scene before his eyes.

He sat at the edge of the bed and tried not to control his thoughts, just letting them float. When he'd examined the room yesterday, he had been looking for something (he wasn't sure what) that he'd assumed would be hidden. But it could be something staring him in the face, something whose meaning or importance he didn't comprehend. It could be something big, like a suitcase, or small, like a key. One of the probable answers was a key. The key to an apartment, a safe-deposit box, a locker . . . the search could be infinite. A key could be hidden in any joint of the furniture, any crack or chink or slot. Rose would have needed only five square centimeters to hide it: every inch of the walls, the ceiling, the floor could conceal it.

But if instead of a key it was some kind of numeric code, it could be written down on any millimeter of every surface, including books, notebooks, agendas. Or it could be recorded somewhere, even in someone's memory. He could stay in that room for the rest of his days and there would still be an unexamined hiding place for a hypothetical thing. More than an hour passed. He got up, closed the curtains and the blinds, put his jacket on, and left.

Welber had been released from the ICU that morning but still couldn't have visitors. The doctor on duty allowed Espinosa to talk to him for five minutes. It was a three-bed room, but only two of the beds were taken. The blinds were down and didn't let in much light. The beds were separated by a partition. The other occupant was asleep or drugged. Welber had at least three tubes hooked up to his body, and several machines blinked numbers behind him. But as soon as Espinosa came in, he looked up with incredibly alert eyes.

"How's it going, buddy? I brought some fruit and flowers for you. Careful not to mix them up."

Welber's mouth was covered with an oxygen mask, which forced him to lift up one side of the mask to talk.

"Thanks, partner," he said with a raspy voice. "I think you'll have to call in someone to replace me."

And, before Espinosa could say anything, Welber gripped the sleeve of his coat, pulling the inspector toward the oxygen mask and saying quietly:

"Espinosa, I saw the guy for a fraction of a second, but I'm sure he looked familiar. I saw him behind the flash of his gun, and the hall wasn't very well lit, but what little I saw looked familiar."

"Someone from the police? Someone from Planalto Minerações?" Espinosa asked.

"I don't know, just something familiar."

The nurse came in with a tray of plastic cups filled with pills.

"I'm so sorry, sir, but he can't speak; he has to keep the mask on the whole time. I'll have to ask you to leave because it's time for his medication."

As Espinosa was leaving the room, another nurse came in, wheeling a cart full of surgical instruments, gauze, cotton, and jars of various sizes, and wearing an expression even more stony than the first nurse's.

He left thinking about what Welber had said. He also had the feeling he was dealing with someone he knew or at least someone who sometimes foresaw his own acts, such as in the incident with Rose. Where had the attacker sprung from? The last he could remember, he was alone with Rose. But she couldn't have been the aggressor. It was true that he had turned his back to her when he went to open the other door. All she had to have done was call and say she'd been kidnapped. Why had she talked, and not the kidnapper? Because there wasn't a kidnapper, of course. What Welber had seen was Rose herself. But it wasn't possible that someone would torture and kill their own mother. Why would she? To eliminate herself as a suspect? Human beings had already shown themselves to be capable of much worse, but that was an inconceivable aberration. The truth, though, was that she had whatever they were looking for. How had she gotten it? Could the phrase "Lucena discovered New York!" have indicated the beginning of a conspiracy between Rose and Carvalho?

Maybe Carmem could clear some things up. The receptionist at Planalto Minerações was no longer as interested or excited to see him as she had been the first few times, but was still pleasant.

"Dona Carmem is in Dr. Lucena's office, but she should be out soon. Wouldn't you like to have a seat, Inspector?"

After forty minutes, Espinosa asked the receptionist again:

"Miss, is Dona Carmem going to be spending the whole day with Dr. Lucena?"

"No, Inspector, it's already lunchtime; she should be coming out soon." She dialed an extension and said:

"Ready, what did I tell you? She's free now."

They talked in the room they had used before. Her sandwich looked identical to last week's; it was the same diet soda.

"You always eat the same thing for lunch?" He tried to start off on an informal note.

"This isn't a lunch, Inspector, it's a ration. So, Inspector, the Hotel Novo Mundo suggestion didn't turn anything up?"

"To the contrary, Dona Carmem, it was very useful—so useful that I need your help again."

"Of course. I'm glad I could help."

"Dona Carmem, who did you discuss our conversation with?"

"Nobody."

"Not even Dr. Lucena? After all, he is your boss."

"I only told him that you'd been here and that we'd talked during my lunch hour."

"He didn't ask what we'd discussed?"

"Not really. He just asked if you were still investigating the death of Ricardo Carvalho. I told him that this time you had come about Rose."

"And did you say anything else?"

"Nothing, really. I just said that you'd looked interested when I mentioned the fact that Rose had stayed in the Hotel Novo Mundo when she moved to Rio."

"And you didn't talk about this with anyone else?"

"No. Nobody."

"Thank you, Dona Carmem. Could I make a phone call before leaving you alone?"

"The receptionist will put your call through."

No news at the station. The Anti-Kidnapping Division still had nothing to report. He had a message from Aurélio saying he'd be eating lunch at one in the usual place. The clock in the elevator lobby said five past one.

While he was standing in the lobby, he imagined Carmem going into Cláudio Lucena's office and telling him in detail what they'd talked about. After all, she was Lucena's secretary, not his.

It took only three minutes to get to the restaurant. Aurélio welcomed him with a big smile.

"I thought my message would miss you."

And turning to the waiter who was passing by:

"Waiter, the same for the inspector."

"Well? I heard from the station what happened at the hotel. How's Welber? Is it serious?"

"They had to remove his spleen—it got hit—but he's a young kid, strong. He'll be okay."

"So, Espinosa, what's going on?"

"I'm not sure; I can't quite piece the facts together." He went on: "What does a rich businessman have to do with an old pensioner in the Zona Norte and a low-class pickpocket? Nothing; those three wouldn't bump into each other even accidentally."

The waiter brought the sandwich and the beer. Espinosa took his first sip without even noticing what he was doing. He didn't seem aware that he was in a packed downtown bar with people shouting all around him; he saw only the imposing figure of Aurélio as he kept talking.

"It's obvious that Rose is the thread that connects all these people and the three deaths. From the first account Bia Vasconcelos gave, Rose disappeared on her way home. This after a call in which she claimed to have something important to report about the death of Ricardo Carvalho. Days after her disappearance, her mother is found tortured and killed without managing to reveal where her daughter was—because she didn't know. Everything indicates that Max was killed and that his body was mutilated and burned for the same reason. Until Rose called and met me, nobody knew where she was. The person who gave me the clue and who unconsciously knew where she could be was Carmem, her colleague and Cláudio Lucena's secretary. It's interesting that Lucena's name appears in the daybook in the phrase "Lucena discovered New York." Pretty obvious she's not referring to Lucena's enthusiasm for the city. Coincidence? I don't know. As you can see, my friend, a mythical darkness is falling."

Before Aurélio could say anything, the waiter approached them.

"Which of you is Inspector Espinosa? There's a call for you. They said it's urgent."

Espinosa came back from the phone taking money out of his wallet and throwing it onto the table.

"Sorry, buddy. Today's still not the day for our lunch. We'll talk later."

He left half his beer and sandwich.

3

Espinosa didn't have to look for long to tell that it wasn't Rose's body. The height was wrong, and the state of decay indicated that the person had been dead for more than three days.

"We knew you were looking for a woman, and since this body was found near that other one . . ."

"That other one" was the body Espinosa supposed, but couldn't prove, belonged to Max. He was relieved to see that it wasn't Rose.

"It's not the one I'm looking for, doctor, but thanks for letting me know."

The news of the girl's kidnapping and the shootout in the hotel had quickly spread throughout the city. The police radio and telephone were still the best ways to leak information.

In the street, he thought about walking back to the Praça Mauá. The way downtown passed through the land of his childhood. He remembered going to the Colégio Pedro II, on the Avenida Marechal Floriano, and walking there every day. From there to the Praça Mauá: another walk he'd taken countless times. It was a good chance to revisit some sites from his childhood, especially because the landscape hadn't changed very much.

Certain institutions contaminate neighborhoods, bringing down the level of housing, inhabitants, and shops. Cemeteries are an example, as if death required a border post between itself and the world of the living. The same thing was true of the Forensic Institute, a frozen legal cemetery that lacked even the transforming tenderness of graveyards. The neighboring buildings looked abandoned except for a few low-rent bars where cheap rum was the only way to restore human warmth.

He went down Rua dos Inválidos toward the Praça da República.

Despite the location and the hour, a pleasant breeze was blowing from no certain direction. Right on the corner of Rua da Relação stood the imposing building of the Central Police, crumbling, as if atoning for the abuses of the dictatorship. The building's function had been assumed by a newer building next door, this one free of notable architectural features. The houses across the street, opposite Santo Antônio Church, had become run-down; there were only about half a dozen of the old furniture stores left, and the colonial houses were only minimally kept up.

At the end of Rua dos Inválidos, he crossed Visconde do Rio Branco toward the Praça da República. He took the narrow sidewalk in the middle of the street (nonexistent during his childhood) that bisected the street running alongside the Praça da República. On the left, the Campo de Santana, with its age-old trees and the squirrels that had survived the predators. On the right, the General Archives and the Museum of Justice, with the arms of the republic in relief on the top of its facade. Next door, the home of the Fourth Precinct, taken over by the Heritage Society, clearly demonstrating that, at least visually, not every police station had to look like the hovel on the Praça Mauá. Directly ahead, the tiny but nice colonial building that housed the Brazilian Geographical Society, just after Rua da Constituição, itself an archaeological find.

He walked down Rua Senhor dos Passos and stopped on the second block at the Cedar of Lebanon, a little store counter in the middle of street with different kinds of fried pastries and juices. He wanted to finish the lunch he'd had to break off. It was almost three, and the long tables where everyone sat next to each other had some seats available. But he didn't want to sit down; he just wanted to fill the hole in his stomach. That he could do standing up, right there on the sidewalk.

He kept walking, overtaken by the smell of tobacco coming from the Syria Cigar Store. It was like smoking a cigarette after lunch, something he still missed. He turned left into Avenida Passos, crossed Presidente Vargas, and came out on Marechal Floriano, directly in front of the Colégio Pedro II. He could even feel the little leather schoolbag whose handle changed every year as the books and notebooks got heavier. I don't carry a schoolbag anymore, he thought. I carry cadavers. He tried to push the image of Rose's mother's fingers out of his head. He stood for a while in front of the stonework facade of his old school, with its iron and wooden doors and cast-iron and marble staircases. How many times he'd run up those stairs, late for class! Rose hadn't called back; rather, the kidnapper hadn't used Rose to call back. Why didn't he call himself? Welber said he looked somehow familiar. Was that the reason he'd made Rose call? Because if he did it himself he'd be recognized? He continued down Marechal Floriano toward Rua Acre. And what if someone was calling his apartment or the station right now? The phone could be ringing as the inspector was downtown, strolling down memory lane. Passing the corner of Rua dos Andradas, he looked to the left and momentarily lost his train of thought. The street was a corridor of little old houses from the middle of the last century, with tiny balconies of wrought iron, the sidewalks almost touching each other on the narrow street, at the end of which the hill of Santo Cristo was lit up by the sun. The beauty of the place was moving. Turning to the right, down Rua Leandro Martins, he experienced a similar sensation. Back then, he said to himself, crimes were extraordinary. Today they were committed in series. Without realizing it, he'd arrived back at Rua Acre, practically at the station.

Espinosa knew the kidnapper wouldn't call during the day. He preferred the protection of the early morning, when he had the added buffer of finding Espinosa groggy and disinclined to effective action—if there was any action he could take. Espinosa knew there was no reason to stay up all night; that would only make him even less effective.

4

The incident in the parking garage had taken place almost a month ago. There hadn't been a Mass for Ricardo Carvalho. Or mourning. Or memorials. It looked as though everyone wanted to forget about him. The only one who had seemed to regret his loss was Rose, and right now she must be more concerned about her own situation. If everyone was satisfied with what had happened to Ricardo Carvalho, why seek out the guilty? When people were making laws, they were trying to express in the human microcosm the order of the macrocosm. The function of the police was to capture deviants. Only a few people were authorized to kill; anyone else who did must be brought to justice. Espinosa didn't think that this particular justification, however fictive, was any better or worse than the others. Sometimes, he made little adjustments on his own.

One of the adjustments he wanted to make had to do with Bia Vasconcelos. Where was it written that they were incompatible? For now, though, he preferred to pursue the possible. He called Alba. He'd forgotten the name of the magnificent receptionist, but she hadn't forgotten his.

"How's it going, Espinosa? When are you going to start?"

"Start what?" he answered, not sure he knew exactly who he was talking to.

"Start working out."

He remembered her name.

"Adriane, I couldn't stand working out for five minutes."

"Depends on the workout, though, doesn't it?"

He smiled into the phone and asked if he could speak to Alba.

"Hey, handsome, what's this about it being dangerous for us to meet?"

"Until some things get resolved, I wouldn't like people to know that you're important to me."

"Am I?"

Espinosa was always surprised by Alba's responses. The fraction of a second he needed to react, pretending nothing happened, was an unmistakable sign for Alba that she'd hit the nail on the head.

"You don't need to answer, sweetheart. Come get me and show me yourself."

When he drew his car up to the door of the gym that night, Alba was already waiting for him. She wasn't wearing her workout clothes; she had on jeans, a blue T-shirt, and blue tennis shoes: her firm breasts hinted that they were loose under her shirt. They kissed as if they'd been together for a long time.

"Do you live alone?"

That question surprised him too.

"Yes," he responded, a little nervous.

"So take me to your house and show me around. On the way you can explain why it's dangerous for us to go out together."

Espinosa told her the story of Rose's reappearance, the kidnapping, the shooting in the hotel, and the phone call.

"I'm scared," he continued, "that the kidnapper might try to force my hand, using something he thinks is important to me."

It was clear that Alba did feel important, more beloved than threatened. Espinosa had to reiterate that the threat was real.

"Alba, I don't know who this guy is, but he's definitely a cold-blooded killer, probably a psychopath. He's already seen us together once and I don't want to take any chances. My apartment is not safe—I even thought he'd tapped my phone. He's not an amateur."

Espinosa finished this last sentence as they were pulling up to his building. He wasn't worried about the guy just then—he was probably busy guarding Rose. Unless they were a team.

Luckily he'd stocked up at the supermarket. The frozen dinners would last another week, and there was still plenty of cheese, cold cuts, and drinks. He even had ice cream in the freezer.

The sexual readiness Alba projected contrasted with the deliberation with which she arrived at intimacy. She wandered around the living room seeming to notice more what was there than what wasn't, until she came to the bookshelf. She smiled. She went to the balcony and turned around, leaning on the railing. Espinosa was still standing in the living room.

"Your apartment is your face."

"What do you mean?" he wanted to know.

"All makeshift, all wonderful."

She sat lazily on the sofa while Espinosa went to get something to drink. In movies that's what the guy did; when he was embarrassed he showed up with a glass in each hand. Not a bad idea when you didn't know what to do with the girl.

It had been a while since a woman had been in the apartment. Espinosa had been afraid that when it happened he'd feel invaded. But that absolutely wasn't how he felt now. He also didn't feel as if he had a visitor. It felt so natural to have her there. And what he liked the most was that he didn't feel as though he had to justify himself to her. In one of his hands he had a beer, in the other a soda. He looked at her on the sofa a little awkwardly, as if he'd been surprised to realize he had been thinking out loud.

It didn't look as if Alba felt uncomfortable in the least, even though she knew next to nothing about him. In any case, she didn't seem interested in his life story right now. She made it clear that she loved the sense that much about him still remained to be written, not because he didn't have a life story but because it was written on a surface that had proven easy to erase.

While he served the beer, Espinosa remembered the night he'd spent with Alba. Things had happened so naturally, facilitated, perhaps, by the drama of the previous day. The role of protector had made intimacy easier. Now there was still something to be scared of. But what the hell. People didn't get together because they were scared, because there was a threat . . .

He wasn't shy. At least he didn't feel shy, just a little out of sync with the prevailing rules. Even animals, when forming couples, follow signals, the code of their species. The problem was that in the human world, depending on the time and place, the codes were extremely changeable, and he always seemed to be in the wrong place at the wrong time.

From the sofa, Alba looked up at him, clearly bemused.

"Espinosa, I think you need to change your battery." She pushed him with her leg and he fell to the sofa on his knees, holding on to the two bottles. He put them on the coffee table and grabbed Alba. Her hair was still wet from her shower; her skin smelled like a woman's. While she was pulling off her T-shirt she asked Espinosa to pull her underwear down to her thighs. After pulling them all the way off, Espinosa, standing, let Alba's feet rest against his stomach for a while. She let him look at her, confident of her beauty. Espinosa remained standing, taking his clothes off slowly, afraid to break the magic, keeping her feet against his body, grabbing her ankles and spreading them slowly and sliding his head between her legs until he lost himself in a tangle of moist perfume.

Espinosa groped in the dark and found Alba's body. Half of it was on top of one of his legs; she was sleeping so soundly that she didn't hear the telephone ringing. With great effort he found the phone at the same time he turned on the lamp. The alarm clock read two-ten in the morning.

5

Just like last time, Rose mechanically read the kidnapper's instructions into the phone, voice uninflected, no doubt with a gun to her head. He gave Espinosa approximately twenty hours to get his hands on the letter, in case he didn't already have it. It should be placed in its original envelope within a brown envelope approximately twenty-five by twelve centimeters, the kind available anywhere. After ten o'clock the next night, he was to wait at home for a call with new instructions. In the event that he tried to get help from the station or the Anti-Kidnapping Division, the kidnapper would know about it even before Espinosa hung up the phone, and the price would be the fingers from one of Rose's hands.

"So it's a letter!" Espinosa tried to mentally reproduce his search in the Hotel Novo Mundo and couldn't remember any envelope. It was true that at the time he didn't know what he was looking for, and he could have missed it. But he surely would have remembered an envelope.

Alba was already wide awake; she looked at his face, terrified.

"What was that? What's going on?"

They were quiet but worried and frightened. Espinosa didn't want to test the kidnapper's threat—he'd already shown what he was capable of. Besides, the kidnapper really could be linked to someone at the station or in the Anti-Kidnapping Division.

"I have approximately twenty hours to find a letter. I'd better take you home."

"You're going to leave now, at two in the morning, to go look for a letter? Are you crazy? What letter?"

"I haven't got the slightest idea," Espinosa said, starting to get dressed. Alba looked completely incredulous but got dressed anyway.

The streets were empty, so he dropped Alba at home and was at the reception desk of the Hotel Novo Mundo before three, trying to convince the night clerk that he wouldn't make any noise. At seven in the morning, after a painstaking search of every possible space in the room, he was absolutely certain that there was no envelope. He'd slept at most two hours and had hardly eaten the day before. He called the hotel restaurant and ordered a complete breakfast.

While he ate he thought about the envelope. From the conversation he'd had with the hotel manager, he had learned that she had hardly left the room during her stay. Just to be safe, she could have left the letter with someone she trusted—if after the death of Ricardo she still trusted anyone. There was a remote possibility that Carmem had the letter. After all, she had suggested the hotel. Another remote possibility was that Bia Vasconcelos had it. Before she'd disappeared, Rose had called Bia to arrange a meeting to talk about something very important related to Ricardo Carvalho's death.

He stopped by his apartment to shower, shave, and change clothes, before going to Bia Vasconcelos's studio.

He arrived unannounced a few minutes after Bia had parked and turned on the coffeemaker. The receptionist announced that Inspector Espinosa was on his way up.

"Inspector, it's been a while."

"Almost a week since we last saw each other."

"Come in, please. You got here at coffee time. Any news?"

"The first mangoes have appeared."

Bia didn't understand immediately what Espinosa meant until he pointed to the mango tree in the garden.

"The last time I was here it was flowering—now the first mangoes are coming out."

Weird guy, Bia thought. His answers are always different from the questions.

"There's actually a lot of news, but not the kind of news that clears anything up—mostly the kind that distorts, and hides, more than it reveals."

Bia filled up two coffee cups.

"For example, Rose appeared."

Bia, holding the two cups and looking at Espinosa, stopped, waiting for what would come next.

"Only to disappear again." Bia gave him one of the cups.

"Kidnapped."

Bia's mouth was half open, she looked at him, not breathing.

"Out of my hands."

She sat; Espinosa was still standing.

"Sit down, please, Inspector."

If Espinosa had meant to surprise her, he'd done it.

"You're saying that Rose came back and then was kidnapped when she was with you?"

"That's right."

Júlio had warned Bia about this cop. Espinosa had come to his house on a Sunday afternoon with a story that could have been as much a product of a delirious brain as an attempt at blackmail. Now the two were seated on the sofa, drinking coffee. He wasn't at all unpleasant—she even had to force herself to remember that he was a cop. If it weren't for the gun that occasionally appeared underneath his blazer, she would have thought he was a university professor, no different from Júlio himself. But it would be imprudent to forget that he was a cop, and a cop on duty.

"How do you think I can help you, sir?"

The question was put with a slight hesitation, imperceptible to anyone who wasn't looking for it, but loud and clear to Espinosa.

"Before her first disappearance, Rose was on her way to your apartment. She'd called you alluding to something very important, so important that she had to meet you that very afternoon. The reason she's been kidnapped now is for a letter she's supposed to have, the contents of which are somehow linked to your late husband. The kidnapper proposed exchanging the letter for Rose's life. But it happens that I don't have the letter, and neither is it in the hotel room where she was hiding. I was hoping that perhaps she brought you that letter before disappearing the first time."

"Inspector, as I told you then, Rose not only didn't bring me anything, but she didn't even meet me. The last time I saw her was at Ricardo's funeral."

The morning light—clean, fresh, and shining—came through the wide window. Espinosa put the coffee cup on the desk in front of him and ran his hands through his hair, as if that gesture closed off an idea. He got up and wished Bia Vasconcelos a nice day. She was disconcerted by the sudden and dry end to the meeting.

"You don't have anything to add to what I've said?" she asked.

The question was intended more to prolong the encounter than to find out anything else.

"Just that she doesn't have much hope of getting out of this alive."

And when he was already on the external staircase that led back down, he added:

"Don't forget to send the mangoes you promised me."

He walked toward the gate, hands in his pockets, as if he were ending a Sunday visit to an aunt.

He got to Planalto Minerações at ten-thirty.

"Good morning."

"Good morning, Inspector. Would you like to speak with Dona Carmem?"

"If I may."

"I don't think she should be busy—Dr. Lucena hasn't gotten in yet."

"Dona Carmem, that inspector wants to talk to you." After a pause, the receptionist added: "She's coming, Inspector. Won't you take a seat?"

No, he wouldn't. The last time he'd taken a seat, he'd waited for forty minutes. The situation now was different—more urgent. He had to find that letter—if he didn't, Rose's life would be absolutely worthless. So he didn't have time to sit and wait. He was about to say this to the receptionist when Carmem appeared in the hallway.

"At least this time you came at a different time. Now we won't have to sit in the cafeteria."

The sentence was accompanied by a well-meaning smile.

They talked in the space that had belonged to Rose, directly in front of Ricardo Carvalho's office. Espinosa briefly summed up what had happened since they'd last spoken.

"As you can see, Dona Carmem, Rose's life depends on a letter I need to hand over to someone after ten o'clock tonight. I don't have any idea where this letter might be. I had two ideas—the first one wasn't right, and the second is that Rose left the letter with you or hid it here."

"She didn't leave anything with me, Inspector. As for hiding it here before she left, I don't think so. In any case, if you want to, we can look around in here. I don't dare go through Dr. Ricardo's office. I could only do that with the permission of Dr. Weil."

"Don't worry, I don't want to invade anyone's privacy, I just want to find the letter, which is Rose's only hope of coming out of this alive."

The space wasn't very big. It was the waiting room for Ricardo Carvalho's office, separated by an internal door, next to which Rose's desk sat, alongside a computer table. The mail piled up on top of the desk bore witness to the amount of time Rose had been gone. In the drawers, nothing that wasn't strictly necessary to her job; in the last one, a few personal-hygiene products and a face towel wrapped up in a plastic bag. Espinosa unrolled the towel, opened and examined every one of the maxipads, made sure there wasn't anything stuck underneath the drawers. Deep down, he agreed with Carmem that it was pretty unlikely that Rose had hidden the letter in that room or in any other at Planalto Minerações.

He left wondering if he should go to the apartment in Tijuca, but decided against it. It wasn't any more likely that Rose had gone to her mother's apartment than that she'd gone back to Planalto Minerações. The letter must have been with her while she was in hiding and she'd decided to stash it somewhere else when she went out to meet Espinosa. Or—the worst-case scenario—the letter had been with her the whole time: in her purse, inside her blouse, in a false pocket, somewhere so close to her own body that the kidnapper hadn't thought to look there. Even when forced to make those phone calls, she hadn't said anything because she didn't want to end her own life.

He went into a stationery store and bought a regular envelope and a brown envelope of the required size. He put one inside the other and stuck them in his jacket pocket. He had a little more than ten hours before the time dictated by the kidnapper, and he couldn't make any plans because he didn't know what he'd have to arrange.

It was no use talking to Max's sister. Welber was his final hope.

6

They hadn't removed the sign prohibiting visits; Welber was still being monitored. His roommate was gone; Espinosa didn't want to know where. In the hall, the carts passed, full of used lunch trays; inside the rooms, the patients took advantage of the moment to nap before the afternoon session: temperature, blood pressure, shots, pills, therapy, and everything else that fills up what remains of the lives of the ill.

As soon as Espinosa came in, Welber's eyes opened with surprising immediacy.

"Espinosa, how great to see you. Seems like my roommate couldn't resist all the good treatment. There's people like that—mistreated their whole lives, and when they're treated well they die. Must be so they don't have to go back to the way things were before."

"Welber, just listen. Don't talk, except at the end."

Welber didn't have his oxygen mask on, but it was still hard for him to talk. Espinosa went over the events of the last forty-eight hours, omitting only the part about Alba. When he mentioned the letter, Welber's eyes sparkled.

"So the reason for all this is a letter," he said in a low voice, to himself.

Espinosa interrupted.

"I don't know if it's the reason for all this, but at least it's the reason for the latest events. I'm not sure what the motive was for the murder of Ricardo Carvalho."

Welber appeared slightly agitated.

"Espinosa, day or night I can't stop thinking about that ghost who shot at us."

"Don't try to force yourself to remember—that's worse. Suddenly, when you least expect it, you'll remember. But please, if that happens before ten o'clock tonight, call me."

Espinosa called the precinct from the hospital. No news. They kept reiterating that it was an isolated kidnapping, not related to the "normal kidnappings in the city." Espinosa was stunned by the phrase: how could cops talk about "normal kidnappings"? Were there normal kidnappings and abnormal kidnappings?

What Espinosa wanted more than anything was to slow down and think intelligently about how to save Rose. Slowing down wasn't such a problem—he was already paralyzed. As for thinking intelligently, that was what he'd been trying to do since the beginning of the case. If at the stipulated hour he still didn't have a concrete plan, he was prepared to go to the meeting with the empty envelope. Really, he didn't have a choice; if he revealed to the kidnapper that he didn't have the letter, the kidnapper would know Rose had been bluffing. The kidnapper would get it out of her by torture. And once he had it, there wouldn't be any reason to let her live. Rose's only hope was the kidnapper's belief that Espinosa had the letter. He'd already killed at least two people; he wouldn't hesitate to kill a third, especially to save his own skin.

He left Gávea and drove around for a while at random. Passing through Copacabana, he reflected that if he didn't have anywhere to go or anything to do he might as well stay home near the phone. On the way, he wolfed down something—ten minutes later he wouldn't be able to remember what. When he got home, the machine's blinking indicated there was only one message. From the bank, inviting him to come learn about different ways to invest the money in his checking account. He didn't feel like it. Besides, the money wouldn't be there long. He erased the message, called the station to let them know he'd be at home, sat down on the living room sofa, and began his wait. Two minutes later, he got up. He couldn't just sit there when Rose's life was in danger. He'd never seen any movie star sitting at home, staring at the ceiling, waiting for something to happen. The kidnapper had said that he'd call after ten. So it didn't do any good to sit around and wait at two.

His colleagues, in a situation like this, would be assiduously interrogating suspects, putting their informants into action, doing what every policeman was trained to do. The only action he'd taken so far was to detain a suspect he'd then immediately released because he "didn't look like a killer" and who, almost certainly, was sleeping the eternal sleep in a cabinet at the Forensic Institute. He knew how rarely the police did anything effective to solve a crime. Ninety percent was a cynical game, and since he wasn't in the mood for that there remained the 10 percent of activity— which he was now performing on the living room couch.

He removed the envelopes he'd bought from his coat pocket, inserted a twice-folded piece of paper into the small one, and placed it inside the brown envelope, which he didn't seal. He left it on the coffee table, with a 9 mm pistol as a paperweight. That was all he could do for the time being.

That day, Carmem had spent her free moments (she had a lot: Cláudio Lucena was out of the office) thinking about Rose and reflecting that she hadn't always been so nice to Inspector Espinosa. She'd only collaborated exactly as much as he had asked, and there was no reason for her to act that way: Rose was her only friend in the company, and the policeman had always been nice and polite.

While she was thinking, she examined Rose's work space again, imagining where she herself, Carmem, would have hidden a letter. It wasn't in her desk, or in the rolling file cabinet her colleague always kept close by when she was working. She took the accumulated correspondence and started to separate out the business letters from the personal letters for Ricardo Carvalho. Among the correspondence addressed to Rose, one envelope especially stood out. It had no return address. What intrigued Carmem was that the handwriting was Rose's own.

Carmem was probably the only person in the company who knew about the affair between Ricardo Carvalho and his secretary. She knew how it had started around two years ago; she knew they met on Tuesdays and Thursdays, even though they hadn't talked about it very openly. If Dr. Daniel Weil had found out about it, Rose would have been fired instantly and Ricardo Carvalho's own situation would have become difficult. Carmem hadn't worried about him, but she had been concerned for her friend. She knew that Ricardo Carvalho was worthless, and she knew that if the word "ethics" was removed from the dictionary, Cláudio Lucena, for one, wouldn't miss it. But she liked Rose, who was a highly competent secretary yet as naive as a newborn babe when it came to Ricardo Carvalho. She had no doubt that the death of Rose's boss and lover had taken her by surprise. And now there was that envelope, apparently sent to herself, appearing at the exact moment Espinosa was asking about a lost letter.

The fact that the handwriting on the letter was Rose's own made Carmem decide to call the inspector. He was the only one in the midst of all the confusion who seemed to be worried about her. He'd left a card with his numbers at work and at home. She tried the first and was informed that Espinosa was out on a case and hadn't come back yet. She tried his home and got the answering machine. She left a message. It was six in the evening and the employees of Planalto Minerações were starting to leave. She thought it would be better to take the envelope with her in case the inspector wanted to see her. It had been a peaceful day with Cláudio Lucena away.

While he was walking through Copacabana, Espinosa was thinking about the confrontation with the kidnapper. At a certain moment, he would trade what the kidnapper thought was the letter for Rose. It was the moment of greatest exposure for both sides. The so-called kidnapping industry had even inspired the birth of firms, domestic and international, specializing in resolving kidnappings—negotiating the amount of the ransom and the conditions under which the hostage would be liberated. In this case, there was no money, only a letter. It was a simple exchange: a prisoner for a letter. Espinosa didn't think things would happen that way. Unless the kidnapper took extreme measures to conceal his identity, he would have to kill Rose. And Espinosa would have to be killed at the moment of exchange as well.

Without realizing it, Espinosa had cut around the Peixoto neighborhood, down a block of Rua Santa Clara, and now found himself directly in front of Júlio's building. Six in the evening. Time for a professor to be home. The parking spot in front was empty, and there was a weak light upstairs. Some people liked to leave a lamp on when they went out, to give the illusion that someone was home. In Espinosa's opinion, the only thing that accomplished was to light the way for the burglar. All the houses on the street were lit up, and in all of them he could make out the bluish light of the television. He shyly rang Júlio's bell, as if he were walking into a church in the middle of Mass. The second time he pressed harder. The door to the house next door opened and a middle-aged woman appeared, looking extremely tired.

"The professor's gone. If you're delivering anything you can leave it with me."

The voice seemed to emerge from a warped wind instrument, devoid of modulation.

"Do you know where he went?"

"No. Or when he's coming back. I just know that they didn't take much with them."

"They?"

"Yes, him and his girlfriend. Do you work with him?"

"I do. Thank you for your help."

Espinosa walked back down Rua Santa Clara to Peixoto on Rua Tonelero. The neighbor's phrase was still echoing: "him and his girlfriend." An absurd idea passed through his mind. He went back home shaking his head, saying no to an invisible interlocutor. He listened to the message on the machine: "Inspector Espinosa, it's Carmem from Planalto Minerações. I found something that might be what you're looking for. Call me at home; I should be there around six-thirty." It was six-twenty. He dialed the number and no one answered. He called back, at intervals that varied from two to five minutes, until six forty-five, when he began to fear that what had happened to Rose had just happened again.

7

Around six-thirty, Welber suddenly became extremely agitated. He pressed the buzzer on his headboard and called out for the nurse. Every time he shouted it hurt a lot, but he kept shouting all the same. It was a long time before someone responded. When a nurse entered the room, Welber was trying to get up and yelling:

"It's him! It could only be him!"

"What are you talking about, son, are you crazy? You can't get up or shout like that."

"It's urgent that I speak with Inspector Espinosa right now." His dry mouth made it even harder to speak. "Call him."

"Calm down, kid. Everything's okay. Relax."

Welber grabbed the nurse by the sleeve of her uniform.

"He's going to kill Espinosa, just like he killed the others and almost killed me."

"Nobody's going to kill anyone, son. Just calm down."

"I saw it, I saw it like in a dream, I saw it perfectly."

"There, there. You must have had a nightmare."

"God damn it, don't you get it? I saw who shot me and who's now going to kill the girl and Espinosa. I must speak to the inspector. It's urgent."

The more determined Welber was to convince the nurse, the more excited he grew, and the more intent she became on convincing him that it had been nothing more than a nightmare.

"What nightmare? You're telling me that getting shot was just a dream?"

The nurse rang the bell and asked for the on-duty doctor to come in. When he arrived, the nurse and her assistant were trying to get Welber to lie down while he kept screaming. They thought they should give him a sedative, but they wouldn't do anything without an order from the doctor. Welber said that if they put him to sleep they would be ordering the death of two people. The doctor proposed that they would get him a phone to plug into his headboard if he would promise to remain calm.

While someone came in with the phone, the nurse hooked back up the serum that had come undone when Welber had started jerking around. The phone connection wasn't direct; it had to pass through the receptionist. Welber gave her Espinosa's home number and said it was a matter of life and death. The operator reported that no one was answering. Welber asked that she keep calling every minute.

"Sir, I can't do that, I have to answer the other calls."

"Miss, if you keep trying you could save two lives. Please."

"All right, I'll alternate the other calls with yours."

After a few minutes, Welber was about to embark on a new crisis when the operator called back.

"Sir, now it's busy. I'll keep trying; as soon as I get through I'll call back."

Even before she opened the door to her apartment, Carmem could hear the phone ringing. It was a quarter to seven. It had to be Inspector Espinosa. That day it had taken her longer than usual to get home. She didn't open the door in time to answer. In her hurry, she left the door open and still had her purse across her chest and two loose bags from the supermarket in the middle of the living room. She immediately called the number she had memorized. Espinosa answered.

"Thank God!" they both said at once.

Carmem told him about the envelope and her certainty that it was addressed in Rose's handwriting. She hadn't opened it. It seemed to have another envelope inside it; and she couldn't read it holding it up to the light.

"Where do you live?" asked Espinosa.

"In Laranjeiras, near Cosme Velho."

Espinosa wrote down the address.

"I'll be there in a half hour, max."

And when he was already hanging up:

"Don't open the door for anyone until I get there."

When the hospital operator finally got through, she only reached Espinosa's answering machine. The tranquilizer they'd put in the IV still hadn't taken effect. Welber was wide awake and under the impression that the difficulty he was having in getting through to Espinosa was a scheme of the operator in collusion with the doctor. Only the older nurse had stayed in the room. Welber made himself comfortable in the bed, yawned a few times. The nurse turned off the overhead light, leaving on the little lamp on the headboard. Welber closed his eyes and seemed to be fast asleep within a few minutes. As soon as the nurse left, he removed the needle from his hand, sat up, pushed the little ladder away from the bed, and got up to look for a phone in the hall. He fell, taking with him everything on the bedside table, as well as knocking over the metal stand that held up the IV. The noise must have awakened the whole floor.

Espinosa took less than half an hour to get from Copacabana to Laranjeiras. He rang the doorbell three times and, when he felt someone looking through the peephole, said his name. Carmem was alone. Both mumbled a greeting, and she took the envelope out of a book.

"It was right there the whole time. When we were looking through her drawers and files, it was on top of the desk with all the other mail. I think it must have been there for three or four days."

While Carmem spoke, Espinosa carefully opened the envelope with the help of a pocketknife. When he removed the second envelope he couldn't contain his surprise.

He sank into the nearest chair. He stared at the letter with wide eyes, mutely, without even reading it again. After a moment, he murmured:

"So that was it?"

Carmem, uncomprehending, looked at him blankly. "Inspector?"

Nothing. No noticeable reaction, until he turned his body toward Carmem and said, almost in a whisper:

"It wasn't a murder. It was a suicide."

In spite of the laconic and almost inaudible communication, the girl was smart and immediately recognized its implication. "Ricardo Carvalho killed himself."

"Carmem, for your safety, it's important that you not read this letter. You didn't hear or understand the information I just revealed. Don't mention to anybody what happened today. You never saw a letter."

He left praising her intelligence and persistence and promised her that when it was all over he would tell her the whole story.

From Carmem's building he headed up Rua das Laranjeiras toward the Rebouças Tunnel. By the time he exited at Lagoa, he'd recovered from half of his shock. He'd hidden the other half from Carmem. Which policemen had recovered the letter? It could only be the patrol crew that had made the first report in the parking garage. Two military police—for ten thousand dollars each they could have made anything disappear: the gun, the car, the body, even the parking garage. But if that was the case, how did Max end up with the gun? Only if, in their hurry to get rid of it, they'd tossed it somewhere and Max had accidentally stumbled across it. The other possibility was that Rose was the first one to arrive on the scene and, terrified by what she found, grabbed the gun and the letter and ran off, then was intercepted by Max, who figured everything out. She could have given Max the revolver and the money, but kept the envelope; there was no other explanation for how she got her hands on the letter. By the time he'd reached Peixoto he'd already come up with five or six versions of the story. But none explained the deaths of Dona Maura and Max. The only thing he knew for sure was that Max had gotten the gun and Rose had gotten the letter. He still had to find out why two people had been murdered on the heels of the executive's suicide.

8

He didn't turn on the lights when he walked in. The only things glowing in the darkness of his living room were the little red and green lights of the answering machine. Nobody had called while he was gone. The light from the street, reflected on the ceiling, indirectly lit up the furniture and other objects. Each one acquired its own density according to how its shadows transformed it into another object, even a person. An innocent chair in the corner of the room suggested a squatting man; the old floor lamp looked like a felt-hatted bandit from an old American movie. But Espinosa didn't believe in ghosts; besides, he was entirely consumed by the confrontation that would take place in the next few hours. While he was waiting, he thought about the case in the light of the new discovery of the letter.

The letter relieved him of the strange feeling he'd had whenever he'd wondered who'd killed Ricardo Carvalho. Nobody had fit the role of the murderer for the simple reason that there wasn't a murderer, which didn't necessarily mean elimination of the murder hypothesis. That letter could be forged, even though he didn't consider it likely, and handwriting analysis could attest to its authenticity. But if it was a relief to lay that mystery to rest, the next two deaths moved from the background up to the front. They were definitely murders. That is, of course, if the burned and mutilated cadaver was Max's, which, at this point, wasn't certain. But nobody, no matter how cynical, could believe that Dona Maura would cut the fingers off one of her hands while hanging herself with the venetian-blind cord with the other. So there was for certain at least one murder. And if no one fit the role of Ricardo Carvalho's murderer, there was surely no one he could imagine in the role of Rose's mother's torturer and murderer. The characters and the set had been transformed, just like the shadows in the living room. There was a little more than an hour left before he could expect to hear from the kidnapper.

Even in his sleep, Welber was mumbling incomprehensibly and shifting in his bed. The sleeping drug they'd put in his IV was enough to take him out of commission at least until the next day, when the nurses and the doctor on duty would be replaced. They were a little concerned that his story might be true. It was lucky that his fall hadn't torn out any of his stitches. They didn't know if he'd been injured internally. A nurse was placed by his side all night, with orders to report any change in his condition and to stop him from trying to get up again.

Espinosa was wondering how Welber was doing just then and thinking how nice it would be to be able to count on him. Espinosa could have been the one hit; all he would have had to do was get to the door before his partner. He could have died, just like he could be killed during the meeting tonight. If he'd been hit a few centimeters higher or to the side, Welber could have been killed or paralyzed. Life would have escaped through the little bullet hole like gas leaving a balloon.

Rose had decided to cooperate with the kidnapper. She never let on that she knew that he had tortured and murdered her mother. The more she thought about the severed fingers described by the newspapers, the more coldly she analyzed how to kill the man. She preferred to make him suffer as he'd made her mother suffer. She didn't speak; she didn't resist; she didn't try useless attacks, physical or verbal; she simply waited for the moment he'd trip up. She didn't know precisely what she would do. It couldn't be anything requiring a physical confrontation—he was very strong and could take her out easily, even if she had a knife or another weapon. She didn't know how, but she was going to kill him.

Around eight o'clock, the man put a handcuff on his own wrist and the other around hers, lying down on his chest on top of the cushion, forcing her to do the same.

"Try to sleep a little—it's gonna be a long night."

He closed his eyes and soon was snoring. His arm looked like an anchor. All she could do was lie next to him awake while he slept. So this was the decisive night. The inspector couldn't know where the letter was, and no matter how thoroughly he searched the room he wouldn't find it. Rose knew the kidnapper wouldn't kill her before finding the letter, but she also knew that he wouldn't hesitate to cut off her fingers to put pressure on Espinosa. The man had a gun he carried inside a bag; it was in the corner of the room, ten feet away. To get there, she'd have to drag him while he slept, and she could barely move his arm a single centimeter.

With half an hour remaining before his deadline, Espinosa rose from the sofa, turned on the lamp, and picked up the brown envelope he'd left on the table. He removed the white paper and the other envelope and copied the letter and the address as best he could, closing both the envelopes, replacing the smaller one in the bigger one, and putting it in his jacket pocket. He hid the originals inside a Dickens novel he was reading. Waiting was more dream than reality, but Espinosa did his best to get his ideas into the most realistic form possible. He tried to piece the story back together, starting with the suicide note and including all the fragmented images, stray conversations, and loose ideas. The letter itself wasn't from a suicide: it was from a businessman. It was hard to believe that someone wanting to kill himself would do so in such a cold and calculating manner. Yet no one except Ricardo Carvalho himself was responsible for his death. There was no murderer to find unless he could be considered to have murdered himself. The motive of the other two murders became clear with the other piece of the mosaic, the million-dollar life insurance policy. That explained the suicide note and Dona Maura's death, and probably Max's as well. All that was left to figure out was who'd done it. He was nervous.

Perhaps the reason Rose had the letter was that she was the first person to reach Ricardo Carvalho's car after his suicide. She would have been in the garage because she was meeting him there at the usual time, on Tuesdays and Thursdays. If that was the case, Ricardo killed himself believing that Rose would find the body, the letter, and the gun, and knew that she would do what he asked. The money was just in case someone else, or the police, got there first. That would mean that Rose didn't know that Ricardo was going to kill himself: she surely would have made a scene, tried to stop him—a situation he no doubt wanted to avoid.

Ideas and images came tumbling out. He wasn't sure why Rose had the letter and Max had the gun. Unless Max's story was true: Rose arrived immediately after the suicide, saw the note, grabbed the gun, the letter, and the briefcase and ran downstairs. When she reached the street, she looked around for the first place she could get rid of the gun—which is when Max encountered her. That explained the story of the businessman's death, but didn't quite account for the murder of Rose's mother and the probable murder of Max. The element that tied the two stories together was Rose, and just then Rose was in the hands of the murderer. The other possibility: Max killed the executive in an attempted robbery; Rose saw him; Max started stalking her and she had to hide. So Max tortured her mother to find out where she was. The letter had been forged, but needed to be seen by somebody, preferably the police, to give the impression that it was a suicide. Later, the letter would have to be recovered and destroyed so that the handwriting couldn't be examined. So he was now trying desperately to get it back. A third hypothesis, even weaker, was that Max and Rose were accomplices—not in the death of the executive but in the use of the letter. But that wouldn't explain a lot of facts, such as Dona Maura, the hotel shootout, the attack in Ipanema, and the fact that both of them were now fighting for control of the letter.

Ten-twenty. No call. Maybe it would be better to get help. It was pretty pretentious to think he could solve a kidnapping case all by himself. True, it wasn't your average kidnapping. There were no vast, or even small, sums being demanded. All the kidnapper wanted was a letter. The problem was that it wasn't a simple matter: the girl for the letter. Espinosa knew this as well as the kidnapper. Once he'd handed over the letter, Rose would live just as long as it took to verify its authenticity. Espinosa was inclined to take the risk. Asking for help from the Anti-Kidnapping Division could mean delivering both himself and the letter to the enemy. They'd find a way to make sure he died "in a shootout with the gang of kidnappers." There was no other way: he had to save Rose at the moment of the meeting or, at the very latest, during the amount of time the kidnapper needed to confirm it was the right letter. If that was what the kidnapper planned to do.

Ten-forty. The ring of the phone startled Espinosa. It was Alba.

"Espinosa, what's going on?"

"Nothing, why?"

"Why, damn it? You mysteriously pack me off in the middle of the night and that's the last I hear of you . . . obviously something's going on."

"I can't explain it now. . . . I have to hang up. . . . I have to leave the line open. . . . I'll call you tomorrow."

He hung up before she could say anything.

At eleven-fifteen, he chose a book to read. He gave up after a few minutes. He was afraid to go to sleep and miss the phone. He couldn't listen to music. The emptiness of the wait could only be filled by his own imagination. Every time he tried to focus on reason he was immediately invaded by fantasy. At two in the morning, he couldn't tell the difference.

9

Rose didn't move while the man slept beside her. She wanted to know who this man was who could sleep so soundly at a time like this. Was he her mother's murderer? Up until now, he hadn't mistreated her, except for holding her prisoner. The physical restrictions he imposed were understandable security measures. It was the second time he had slept handcuffed to her. The first time, she'd considered trying to seduce him. The situation was right. But she'd given up the idea. Trying to seduce him was like trying to seduce a fish. His wedding ring indicated some interest in women, but in the present circumstances, it was clear, he was so blindly obsessed with something else that he couldn't possibly see her as a sexual object, in spite of the intimacy provoked by their physical proximity. He hardly spoke; when he did, it was to transmit precise instructions. He'd never tried to have a conversation. Not only was he not interested in her sexually, he wasn't interested in her as a human being. Maybe this was because he himself didn't seem very human.

She didn't know what she would get out of seducing him anyway. Would he suddenly fall in love with her and let her go? Grateful for the terrific fuck, would he remove her handcuffs and send her home? The idea was ridiculous—the gorilla wouldn't have set up this whole thing only to end up ceding to the victim's charms. A few girlishly modest gazes wouldn't be enough for him; he was no Max. But even if she didn't have any hope of freedom, she could at least buy herself some time. Everything indicated that this was the decisive night; no matter how it ended, he wouldn't leave her alive as a witness. The idea repulsed her, but it could mean her survival.

arm and left it hanging off the handcuffed one. He used the hand between her legs to force her to her feet, in spite of the handcuffs, and pulled down her jeans and underwear as she did so. Then he got rid of his pants and boxers. When Rose squatted over his cock, feeling it enter, she let it slide in slowly. They fucked handcuffed together, shirts caught on their shackled arms. Rose moved up and down; the two looked like a well lubricated piston. She came, shot through by pleasure and rage. She remained seated, motionless, torso erect, head up, rejecting the man's gaze. She didn't want to move; she couldn't let the blood flow out because then he'd slip out of her. She kept contracting rhythmically for a long time, until she felt the man come inside her. At no point did they embrace or kiss; all their energy was concentrated. When they started again, the man's body was bathed in sweat; each took their turn wiping the sweat from their faces with the T-shirts knotted around the handcuffs. Neither had said a word. It would have been impossible to mingle the pleasure of speaking with the pleasure of fucking. Instead they moaned, snorted, screamed, gagged. They took it slower the second time. The man sweated from all his pores; his hair was soaked and he puffed and panted. When they were done, Rose let her body relax, reluctant to unglue herself from him. She didn't get off, but sat on his chest, near his neck, as if he were a saddle, pressing his face between her thighs. She stayed in that position for a while, letting him take in the acid smell of her sex. She started again slowly, rubbing herself along his whole body, greased by their sweat. She couldn't say how long she stayed like that, or how long afterward it was that she felt him grow hard again, but not enough to penetrate her. She kept rubbing him. Now both of them were sweating profusely. The man tried to get an erection, but the effort was futile. On her knees, with his head between her thighs, Rose lubricated his face vaginally, letting his nose penetrate her until he couldn't breathe. Without moving from where she was, she turned around, slid her head between his legs, licking and sucking, until she could once again sit on him. She had to keep up the rhythmic motion, slowly, so as not to lose her position. Time stopped. There was only a circular movement accompanying the measured movement of her body. The man's muscles were stiff; the veins in his neck popped out; he squeezed himself like a fruit offering up its juice. The cushion was completely soaked. They came amid groans and panting. Rose fell back onto the floor. Her cushion had slid quite a ways. She felt the pleasant coolness of the wood underneath her body. She sat staring at the ceiling for a few minutes; the man was still by her side. The sweat had already completely dried when she turned to him; she needed to go to the bathroom. Kneeling at his side, she saw that his face was blue. She checked to see if he was breathing; he was dead.

10

Espinosa awoke to the sound of the telephone ringing. Stretched out on the living room couch, completely dressed, he felt for the phone while he thought of Rose conveying the kidnapper's orders. He didn't immediately notice that it was light outside. He only woke fully when he heard the voice of the on-duty officer saying his name.

"Espinosa, sorry about calling you at this hour, but there's something going on over by your house. A woman was found screaming inside an apartment, handcuffed to a dead guy, both butt naked, and the woman keeps demanding to talk to Inspector Espinosa from the First Precinct."

The address was on Rua Barata Ribeiro, close to his house. It was six in the morning.

An old building with more than a hundred one-bedroom apartments—a well-known address in the Copacabana underworld. Two patrol cars from the military police were parked on the curb. And two cops were drinking coffee in the bar next door. Espinosa asked what floor it was and if the girl was still there. In the lobby, people weren't leaving for another day at the office; they were coming back from another night out and yet another anonymous hookup. He went up in the elevator with a soldier from one of the patrol cars.

"Damn, the guy died the way I'd like to go; I just don't get what's with the handcuffs."

When he entered the apartment, a sergeant from the military police was trying to get Rose to go with him to the hospital. She was curled up in the corner, wrapped in a sheet someone on the floor had doubtless loaned her. She was mumbling gibberish. Next to the window, covered by a sheet filled with cigarette burns, was the dead guy. His feet were sticking out. Espinosa lifted the sheet and saw the face of Aurélio.

Details he'd forgotten came surging out of his subconscious, details he himself had provided at the lunches Aurélio had kept suggesting. The ex-policeman's experience, the insurance company's investigation, the information he'd gotten during his lunches with Espinosa made Aurélio, now, retrospectively, the obvious suspect . . . and such an impossible one.

Rose didn't look up when Espinosa came into the room, and even when he squatted in front of her she didn't seem to recognize him. She trembled as if she was cold, clasping the sheet against her body. On her wrist was the red mark left by the handcuffs.

"Rose, it's me, Espinosa."

And she said mechanically:

"Inspector Espinosa from the First Precinct."

"Rose, it's Inspector Espinosa, don't you remember me?"

"Inspector Espinosa from the First Precinct."

"Yes, it's me, remember?"

"Inspector Espinosa from the First Precinct."

A lieutenant from the military police walked up to him and put his hand on Espinosa's shoulder.

"Inspector, I've seen this before. She's stunned, she's talking nonsense. The best we can do is take her to the Hospital Pinel. They'll know what to do there."

"Pinel? Do you think she's gone crazy?"

"It's a kind of craziness. The person keeps saying meaningless things, like they are out of their minds. . . . You'll see she really is. Sometimes it goes away; sometimes it never does."

"Wouldn't it be better to wait awhile? She may come to."

"Inspector, in my experience, the sooner they take care of her the better."

"All right. I'll come with you. She may remember me on the way there."

He picked up the clothes tossed around the room. The lieutenant helped dress her. They left behind her underwear; that could get complicated. They put on her jeans and her still-wet and twisted T-shirt. Together with Aurélio's bag, they found her purse with her belongings, her wallet, credit card, keys, hairbrush, lipstick, and other trivial items. Rose left the room without seeming to notice the cadaver on the way. She didn't look directly at anything or anyone; what she did look at she didn't seem to see. She didn't offer any resistance. When she got in the back seat of the police car, with Espinosa holding her hand, it was as if she'd never seen him in her life, even though, once they got to the hospital, she kept repeating to the doctor: "Inspector Espinosa from the First Precinct."

He left his office and home numbers with the people on duty at the hospital and asked the lieutenant to take him back to the crime scene to get his car. From there he went straight to the Hotel Novo Mundo to pick up clean clothes and toiletries for Rose. He asked the cleaner to separate out some outfits from the closet and select some things from the medicine cabinet in the bathroom. He put it all in a travel bag and had the rest stored in the baggage check at the hotel. Back at the hospital, he dropped off the bag with the attendant and once again left the numbers where he could be found.

His clothes were a disaster, he hadn't shaved, his face made it clear that he'd hardly slept at all, and his stomach was empty and nauseous. He had a café au lait and some bread and butter at the corner bar. Aurélio's body would be taken to the Forensic Institute. He got in his car and went home.

The phone was ringing and the red light of the answering machine was blinking. When he picked up, he heard a shout and then Welber's voice:

"Espinosa, thank God! I tried to warn you yesterday but they put something in my IV." He stopped to breathe. "Espinosa, the guy who shot at us was Aurélio. His face came to me as clearly as in a photograph. Espinosa, are you listening to me?"

"Yes. Don't worry, Welber. He's dead."

"Did you kill him?"

"No. It's a long story. I'll come by later to tell you."

"Are you all right, Inspector?"

"Almost as well as you, buddy. See you later."

When he took off his jacket, he saw the envelope with the fake letter he'd prepared for the meeting. He went to his room and took the original out of the Dickens. That letter was worth a million dollars for Bia Vasconcelos or the insurance company. Of the four people who knew what it said, two were dead and one was, for the time being, half dead. It was up to Espinosa to decide what to do with it. He looked at the envelope for a long time. He would prefer not to.

ABOUT THE AUTHOR

LUIZ ALFREDO GARCIA-ROZA is a critically acclaimed bestselling novelist who lives in Rio de Janeiro. The other books in his crime trilogy, *Lost and Found* and *Southwesterly Wind*, will also be published by Henry Holt.